REMBRANDT'S GHOST

The dark blue Audi pulled onto the wide sidewalk beside the old Strand Station, a shadowy figure at the wheel. Twenty, perhaps thirty seconds and it would be too late. Finn's roving eyes found a low wrought-iron gate beside a door, a pair of neglected rubbish bins, and a little pile of builders' junk. God bless you, Miss Turner from Northland High School, wherever you are. Tumble.

"Jolly good!" yelled Finn at the top of her lungs. She went into a simple tuck and roll, her hand reaching out blindly, fumbling, grabbing the length of old narrow plumbing pipe. She came out of the somersault, facing back the way she'd come, and swept the pipe around as hard as she could, aiming for the kidnapper's knees. The pipe connected, and she felt the shivering, wet crunch of impact run up her arm. The man screamed and dropped his newspaper and umbrella. She saw that there really was a gun in the man's hand—a flat, chunky-looking automatic. Then chaos.

ALSO BY PAUL CHRISTOPHER

Michelangelo's Notebook
The Lucifer Gospel

REMBRANDT'S GHOST

PAUL CHRISTOPHER

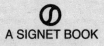

A SIGNET BOOK

SIGNET
Published by New American Library, a division of
Penguin Group (USA) Inc., 375 Hudson Street,
New York, New York 10014, USA
Penguin Group (Canada), 90 Eglinton Avenue East, Suite 700, Toronto,
Ontario M4P 2Y3, Canada (a division of Pearson Penguin Canada Inc.)
Penguin Books Ltd., 80 Strand, London WC2R 0RL, England
Penguin Ireland, 25 St. Stephen's Green, Dublin 2,
Ireland (a division of Penguin Books Ltd.)
Penguin Group (Australia), 250 Camberwell Road, Camberwell, Victoria 3124,
Australia (a division of Pearson Australia Group Pty. Ltd.)
Penguin Books India Pvt. Ltd., 11 Community Centre, Panchsheel Park,
New Delhi - 110 017, India
Penguin Group (NZ), 67 Apollo Drive, Rosedale, North Shore 0745,
Auckland, New Zealand (a division of Pearson New Zealand Ltd.)
Penguin Books (South Africa) (Pty.) Ltd., 24 Sturdee Avenue,
Rosebank, Johannesburg 2196, South Africa

Penguin Books Ltd., Registered Offices:
80 Strand, London WC2R 0RL, England

First published by Signet, an imprint of New American Library,
a division of Penguin Group (USA) Inc.

First Printing, July 2007
10 9 8 7 6 5 4 3 2 1

Ⓟ REGISTERED TRADEMARK—MARCA REGISTRADA

Printed in the United States of America

PUBLISHER'S NOTE
This is a work of fiction. Names, characters, places, and incidents either are
the product of the author's imagination or are used fictitiously, and any
resemblance to actual persons, living or dead, business establishments,
events, or locales is entirely coincidental.

The publisher does not have any control over and does not assume any
responsibility for author or third-party Web sites or their content.

To Gabriel, an American boy in accordance with whose classic taste the following narrative has been designed, *Rembrandt's Ghost* is now, in return for numerous delightful hours, and with the kindest wishes, dedicated by his affectionate grandfather, the author.

If sailor tales to sailor tunes,
Storm and adventure, heat and cold,
If schooners, islands, and maroons,
And buccaneers, and buried gold,
And all the old romance, retold
Exactly in the ancient way,
Can please, as me they pleased of old,
The wiser youngsters of today:

—So be it, and fall on! If not,
If studious youth no longer crave,
His ancient appetites forgot,
Kingston, or Ballantyne the brave,
Or Cooper of the wood and wave:
So be it, also! And may I
And all my pirates share the grave
Where these and their creations lie!

—Robert Louis Stevenson,
Treasure Island

1

Fiona Katherine Elizabeth Ryan, late of New York City and, before that, Columbus, Ohio, known as Finn to her friends and loved ones, stood at the window of her little flat above the restaurant on Crouch End Broadway in North London and watched Emir, the tobacconist on the far side of the street, roll up his shutters, opening his shop for the early-morning customers standing dripping and dreary, waiting at the bus stop on the rain-dark sidewalk in front of him.

Of course in England a sidewalk wasn't a sidewalk—it was a pavement. A Broadway wasn't a place where they had theaters—it was a High Street. And the locals weren't the ones with an accent—Finn was. She sighed and swallowed the last of the mug of tea she'd just zapped with her immersion heater. It tasted like burned acorns. It was seven in the morning, it was April, and it was raining. Of course it was raining. In London, if it wasn't snowing, it was probably raining no matter what time of the year it was.

Finn sighed again. London wasn't what she'd expected at all. After her adventures in New York and her fugitive escapades in the Libyan desert and the depths of the Caribbean the year before she'd been ready for some serious work and study in an environment of culture and sophistication. Her job as a client adviser at the prestigious Mason-Godwin Auction House was supposed to take care of the sophistication, and living in the city that was still the center of the art world was supposed to take care of the culture.

Sadly, it hadn't worked out that way. "Client adviser" at Mason-Godwin meant looking good in high heels and a short black cocktail dress on Sale Nights, finding out beforehand what a potential buyer's bidding range, alcohol capacity, and net worth were, and fetching coffee, tea, and biscuits during daylight hours for the office's high muckety-mucks, like the Ghastly Ronald, managing director of Mason-Godwin.

As far as sophistication went, it appeared to Finn that London had more Starbucks than Seattle, more KFCs than Kentucky, and its own version of *American Idol*. A burger and fries at Pick More Daisies, the self-styled California restaurant directly below her, cost eleven pounds—twenty-five bucks when you added the tax and tip. On top of that, she was paying more for a two-room flat with a hot plate and a bathroom down the hall in Crouch End than she had for her tidy little apartment in Manhattan. In a word, London was a rip-off.

Sighing again Finn slipped on her raincoat, grabbed her telescoping umbrella from the shelf by the door, and went downstairs to join the group of commuters waiting for the number 41 bus and the long ride down the hill toward the distant Thames and the City.

A little more than two thousand years ago, a small village appeared at the intersection of two Roman roads that converged just west of the port town of Londinium. This was the original Mayfair, named for the country market and annual pagan religious festival held there every spring.

Between 1720 and 1740 the entire village was expropriated and developed by the Grosvenor family and the Earl of Chesterfield, who was famous for putting velvet collars on his coats and the invention of the modern upholstered couch. By 1800 it was the most fashionable place to live in London with wall-to-wall stately mansions on its score of elegant cobbled streets.

By the turn of the new millennium, it had gone through a number of transformations, including some random bomb hits during World War Two, inevitable stock market crashes that turned the mansions into flats and apartments, and economic upturns that turned the street frontage into some of the priciest property on the planet, with rents paid by everyone from Fortnum and Masons to Prada and Dolce & Gabbana.

In the middle of it all was Cork Street, a single long block running between Clifford Street and Burlington Gardens, just a stone's throw from Piccadilly and ending at the exit of the Burlington Arcade, where James Bond purchased his Mont Blanc pens and around the corner from the shop where he bought his handmade Morland's cigarettes.

There are twenty-three art galleries on Cork Street selling everything from old Dutch Masters to Basquiat's little scrawls and Keith Haring's gentle doodles. More than a billion dollars' worth of art on the current market, depending on how gullible you are, representing every major artist in the world, alive or dead, all packed into less than two hundred yards. And in the middle of all that, at 26–28 Cork Street is the firm of Mason-Godwin, fine art auctioneers, which was established in 1710, thirty-two years before Sotheby's had its first little sale of old books for a total take of less than three hundred pounds—a fact that the management of Mason-Godwin was almost sure to impart at the drop of a hat to anyone willing to listen.

The premises had originally belonged to a firm of decorators and furniture makers specializing in clients with titles in front of their names. That firm eventually went bankrupt due to the unfortunate habit of those titled clients not paying their bills on time, if at all. After that, the large workrooms and warehouse floors were broken up into flats and apartments for the wealthy, then offices for the not so wealthy. A decade before World War Two, the property was purchased by a pair of closeted gay confectioners, who turned the property into a chocolate factory and showroom manufacturing a particularly popular bittersweet mint concoction known as Turner & Townsend's Minto-Bits.

The two men and their company thrived until war came and knocked the stuffing out of the chocolate business. Sugar was rationed early and people had better things to do between 1939 and 1945 than either making or consuming Minto-Bits or the equally popular Hinto-Minto Collection. Mason-Godwin on the other hand did extremely well before, during, and after the war, buying and selling with equal zeal from both oppressed and oppressor, generally through Swiss intermediaries. In 1946 Mason-Godwin, bloated with cash and unsold inventory and looking to expand, snapped up the building on Cork Street, which was just beginning its paint-spattered climb to fame. The rest was history. All of this information, with the exception of Turner's and Townsend's sexual predilections, and the pre- and post-war art market in Switzerland, was included in the orientation brochure given to Finn when she joined the firm.

Mason-Godwin, which hadn't had either a Mason or a Godwin on its staff for more than a hundred years, wasn't as large as Sotheby's or, heaven forbid, the upstart Christies, but at least its heart was pure. It had always auctioned art and nothing but art, unlike Sotheby's, which sold everything from real estate to old wristwatches, or Christies, which had recently stooped to selling off props from old television shows, including Captain Jean-Luc Picard's first-season *Star Trek, Next Generation* uniform complete with authentic Patrick Stewart sweat stains. According to the Ghastly Ronald, *Ars Gratia Artis*—Art for the Sake of Art—had been the motto of Mason-Godwin for a hundred years before MGM even existed.

The main floor of the old Georgian-fronted building held a small, elegant reception area furnished with antiques and a rotating series of impressive but relatively unimportant Royal Academy painters from the nineteenth century, meant to show the prospective buyer or seller that Mason-Godwin didn't have a frivolous bone in its body and took the job of flogging your pictures seriously. Beyond that was a large preview gallery with white walls, track lighting, and a sprinkling of uniformed guards to show you how secure Mason-Godwin was. At the rear of the building was an immense cavernous room that had once

been the actual factory for Turner & Townsend
and which Finn could almost swear still smelled
faintly of Minto-Bits. This was the actual auction
floor or, as a few office wags referred to it, the
money room. Phone banks on the left for call-ins,
freight elevators, prep rooms on the right, and a
giant viewing screen behind the actual auctioneer's podium in the center. In the middle of the
room were three hundred fifty very comfortable
chairs for the people holding their little paddles
and upping the bids—and M-G's commissions—
with every passing minute on Sale Nights.

On the first floor above was the Research Department, where a score of young men and
women worked to establish provenance for art
being auctioned, and the small offices where Finn
and a dozen other young women like her in Client
Advisory worked the phones, making sure prospective buyers were comfortable in their hotels if
they were from out of town, or had received their
catalogues. Occasionally client advisers would even
briefly get to see a work of art being brought in
for evaluation, but their job was to quickly assess
and dismiss, or immediately send the person up
to one of the experts on the third floor, where
everyone seemed to have names like Philoda,
Felix, or Alistair or, in one instance, Jemimah, and
have degrees from places like St. Edmund Hall at
Oxford or Trinity College at Cambridge. The
fourth, fifth, and sixth floors were given over to

the more mundane part of the business that involved cleaning, restoring, framing, and warehousing of the Mason-Godwin inventory.

Finn, she'd soon realized, had been hired as a client adviser to take care of American prospects who sometimes felt uncomfortable and off their turf in London and who appreciated her nice, familiar Midwestern drawl. She also had the other central asset of a CA: she was stunningly beautiful. Her model's body, her green-eyed Irish features, and her long red hair seemed far more important than her knowledge of art or her formal education in the subject. The fact that she had a BA in anthropology and a master's in art history from NYU as well as a year's study in Florence barely seemed to matter at all. She was a fluffy part of a well-oiled machine that took roughly twenty percent of the hammer price of a work of art from the seller going in and an equally elastic twenty percent "Buyer's Premium" from the new owner going out.

A Jean Dubuffet for instance, two feet by three feet, oil and enamel on canvas that sold for 111,000 U.S. dollars would actually cost the buyer $140,000 since M-G added its commission on the front end, which would in turn cost the seller an extra $28,000 since the sales commission was computed on the total amount going out. The result was that Mason-Godwin made a total of $56,000 for the simple act of introducing the buyer to the seller,

or almost half the hammer price. Not to mention
the sale of catalogues, the publication of which
was a tidy business on its own. It was rather like
selling someone his own shopping list with an
even heavier black market trade in slipping ad-
vance copies to "special clients"—"special" meaning anyone who asked and who was willing to
pay a hefty premium to get a catalogue a fortnight
before everyone else.

This, then, was the delicate balancing act of the
art auctioneer, the slick, ultra-high-end confidence
trick of convincing the seller that he no longer
needed the item, and the buyer that he must have
it at any price. The higher the better.

If both parties were given the impression that
their needs had been met they'd probably, eventually, be convinced to switch roles, buyer becoming
seller and seller buyer in a dance that could last
a lifetime and sometimes longer, a single work of
art making its way through the M-G list of contacts and clients, shedding commissions every
time.

The Ghastly Ronald boasted that he'd shifted a
single Turner sunrise eleven times during his career with Mason-Godwin, making more than a
million pounds in commissions for the firm. In
other words, it was all a scam. In the past year,
Finn had discovered that in the art world, the
painter and the painting were nothing more than
commodities, like orange juice or sugar beets, and

that the art market, like the stock market, was an
invention with about as much substance and in-
tegrity as a stink in a high wind as her father used
to say. Sort of.

Finn took the awkward-looking bright red
double-decker bus down to Euston Station, then
switched to the Underground riding the Victoria
Line down to Green Park. She came above ground
into the drizzling rain again, walked to Albemarle
Street, then purchased the largest possible container of coffee and a blueberry muffin from the
local Prêt-a-Manger shop. Carrying her breakfast
she zigzagged through the narrow streets to the
discreetly canopied entrance to Mason-Godwin,
careful to shake out her umbrella and collapse it
before stepping through the brass-and-glass doors
and onto the bloodred and black Oriental carpets
covering the polished wood floors of the oak-
paneled reception area.

It was now eight o'clock in the morning and
after an hour on various overheated London
Transport vehicles crammed with various overheated passengers, Finn Ryan was not in good
spirits. Her mood wasn't made any better by the
sight of Ghastly Ronald standing at the ornate
Louis the Fifteenth escritoire that passed as a reception desk, chatting up Doris, the plain-Jane
battle-ax who acted as the first line of interference

for anyone entering the sacred halls of Mason-Godwin.

The Ghastly Ronald's real name was Ronald Adrian DePanay-Cottrell, better known as Ronnie and sometimes behind his back as Lady Ron. According to Ronnie he was somehow related to the queen but he could never quite explain the connection. He had a plumy Oxford accent, a degree in something he never talked about, thinning black hair, wet lips, and intelligent, dark eyes that always seemed to be in motion. He had the kind of lanky loose-boned body that belonged in a *Monty Python* skit, but the John Cleese–Ichabod Crane look was muted by the expensive Crockett & Jones calfskin oxfords, the even more expensive Anderson & Sheppard pin-striped suit, and the creamy silk Dege & Skinner club tie in dark blue with little tiny crowns on it, hinting once again at a royal lineage that Finn was positive the Ghastly Ronald didn't really have any claim to at all.

Ronnie and Doris glanced up as Finn came through the doors, both looking at her with mild disapproval as though she'd blundered clumsily into some intimate and important conversation. Finn instantly felt self-conscious, which was the whole point of course, and her self-consciousness instantly turned to resentment. The whole nose-in-the-air snobbishness of Mason-Godwin and a thousand years of English aristocratic arrogance were beginning to wear a little.

"Ah, Miss Ryan," said Ronnie, "arriving for work, I see," as though she were tardy, which she wasn't—not by a full half hour.

"Ah, Mr. DePanay-Cottrell," she responded with some dry ice in her tone, leaning a little heavily on the "Mr." knowing just how much Ronnie yearned for something else like "His Grace" or "Baron" or "my lord'" or even a bare-bones "sir." Not in this lifetime, Finn thought.

"One should eat one's breakfast at home, Miss Ryan, not spread crumbs across one's desk at one's place of employment."

Finn wondered how often Ronnie could use the word "one" in a single sentence. He really was profoundly irritating.

"Not when one has to make allowances for one's ride on London transport that takes an hour, one doesn't," Finn answered.

"Tooting, isn't it? Stepney?"

"Crouch End."

"Crouch End. Indeed." Ronnie of course lived in a house in Cheyne Walk once occupied by the American painter James McNeill Whistler and his famous mother.

"Indeed it is," said Finn. She gave Ronnie her most insincere smile and turned away. She'd had enough of him for one morning; he'd probably soured the cream in her cooling coffee.

"No crumbs, Miss Ryan!" Ronnie called as she started to climb the stairs leading up to the floor above.

"Not one!" Finn called back without bothering to turn around. "Twit," she murmured under her breath. She reached the landing and headed down the corridor to her office.

2

Finn's office was a cubicle among cubicles at the windowless rear of a rabbit warren of rooms and corridors on the second floor of Mason-Godwin. Being in England, it wasn't called the second floor; it was the first floor, while the first floor was called the ground floor, which made sense but was still a little annoying. Living in England was sometimes a little like living inside a page from *Alice in Wonderland*, and that made sense as well, she supposed, since Lewis Carroll wasn't the author's real name and he hadn't really been a writer. He had been an Anglican minister and a mathematics professor at Oxford.

England was a confusing place full of confusing people. According to her mother, dead barely a year ago now, England, like the rest of Europe, suffered from enduring the burden of too much history. As she put it, "It makes them all a little eccentric, dear. As a civilization they tend to make everything as complicated as possible, from people to pornography." Finn didn't know much about the pornography part of it beyond the flyers for hookers and their various specialties found pasted inside every phone booth, but the eccentric people part certainly was true enough. She reached her office, had her muffin and coffee, and tried to forget about Ronnie and everything he stood for, burying herself in work.

For Finn, work that day consisted in poring over old catalogues from past sales, noting trend changes and amounts for repeat clients likely to attend the next sale due at the end of the month. The end of April sale was a bad one; instead of concentrating on a simple theme like, say, "Between the Wars British Contemporary Painters 1918–1939," the sale was a spring-cleaning auction that covered everything from a half dozen "School of Delft" paintings that were part of unsold inventory from the fifties to a small Cézanne that Ronnie had been keeping off the market while the prices rose.

Inventory—a dirty word in the auction industry, but an important one. Not many people knew just how speculative the art market was. All of the big houses had been doing it for hundreds of years—buying pictures and other items for themselves, not clients, then slipping lots under the gavel when cash was needed or the market was right, taking full price and not just commissions.

This April was no exception; more than half of the items in this year's sale were from the storerooms upstairs. The scuttlebutt was that Ronnie had spent far too much over the past year acquiring paintings of questionable provenance or even authenticity. Finn knew for a fact that Lady Ron had recently picked up a fifteenth-century bust of Piero de' Medici supposedly done by the Leonardo contemporary Mino da Fiesole that turned out to be a very well-made forgery by Giovanni Bastianini sometime in the 1850s. The difference between the two sculptors was the difference between platinum and pig iron. The cost of Ronnie's mistake was going to have to be made up one way or the other. He wouldn't dare sell the fake as a real Fiesole, so he'd probably wind up attributing it to "Renaissance School," but he'd take an enormous loss.

By twelve-thirty she'd finished the Ds on the computerized client files, then broke for lunch. She went for a slice of pizza at the Europa since she couldn't afford the upscale Irish stew at Mulligan's down the street, then came back to her desk and started on the Es. By four she was wishing she smoked just as an excuse to get outside for some air, rain or not. She was saved by a call from Doris downstairs. As usual, the receptionist's whining voice grated on her nerves.

"We've got a walk-in with a parcel wrapped in string. I told him we didn't do spot evaluations but he insists it's a Jan Steen. I thought I'd send him on to you. Can't miss him, dear, he's wearing one of those silly sweatshirts with Harvard across the front. Purple. And he's wearing scruffy-looking trainers as well."

In other words, not the type who'd have a Dutch Master from the seventeenth century under his arm. The tone in Doris's voice was dismissive. She was passing a nuisance on to Finn.

"He's American?"

"No, British. He was very insistent. Asked to see Mr. DePanay-Cottrell, but I informed him that you'd have to do, Miss Ryan. Deal with him please." Doris hung up without giving her a chance to respond. The name of the university on the man's sweatshirt had sent him in Finn's direction. She quickly checked the computer inventory to see if Steen's name appeared. It did. A small scene of villagers dancing around a Maypole had made a hammer price of slightly less than a million pounds sterling, well over a million dollars U.S. Jan Steen had always been a blue-chip artist, even in his own lifetime.

Two minutes later a figure appeared in the doorway of her office. Just as Doris had described:

purple Harvard sweatshirt, bruised Nikes, and a scruffy-looking package under his arm wrapped in brown paper and tied with what a Midwesterner like her would have called binder twine, the stuff you wrapped around bales of hay. As well as the sweatshirt and runners, he wore a pair of stained blue jeans worn at the knees. Definitely not the type to have a Jan Steen or any other masterpiece under his arm.

What Doris had not mentioned was that the man was disturbingly handsome. He had a lean, tanned face under a thatch of sun blond hair and the body of an Olympic swimmer. He also had huge, bright blue eyes blinking pleasantly behind a simple pair of Harry Potter wire rims. Both the man and the package he held were lightly spattered with rain. He wasn't carrying an umbrella. He looked a little older than she was, mid-thirties or so.

Finn smiled. She didn't know what else to do. "Can I help you?"

"I've got this painting," he said, taking the package out from under his arm and holding it out to her. His voice was definitely Oxford—the real thing, not the walnut-in-the-cheeks adenoidal version poached by Lady Ron. The parcel was oblong, twelve by sixteen, just about right for a Jan Steen. He laid it carefully on the desk.

"Please sit," said Finn, gesturing toward the only other chair in the office. "My name is Finn Ryan, by the way." She smiled again.

"William Pilgrim," he said. "Billy. You're an American."

"Columbus, Ohio."

"Good-bye, Columbus."

"Philip Roth."

"His first book."

"Ali McGraw and Richard Benjamin for the Hollywood version. My mom made me watch it on TV once."

"Well," Billy Pilgrim said smiling, "I think we've exhausted that vein of conversation."

"The painting," said Finn.

"The painting." He nodded.

She unwrapped it. Oil on canvas, no frame, the canvas stapled to the stretcher with rusty iron half-moons. It was a representation of another village scene, this one with a half dozen beer swillers sitting on a bench under a tree. Just the kind of thing the artist was famous for. The signature on the bottom was a group of initials: JHS, Jan Havickszoon Steen.

"Very nice," said Finn. Nice but not right.

"Not by Jan Steen," said Pilgrim, picking up her tone.

"I don't think so, no," agreed Finn.

"Why not? It's been in the family forever. Dutch ancestors. Everyone always called it a Jan Steen."

"A Jan Steen of this size probably would have been painted on an oak panel," Finn explained. "If it *had* been painted on canvas, it would have been tacked or glued to the stretcher, not stapled. It would also almost surely have been restretched and relined over three centuries."

"Oh dear."

"And the signature is wrong. He signed his paintings as J. Steen, not with his initials. He hated the name Havickszoon for one thing. It's not all bad news, though," she added.

"Oh?"

"If you're lucky, it might be a Keating."

"Keating?"

"Tom Keating. A British master forger from after World War Two. His forgeries are worth a lot of money on their own now. He specialized in Dutch Masters."

"But not as much as a Jan Steen would fetch."

"Not by a long shot," said Finn.

"You seem to know a great deal about it," said Pilgrim. There was nothing accusatory; he just seemed curious.

Finn shrugged. "I did a double major for my BFA. Dutch golden age and Renaissance painters. I had a professor who did his doctoral dissertation on Jan Steen."

"Steen stuck, so to speak," said Pilgrim, smiling.

Finn laughed. "So to speak." Billy Pilgrim seemed to be taking his disappointment well. She started wrapping up the little painting again. "I can give you a number at the Courtauld Institute to call about Tom Keating if you'd like. They'll give it a look."

Pilgrim thought for a moment, then shook his head. "No, that's all right, Miss Ryan. I quite like it, and if it's not worth a great deal of money, I think I'll keep it. Hang it up in the salon."

"Salon?" Finn asked. He didn't look like a hairdresser but maybe he meant something else. In England they spoke English, not American.

"I live on a boat," the blond man said. "The *Busted Flush*."

"Funny name," said Finn, tying the string back around the parcel. "Trouble with the toilet?"

It was Billy Pilgrim's turn to laugh. "It's a poker term," he said.

Finn nodded. "As in royal flush."

"A busted flush is a flush you fail to complete—ten, jack, queen, king without the ace. In my case it's a literary term as well. It was the name of Travis McGee's boat in the John D. MacDonald series. I did my dissertation on MacDonald as a matter of fact."

"As in doctoral dissertation?"

"That's right." Pilgrim blushed apologetically. "I was a bit of a prodigy actually. French literature for my bachelor's, as you call it, Spanish for the postgraduate, and modern literature for the doctorate." He made a little snorting sound. "Not good for much, really, when you get right down to it. I thought about teaching, but then I thought about it again and decided I preferred messing about in boats a great deal more, so there you are."

Finn realized that any business part of the conversation had run out and she wanted to keep on talking with him anyway. "Who's Travis Magee?"

"Good Lord!" Billy exclaimed. "You're an American! It's like saying you never heard of John Wayne." He paused. "You really don't know?"

"No idea."

"Did you ever see a film called *Cape Fear*?"

"Sure. Robert De Niro and Nick Nolte."

"Gregory Peck and Robert Mitchum actually, but that's another story." Pilgrim frowned. "The point is the man who wrote the book it was based on was John D. MacDonald. He also wrote twenty-one Travis McGee novels, each one of them with a color in the title. *Darker Than Amber, The Green Ripper, The Deep Blue Good-by*."

"And McGee lived on his boat, the *Busted Flush*."

"Yes. A houseboat. Slip F18, Bahia Del Mar, Fort Lauderdale."

"You live in a houseboat, then?"

"No. Hout Bay 40 with a Marconi Rig. One of the South African designs, before Dix went to Virginia."

Finn didn't have the slightest idea what he was talking about, but she enjoyed listening. "This

Travis McGee is a fictional character we're talking about?"

"Yes."

"You seem to know all the details."

"He was an ex–football player with a bad knee who went around 'salvaging' stolen property and rescuing damsels in distress. Robin Hood and Mike Hammer combined. The archetype for the lovable rogue in American literature. The man every red-blooded Yankee secretly yearned to be. The *Playboy* magazine ideal."

"Just the sort of guy a red-blooded Yankee girl would loathe and despise," Finn said with a laugh.

"Perhaps so," Pilgrim sighed. "But he was a man of his time and he had an enormous cultural effect. He was your Daniel Boone and Davy Crockett, John Wayne, Huck Finn, and Tom Sawyer all rolled into one. The last great American adventurer, the first great American antihero." Pilgrim flushed again. "I've been lecturing."

"Maybe you should have been a teacher after all," said Finn.

"Good Lord, what a horrible suggestion!" said Pilgrim. "All those children with runny noses and Gameboys in their satchels. I'd go mad!" He stood up. "I'm afraid I've taken up too much of your time, Miss Ryan. I'm terribly sorry."

"It was a pleasure, Mr. Pilgrim, the high point of my day, to be honest." She stood and handed him his rewrapped painting. They shook hands. His grip was warm and strong without being overly masculine. He had calluses. These hands worked for a living. She liked that. She liked Billy Pilgrim. She wondered if it would frighten him off to ask him out for a drink or something. She'd never been very good at that kind of thing.

"Thank you for your time, Miss Ryan. You've been most kind." He stood there looking a little adolescent and awkward.

"No problem, really. And it's Finn. Miss Ryan sounds like a kindergarten teacher."

"You could teach the little creatures all about *Menheer* Jan Steen," said Billy.

"And then wipe their runny noses."

"Gad." He looked appropriately horrified and then smiled, his face lighting up and his eyes twinkling.

"Off to the *Busted Flush*?" She was groping now, and beginning to feel like an idiot.

"Not quite yet. I've a flat in town. Appointment in the City tomorrow. Solicitors and such. I've been trying to sell a little seaside property of mine in Cornwall." First the painting, now a house. It sounded as though he was going somewhere.

"Cottage?" Finn asked.

Billy nodded. "Something like that."

"Going on vacation?"

"I thought I'd take a bit of a cruise."

"Away from the rain?"

"Hopefully."

"Any particular destination?"

"I haven't given it much thought."

"What would Travis McGee do under the circumstances?"

"Make himself a Boodles martini and talk to Meyer about it."

"Meyer?"

"His philosophical friend a few slips over at Bahia del Mar. He had a boat called the *John Maynard Keynes*."

"He must have been an economist."

"Something like that. It's never really made clear in the books."

"A Wall Street type?"

"Yes, a retired one."

Now they'd really reached the end of the conversation.

"Well . . ." he said.

"Well . . ." she answered. "It was great fun meeting you. Perhaps I'll see you again." Last chance. If he didn't pick up the hint it would all end right here, a road not traveled at all.

"I do hope so." A polite smile, a little shy, and then he turned and he was gone. Finn dropped back into her chair. The English Travis Magee had just ridden off into the rainy sunset. To top things off Ronnie appeared in her office doorway ten minutes later. He looked like her grade school nerd friend Arthur Beandocker having one of his asthma attacks. His face was tomato red above the knot of his expensive tie, his eyes were bulging, and a vein on his temple was throbbing like a kettledrum.

"His Grace was here and I wasn't informed." His voice was as choked as the look on his face.

Finn stared. "Who?"

"His Grace, the duke, of course!"

Finn had a sudden image of Ronnie greeting John Wayne at the entrance to Mason-Godwin. "There hasn't been any duke here."

"Doris sent someone to you named William Pilgrim, correct?"

"Billy. A boat bum according to him."

"Billy, as you call him," said Ronnie with a shiver, "is Lord William Wilmot Pilgrim, Baron of Neath, Earl of Pendennis, Duke of Kernow."

"He said his name was Billy. He never mentioned being all of that."

"What did he want?"

"He had a painting he wanted evaluated."

"What did you tell him?"

"He thought it was a Jan Steen. It wasn't. It was a reasonably good fake."

"You aren't qualified to tell a Jan Steen from a forgery, Miss Ryan. That is why we employ experts in the field."

"It was fixed to the stretcher with staples, Ron."

"That doesn't mean anything! It would have been relined!"

"But it wasn't," Finn answered calmly, biting her tongue. "It was on the original canvas. A dead giveaway, as you know. An original Steen canvas would be three hundred years old. Unlined it would have rotted away decades ago. It was a fake. There was no question about it. The signature was wrong as well. It might have been a Tom Keating done on a bad day, but that's it."

"You told him this?"

"Of course. Why would I lie?"

"It was not your place to tell him anything. I should have been informed. His Grace the duke is potentially a very valuable customer and not to be dealt with by a lesser employee of the firm."

"A lesser employee?" Finn said coldly.

"His Lordship requires a certain level of deference and respect you are unable to provide, I'm afraid," said Ronnie with a sniff. Finn resisted the urge to kick the pompous idiot where it would do the most good. Instead she stood up from behind her desk and shrugged into her raincoat.

"I'm going home," she said. "Back to my lesser flat in Crouch End." She picked up her umbrella.

"You'll do no such thing!" stormed Ronnie. He moved to stand directly in her way. He glanced at the expensive, wafer-thin Patek Philippe that glittered on his wrist like a large gold coin. "It's not gone five yet."

"I'm going home," repeated Finn. "And if you don't get out of the way, I'm going to do exactly what my self-defense coach at school told me to do to people like you."

The tomato look deepened on Ronnie's face, but he stood aside. "I'll have you sacked!" he hissed as she pushed by him.

"Sack you," she muttered, heading down the stairs. She'd had enough of Ronald DePanay-Cottrell, enough of Mason-Godwin, and enough of the whole damn country.

True to his word, there was a message from Doris on her answering machine by the time she got back to her flat. She'd been summarily fired. A final paycheck would be mailed to her and the Home Office notified of her unemployment status in regard to her work visa. All very cold and efficient. There was also an envelope put through her letterbox from a London lawyer. The perfect end to a perfect day. To console herself she went down to the restaurant below and splurged on a twelve-ounce Daisy Cheese Daddy with coleslaw, chili fries, and a side of guacamole. To hell with the South Beach Diet and to hell with bloody England.

3

SIR JAMES R. TULKINGHORN, Q.C., KCBE.
Barrister & Solicitor
47 Great Russell St, No. 12, London WC1.

Telephone: 020 7347 1000 Cable: Tulkinglaw

Dear Miss Ryan:
It would be to your particular advantage to attend a meeting in my chambers tomorrow afternoon at 2:00 p.m. Should you decide to appear please be so kind as to bring some form of picture identification with you, preferably a valid passport. Until then I shall remain
Yours truly,

James Tulkinghorn, Esq.

The letter was signed with an illegible scrawl. It was dated the previous day and had been hand-delivered; there was neither stamp nor postmark. It looked as though the signature had been scratched with a quill; there were little spatters of ink sprayed around on the creamy, linen stationery. The man's name, the letter, and even the address were all like something out of Dickens. She knew that because she now sat three doors down from it at the local Starbucks. Tulkinghorn's office was above an antiquarian bookstore named Jarndyce, which looked equally Dickensian with its small, dusty display window and its dim lighting. According to a plaque on the wall, the famous Victorian children's book illustrator Randolph Caldecott had once lived there.

She slid the letter back into its envelope and placed it in her shoulder bag beside her passport. Not for the first time, she found herself wondering what she was doing here. She'd never heard of this man Tulkinghorn and she had no idea what particular advantage there could be in meeting with him. On the other hand, with the sudden passing of Mason-Godwin from her life she didn't have much else on her plate right now, except for getting out of Dodge.

Remarkably, the rain had moved on to some other unlucky part of Britain, at least for the time being. It was sunny and warm so she'd chosen one of the little café tables outdoors. She drank her Americano and nibbled on a biscotti as she looked around. On the far side of Great Russell Street a little farther down the crowds were gathering in the big open courtyard in front of the British Museum, standing like some enormous transplanted Greek temple in the middle of London.

Outside the wrought-iron fence the huge polished black German tour buses with their dark-tinted windows gleamed like giant beetles, tourists spilling out of them onto the sidewalk like pale little maggots in Lederhosen. They chattered excitedly and scuttled across the sun-bright courtyard, vanishing into the gloomy depths behind the row of giant columns, intent on an afternoon of "kultur" peering at the famous Rosetta Stone, the famous Bog Man, and the infamous Elgin Marbles; this after all was one of the settings for *The Mummy* and its sequel. If it was good enough for Brendan Fraser it was good enough for a *hausfrau* from Stuttgart and her husband, *nicht whar*? Finn made a little snorting sound and took a sip of her coffee. She'd spent too long under Lady Ron's thumb; she was getting as cynical as he was.

"Hello." It was a familiar voice. She looked up, shading her eyes in the bright, early afternoon sun. It was Billy Pilgrim or, more properly, His Grace the duke of whatever and all the rest of it. This time there was no Harvard sweatshirt. He wore a well-tailored suit, a nice oxford-cloth shirt in pale blue, and a tie to match. The shoes were shiny, the hair was brushed, and the cheeks and chin were clear of stubble.

"You clean up well, my lord," said Finn.

"You know, then."

"I was told in no uncertain terms. In fact I was fired for not knowing your pedigree," she said, unable to keep the chill out of her voice.

"Oh dear!" The blond-haired man looked horrified. He dropped down into the chair across from her. "I can talk to them if you'd like, explain the circumstances . . . make them understand." Finn caught the edge in the last words. The pedigree she'd mentioned had weight and he knew it.

She shrugged off the suggestion. "No sweat. It had to happen sooner or later. I couldn't take much more of that place."

"But still, I mean, really . . ."

"It's okay." She paused, looking at him squarely. The silence went on. Across the street somebody yelled something in very loud German. It sounded like a drill sergeant giving an order instead of a mother calling to her children. Finally Finn spoke. "This isn't a coincidence, is it, meeting like this?"

Pilgrim blushed redly. On him it was cute. She remembered the name of his boat, the *Busted Flush*. With a "tell" like that he'd be a lousy poker player.

"No, I'm afraid not," Pilgrim answered.

"You knew I'd be here?"

"Not this particular spot, but I knew you were coming to Great Russell Street this afternoon, or at least I hoped you would be."

"How?" Then she made the connection. "Tulkinghorn."

Pilgrim nodded. "Sir James is my family's solicitor. One of them at any rate."

"And coming to the auction house, that didn't just happen, either."

"No. You are mentioned as a beneficiary in a relative's will as I understand it. The circumstances are a little peculiar. I wanted to see who you were."

"Did you know the painting was a fake?"

"No." He laughed. "I was always told it was a Jan Steen. I should have known better. Half of my mother's jewelry was paste as well." He smiled shyly. "Ours is a hollow dukedom, I'm afraid. Not like the old days back in the twelfth century, plundering with Richard the Lionheart, whacking the Saracen hordes and all that." He laughed.

"Sounds like fun," said Finn. "So you really did want to sell it? The painting, I mean."

"Rather." He nodded emphatically. "The *Flush* could use a refit and a hull scraping, not to mention the family pile on the coast. Falling to bits it is. Even the National Trust doesn't want it, and it's up to its ears in the tax. *Meur ras a'gas godrik dhe'n wiasva ma!*" The last had a rolling, rhythmic sound like music. It was beautiful, like something from *The Lord of the Rings.*

"What language is that?" asked Finn, delighted.

"The language of Pendragon and Trebarwith Strand, the language of Tintagel and King Arthur."

"Cornish."

"It is and I am," said the duke. He held out a hand across the little table. "Am I forgiven for my deception?"

"I suppose so, Your Grace," Finn answered. She shook his hand.

"It's still Billy," he said. "No one calls me Your Grace except Tulkinghorn and my great-aunt Elizabeth."

"Your great-aunt Elizabeth?"

"The queen," said Billy.

"You're kidding!"

"Unhappily I am not. A great disappointment to all my cousins, I am, to be sure. I am one of that vast spawn of Victoria and Albert, discounting a few indiscretions along the way as I am given to understand. I should have amounted to more. I don't even play polo!"

"How dreadful."

He waggled his fingers. "I'm left-handed. They don't allow left-handed polo players with the exception of cousin Charles."

"The prince?"

"That's the one." He grinned. "No left-handed airline pilots, either."

"I never thought much about it."

"The world's largest invisible minority. Terribly oppressed we are, except for Bill Gates. He's left-handed as well."

"So is Bill Clinton."

"True, but then again, so is George Bush the Elder."

"Michelangelo," said Finn.

"Leonardo da Vinci," countered Billy Pilgrim.

"Kurt Cobain."

"Who?"

"A dead musician," explained Finn.

"Great-Aunt Elizabeth."

"I didn't know that."

"Queen Victoria as well. Second cousin William. It runs in the family."

Finn laughed. "We're getting silly. We should stop."

"Agreed." Billy glanced at his watch, a big heavy thing in a steel casing that would have looked appropriate on a diver. A long way from the thin little bauble worn by Ronnie. "It's just gone two. Sir James will be waiting. Finished your coffee?"

Finn nodded and stood up. They headed down the sidewalk to the narrow doorway leading to the offices above the bookstore at number 47.

"What are these peculiar circumstances you mentioned?" asked Finn as they climbed the dark stairs.

"I'm not entirely sure. Tulkinghorn was a little evasive on the telephone."

They reached the second floor and went down a short corridor. Tulkinghorn's was the first door on the right. Billy opened it and ushered Finn into the room. If the lawyer's letter had been out of Dickens, the man's office was positively Edwardian.

There were three rooms in all, a boardroom to the right, a small, book-lined library to the left, and the actual office in the center of the suite. There was no room for a secretary. A large oak desk with an inlaid, dark red leather center stood between the two large windows that overlooked Great Russell Street. The walls on either side of the windows were decorated with dour hand-tinted foxhunting prints.

There was a thin, worn rug on the wide-planked polished floor and a brick fireplace on the left. An electric fire brooded coldly in the hearth. Everything was paneled in dark-framed squares of exotic woods like lime, black walnut, and Brazilian cherry. The old-fashioned office chair behind the desk was upholstered in the same deep morocco leather as the desk inlay. There was an old-fashioned inkstand on the desk, complete with an onyx base, and an ebony straight pen with a bright gold nib. There was a green-shaded desk lamp on the left and a pipe rack and a tobacco jar on the right. The tobacco jar was blue Delft with a brass lid and the painted figure of an Indian in a headdress. There was a crest on the side facing Finn showing three letters, VOC, intertwined.

The man seated in the chair was dressed in a dark suit and a shirt with a high collar. He looked like something out of a Merchant Ivory film; an Edwardian face to match the furniture: dark gray eyes above sagging pouches of seamed skin, long cheeks, thin, bloodless lips, and thinning iron gray hair swept back from a broad, heavily lined forehead that at the moment served as a resting place for a pair of very heavy-looking horn-rimmed reading glasses.

"Sir James," said Billy.

The man creaked up out of the chair and bowed slightly. "Your Grace," he replied. He held out his hand and Billy shook it. Tulkinghorn was in his seventies at least, the hand skeletal and gnarled with arthritis. Finn noticed how gently Billy took it in his.

"This is Miss Fiona Ryan," said Billy, introducing her.

"Finn." She smiled, and took the old man's hand lightly. Tulkinghorn lowered himself into his chair and gestured toward the leather armchairs set in front of his desk. There was no small talk. The gray-haired man looked down at a pile of papers on his desk, adjusted the reading glasses, and pursed his thin, unhappy-looking lips. This, Finn thought, was not a man who smiled very much and probably never laughed.

"This present matter is in regard to your cousin on your mother's side, Your Grace, a Mr. Pieter Boegart, residing at, among other places"—here he glanced down at his desk and rustled through the papers—"flat nine, 51 South Street, Mayfair, W1."

"He disappeared as I recall," said Billy.

Tulkinghorn nodded. "Quite so. Precisely twelve months ago. Somewhere in the Far East as I recall, Sarawak or Brunei or some such." Tulkinghorn slid open a drawer in his desk and took out a three-by-five color photograph. It looked like an enlarged copy of a passport picture. It showed a middle-aged man with a narrow face, thinning red hair, and a full beard. He looked like a Viking.

"A bit of an adventurer," Billy said.

"That is certainly one way of describing the man," murmured the lawyer, clearly insinuating that he had some other word for him. "At any rate Mr. Boegart left instructions for me in the event that he had not returned to London within a year or had not somehow contacted me to change those instructions. These instructions were also to apply in the event of his death by violence rather than natural causes. The year was up Wednesday week."

"How old was . . . is this Boegart person?" Finn asked.

"Mr. Boegart is fifty-eight, or he was as of the third of this month."

"And what does he have to do with me?"

The old man neatened the pile of papers in front of him. His lips thinned a little more and his frown deepened. He reached out to the pipe rack, chose a curved briar, and filled it from the jar. Reaching into the pocket of his jacket, he removed a plain kitchen match and lit it on a sulfur yellow thumbnail. He puffed, filling the air with aromatic smoke.

He took the pipe out of his mouth and coughed briefly. Then he spoke. "As I understand it, Mr. Boegart was your mother's lover for a number of years, her paramour, so to speak." Tulkinghorn cleared his throat again, looking uncomfortable. "Mr. Boegart was of the opinion that there was some chance that he was in fact your father." He sat back in his chair.

"What?" Finn exclaimed.

"Good Lord," said Billy.

"Um," murmured the old lawyer around the stem of his pipe.

"I don't understand this at all," said Finn, recovering a little. "I mean, it's crazy. My father was

Dr. Lyman Andrew Ryan, and he was a professor of archaeology at the University of Ohio."

Tulkinghorn fussed with his papers, muttering to himself. He resurfaced, nodding. "Yes, here we are," he said. "According to my information, your father was a senior visiting fellow at Magdalene College Cambridge, which was in fact his alma mater."

"That's right. He was there during World War Two. They asked him back to teach sometime in the sixties."

"Nineteen sixty-nine to be exact," said Tulkinghorn. "He spent ten years there, off and on between digs. He returned to the University of Ohio in the summer of 1979 to head up their department of archaeology."

Finn nodded. "My mother wanted me to be born in the States."

"Indeed," murmured Tulkinghorn. "Be that as it may, Pieter Boegart read archaeology at Magdalene from 1970 to 1973. Lyman Ryan was his tutor and thesis adviser. Between 1973 and June of 1979, he was a lecturing assistant to your father as well as field supervisor on several of his digs in Central America."

"He knew my father. That doesn't make him my mother's lover."

"No," Tulkinghorn agreed. He put the pipe down on his desk and opened the center drawer. He withdrew a small package of letters held together by a thick rubber band. The letters looked old. The envelopes were pale green, her mother's favorite color. "These make Pieter Boegart your mother's lover." He used one bony index finger to push the pile of letters across the desk toward Finn.

She stared at them. "What are they?"

"Love letters. Billets-doux as the French like to call them. From your mother to Mr. Boegart. They are all dated and they are quite explicit, I'm afraid."

"You've read them?"

"Mr. Boegart insisted when I expressed concern at his bequest."

"Why would you express concern?" Finn asked sourly, her eyes still on the package in front of her.

"Miss Ryan, Pieter Boegart is a majority heir to one of the largest shipping lines in the world. Netherlands-Boegart actually *is* the largest container corporation in the world. The fortune is immense. To consider paternity, let alone accept it, is a serious legal matter. You could well become what is commonly referred to as, I believe, as a spanner in the works."

"A what?" Finn asked.

"A monkey wrench in the gears," Billy translated quietly.

"A problem," said Finn.

"Indeed," said Tulkinghorn, glancing at Pilgrim over his reading glasses.

"Why did Boegart think I was his child?"

"The timing," replied the old man. "According to Mr. Boegart, his relationship with your mother ended in August of 1979, shortly before she left England with your father. You were born in May of 1980, some nine months later. You were, um, almost certainly conceived in this country. At Cambridge, presumably."

"That doesn't mean it was him."

"The letters would indicate that your father, Lyman Ryan, was incapable of paternity."

"What is that supposed to mean?" Finn asked. "My father was infertile?"

"No," said Tulkinghorn. He looked excruciatingly uncomfortable now. "It would seem from the letters that he was incapable of the act"—he paused and raised a hand to the knot of his tie—"the act of coitus."

The word was so archaic and clinical that Finn would have laughed out loud if the whole thing wasn't so awful and so bleakly intimate.

The old man went on. "It would also appear that he tacitly condoned the relationship between Mr. Boegart and your mother." He paused. "There was a difference in age, as I understand it."

"Twenty years," Finn said flatly. When her parnets had met, her father had been in his early forties, her mother barely twenty-one. A May–December marriage, teacher and student. Ten years later it was her mother's turn. She had been now thirty-one, the young student, Boegart, only twenty.

Finn stared at the photograph on the desk in front of her. Her father had no red hair or freckles, but her mother's hair had been a deep auburn, and in the summer, there was always a delicate sprinkling of freckles across the bridge of her nose. It was possible, maybe even probable. There was a terrible irony to it all. In a few moments she had learned more about her parents than she had ever wanted to know. Things no child *should* know. "Why are you telling me this?" Finn said angrily.

"I'm sorry," said Tulkinghorn. "I mean neither to offend nor to anger. Your blood relationship with Mr. Boegart is irrelevant with regard to his own will and your status as a beneficiary. Any claims to the rest of the Boegart holdings, most of which are in trust, will most likely require some form of confirmation. DNA analysis, that is. I felt that you should be forewarned. News of this will inevitably reach the press. There will be consequences."

"I'm not making any claims to anything," said Finn.

"Quite so," Tulkinghorn said with a nod. "Be that as it may, Mr. Boegart's instructions to you both are quite clear."

"Instructions to us both?" Billy prompted.

"The bequests are cojoint. They involve three items."

"Which are?" Finn asked.

"A painting, which is in the next room, a house, which is in Amsterdam, and the SS *Batavia Queen*, which at last report was somewhere off the western coast of Sarawak."

4

Conrad "Briney" Hanson, captain of the break-bulk freighter *Batavia Queen*, dragged on his Djarum Filter, inhaling the clove-spiced smoke deeply before expelling it with an exasperated sigh, squinting in the harsh tropical sun. He stood on the flying bridge of the old rust bucket, leaning with his elbows on the salt-corroded rail, looking forward.

The bow had swung around on the anchor in the ebbing tide, and three-quarters of a mile away he could see the thick virgin jungle of Tandjung Api. In the distance he could see the white flush of the low waves breaking on the curving sandy beach. It looked deceptively calm but he knew it was an illusion. At low tide this was foul ground with barely six feet of clearance over a long shoal ridge.

If the old fool of an engineer didn't get the engines running soon they'd be trapped here for hours if not actually grounded. He could hear McSeveney belowdecks hammering away with something heavy and cursing in a mixture of Malay pidgin and foulmouthed Scots brogue that would confound even the most knowledgeable linguistic expert.

The dark-haired, deep-tanned captain took another drag on his kerak native cigarette, then snuffed it out in the sand-filled tin can duct-taped to the pipe rail for just that purpose. He glanced down to the fo'c'sle deck, baking hot in the sun. Eli, the powerful-looking, bare-chested able seaman from Mozambique, was painting things while his skinny friend Armand scaled rust. Eli was as black as the inside of a piece of coal, and Armand, who hailed from somewhere in the Balkans, was pale as a vampire and always wore a strange vinyl Cossack hat with ear flaps to keep the sun off his shaved head. They were a strange pair: black Eli with his tattoos and the long wormlike scars across his back that he never talked about; Armand with his pale skin and his hat.

Briney Hanson stared out toward the jungle. Who was he to call them strange? What was a good Danish boy from Thorsminde doing out here in the land of headhunters and China Sea pirates, hauling shipments of fluorescent lightbulbs and bicycles from Bangkok to Shanghai or cocoa powder, handbags, and car parts from Kaohsiung to

Manila? A man who spent his days weaving through the reefs and islands and his nights occasionally fighting off stolen fishing boats full of Abu Sayyaf terrorists or MILF fanatics waving RPG rocket launchers and Chinese AK-47S. Not to mention driving the ancient converted World War Two corvette through the odd typhoon, monsoon, or tsunami?

The answer to that was relatively simple. He didn't like herring. He didn't like how they looked, tasted, or smelled, especially pickled, and he certainly didn't want to spend his lifetime catching them like his father. He'd always been in favor of a simple live-and-let-live philosophy; he'd stay away from the herring and the herring would stay away from him.

After that the rest of the unraveling was easy. Five years in the Royal Danish Navy right out of high school, three in icebreakers, two in supply ships, able seaman in the Danish Merchant Marine, mostly on cargo ships and livestock carriers, working his way up steadily through the ranks until he had his master's papers, then losing everything in a drunken knife fight in Kowloon. Waking up in a Manila flophouse having his pocket picked by a ten-year-old boy, a conversation in a waterfront bar with the leather-faced captain, Nick Lumbera, signing on with him as mate aboard the *Batavia Queen*, then replacing him when dear old Nicomedes died of a stroke in the midst of a force-nine gale in the Malacca Strait. The *Queen* was carrying a bellyful of mentholated cough drops to Bombay, the whole ship smelling like a bad cold.

He'd brought the ship through the gale and the strait with Lumbera safely stowed away in the hold's cold room and delivered the cough drops to Bombay on schedule. Pleased, the ship's owner, the Shanghai-Sumatra Shipping Corporation, a tiny subsidiary of the Boegart maritime empire, asked Briney if he'd like to stay on as the ship's master without too many questions being asked. After all it wasn't easy to find qualified people willing to endure the grueling backwater tramp through two dozen primitive shallow water ports. He'd taken the job with almost no hesitation since it was unlikely he'd ever be offered anything better.

That was a decade ago. In a few years from now, he'd be able to call himself middle-aged. He had nothing saved, no pension, no family. The *Batavia Queen* was almost seventy and reaching the end of her useful life. Without a prohibitively expensive refit, it was only a matter of time before Hanson was given the order to take the old girl to her grave at Alang, that bleak spot on the Indian coast known as the Beach of Doom. It would be the end of his useful life as well. His own wrecking beach would most likely be at the bottom of a bottle in a sweltering room above a Rangoon bar. He butted another cigarette in the sand can. It was amazing how easy it was to get from there to here, from then to now.

"Jakolin mo ako!" The watertight manhole on the portside of the main deck directly below the flying bridge crashed open and McSeveney appeared, the narrow, darkly freckled face streaked with grease, his hair bunched in a nylon net made out of one leg of a woman's panty hose. *"Putang inang trabaho ito! Ya wee houghmagandie Jockbrit! Ya bluidy ming mowdiewark sasunnach sheepshagging shite-skitter!"* He hawked and spit a gob of something semisolid over the side of the ship. *"Cack-arse ham-shanker!* Gives me the *diareaky,* it do, *tam-tit fanny-bawz* thing!" He kicked the mushroom vent at the base of the deckhouse. *"Yah Hoor! Yah pok-pok Ang okie mo amoy ang pussit!"* He paused. *"Cao ni zu zong shi ba dai!"* he added in Mandarin, just in case there was any doubt.

Hanson knew that Willy could curse for an hour without repeating himself. "Problem, Scottie?" he called.

McSeveney peered up at him, his beady black eyes squinting. He looked like an enraged gopher in an ancient pair of striped coveralls. "I hate being called that, as you well know!" Willy snarled, his Edinburgh accent sharp as vinegar and thick as molasses. "That man was no Scot, he was a bluidy Canadian, and this is no *cludgie* starship—that's fer dammit sure. So you can shut yer *geggie!*'' He hawked over the side again and stared belligerently up at Hanson.

William Tung McSeveney was, according to him at any rate, the result of the unlikely mating of a red-haired Scottish clerk working for Jardine-Matheson tallying opium profits in the 1800s and a whore from Macau named Tung Lo May, a name that always reminded Hanson of something you might find on a Chinese take-out menu. The combining of the nationalities continued enthusiastically for several generations, the final result being Willy, raised in the slums of Fountainbridge in a Chinese laundry and enrolling in Sea Cadets at Bruntsfield School where Sean Connery had gone some years earlier. His only dream had been to get out of Auld Reekie, the Smoke, Edinburgh, as rapidly as possible. At fourteen he'd signed on the SS *Lanarkshire* as an unlicensed engineer, fourth grade, bound for Africa and Asia. He'd never set foot in Scotland again, working on fifty different Straits Trade ships from Hong Kong to Rangoon until he finally found a home and a set of old Scotch boilers on the *Batavia Queen*.

The *Queen* was older than anyone aboard her. Originally built as a Flower Class Corvette K-49 at the Vancouver Shipyards on Canada's west coast, she was lent to the Royal Australian Navy and spent the war years dodging Japanese torpedoes and carrying troops through MacArthur's Philippines from Darwin to Rabaul. After being paid off at Subic Bay at the end of the war, she was bought by Burns Philips, given the name she still bore, and spent the next twenty years as an interisland trading ship, her belly torn apart to create a crude cargo hold.

In the sixties she was transformed again—this time into a salvage and survey tug traveling the same routes in search of wrecks and sunken ships from the war that could be raised and floated for scrap. The scrap business eventually self-destructed and the *Queen* went back to being an interisland trader once more, being passed from owner to owner over the years like an old streetwalker in decline, eventually finding herself carried on the Boegart List almost as an oversight.

Barely two hundred feet long and thirty-three feet wide, she had a draft of eleven feet when the pumps were operating. Originally equipped with depth charges, a four-inch gun forward, antiaircraft pom-poms, and a pair of twenty-millimeter cannons, she'd long ago been stripped down to a rusty hulk with only an old twelve-gauge in the captain's cabin for protection and a few other bits of weaponry hidden here and there just in case. Originally designed for a crew of seventy, she now got along with eleven, from Hanson on the bridge to McSeveney in the engine room and his hulking, mute Samoan wiper, Kuan Kong. There was a single lifeboat in case of emergency: a twenty-seven foot vessel dogged down on makeshift davits in the stern, where the depth charge rails had once been fitted. At best she could barely make twelve knots' headway but usually cruised at closer to seven.

Originally painted in blues and grays, the *Queen* had suffered through a number of color changes over the years from black to green to dull red and back to black again, the superstructure white, the funnel scarlet with a large black B, and everything streaked with rust. The bow and stern quarters and the bridge were wooden-decked and desperately worn while the rest was riveted plate steel. It was a credit to her builders that she was still afloat after almost seventy years of battling through wars, storms, and pounding seas, even though she obviously and sometimes noisily showed her age.

Almost as though in defiance of Hanson's bleak line of thought, there was suddenly a racketing roar from the bowels of the ship as the ancient copper-pot cast-iron steam engine rumbled into shuddering life. A few seconds later, McSeveney's voice came echoing up through the wheelhouse speaking tube.

"Captain! D'ye ken that lovely sound?" he called.

Hanson stepped off the flying bridge and into the small shelter of the wheelhouse. "Thank you, Willy!" he said, bellowing into the old-fashioned funnel-necked instrument. He rang the engine room telegraph himself, repeating the request into the speaking tube. "Ahead slow. Let's get off this reef."

A few seconds later the churning propeller dug in and the *Batavia Queen*, like the reluctant dowager she was, began to move out to sea again.

5

One hundred thirty miles farther up the coast, the notorious pirate known simply as Khan, or sometimes as Tim-Timan, the Faithful One, rested in his temporary home—a native *rumah*, a house built on sticks in the estuary of the Rejang River's northwest channel. His fingers, heavy with gold rings, played with the necklace he wore like worry beads. The necklace was strung with dozens of human teeth, some yellow and dark with age, others whiter and much more recent. One or two still even had gnarled dangling bits of nerve and pulp attached. The necklace had been a gift from his grandfather on his mother's side, the infamous *penghulu*, Temonggong Koh.

From his swinging hammock on the wide verandah Khan could see the other houses of the riverbank village, *rumahs* like his. A few were open-sided bungalow-style barracks built by the

Japanese during the war, and there was even an old longhouse or two like the one his grandfather had been raised in, filled with smoke and laughter and the ghosts of the men, women, and children whose shrunken, withered heads were lined up on the rafters, row after row of trophies from a savage past.

Like many modern members of his tribe, Khan was part Malay, part Chinese, and part indigenous Melenau native, but unlike any other Khan could claim direct descent from the original White Rajah himself, Charles Brooke, the adventurer who came to Sarawak in the mid-1800s and whose family had ruled like Oriental potentates for a hundred years. Not only could he claim it, but he could prove it, for although his brutal features were those of a Chinese-Malay half-caste, Khan had bright blue eyes—blue eyes capable of casting spells, seeing through lies, and envisioning the future, or so some superstitious subjects of his pirate kingdom believed. It was an idea that he encouraged and sometimes even half believed himself.

A brief squall pushed in from the ocean and suddenly the air was full of hissing rain that rattled on the old tin roof of the *rumah* like handfuls of thrown pebbles. Khan slipped out of the hammock and walked to the edge of the covered porch, looking out over the rain-tattered river. His feet were bare on the woven mats that covered the floor and he wore only a simple black-checked sarong. He was thick-bodied and tall, hard muscles rippling, his gold-brown skin gleaming with a faint sheen of perspiration. His hair was jet-black, cut in the severe bowl-and-bang style of his ancestors. He was *iban*, a sea dyak, and every inch a warrior *penghulu* of his clan.

He picked up the cup resting on the verandah railing and took a swallow of the fiery *tuak* rice wine it contained, swishing the harsh liquor around in his mouth, then spitting it out over the railing and into the river below. The rain began to slow, the sound of it on the roof above him tempered to the slow drumming of angry fingers.

Once upon a time, it had seemed that Khan might have traveled on a different path. He was James How Ling Singbat Alaidin Sulaiman Khan back then, the younger son of Sarawak's minister of health under Stephen Kalong Ningkan, a privileged young man who had attended the prestigious Lodge School, won entry into Phillips Academy Andover in America and then went on to Harvard and a combined degree in business administration and international law.

During his long time abroad—more than a decade—letters from his family told of change in his homeland, none of it for the better. Corruption set in like a disease, infecting everything it touched. His father had been ousted from his post, his lands and money taken, and finally his dissenting voice silenced by the swinging blade of an assassin's parang in a Kuching alley.

Returning to his native land, he found his mother dying of despair, his older brother now a high-ranking and corrupt civil servant in the Judiciary, and the country committing slow suicide under the self-serving regime of Haji Abdul Taib Mahmud as her natural resources were auctioned off to the highest bidder, her forests and rivers destroyed, and her people abused and slaughtered. Then his mother died and he was alone.

Taking the few remaining assets that were left to him, James How Ling Khan fled to the upriver jungles of the Rejang, renewing friendships and native family ties, forging a pirate empire that had no allies only enemies, preying on the ships of any nation foolish enough to pass within range of his wrath and his fleet of marauding gunships spread out from Sumatra to Zamboanga in the Sulu Sea, lurking like sea snakes in hidden river bases just like this one.

There was other business as well; there were endless shipments of North Korean methamphetamines and counterfeit American currency to move, raw opium from Vietnam, slipper orchids from Sabah, sometimes special human cargo quietly left on the lonely beaches along Northern Australia's Gulf of Carpentaria, and always, and very profitably, guns and other weapons ferried

to the Kumpulan Mujahidin Malaysia terrorists,
Darul Islam, Abu Sayyaf, Moro National Libera-
tion Front, Jemaah Islamiya, and anyone else prepared to pay Khan's exorbitant freight rates.

Through the beating pulse of the rain Khan
heard another, deeper sound that resolved itself
into the familiar, lumbering thunder of his personal boat, *Black Dragon*, one of a half dozen
World War Two "Karo-Tei" subchasers he'd discovered, forgotten and derelict in an old camou-
flaged pen on an uninhabited island in the Sulu
Sea. Based on stolen plans for the prewar American "Six-Bitter" Coast Guard ships, the Karo-Tei
were sixty-foot-long shallow-draft cutters powered by twin eight-hundred horsepower aircraft
engines and capable of speeds up to thirty-eight
knots.

The small ships were heavily armed with twin
twenty-millimeter cannons and an aft machine-
gun tub. They were completely constructed from
wood, which made their radar shadows almost
invisible, and they carried a crew of fifteen, more
than enough men to capture any unarmed vessel
afloat in any weather. They were the deadliest
weapons in Khan's arsenal, and over the years, he
had made them even more fearsome with
Russian-made RPG rocket launchers, sophisticated
navigation electronics as good as or better than
those of any ships sent against him, and refur-

bished engines that made him fleet as the wind
and just as hard to see or catch.

The narrow, V-hulled boat appeared out of the
misty rain, nosing gently through the shallow waters of the estuary, her flat gray and stealthy paint
job making her as elusive as smoke. Khan smiled
coldly as she approached, powerful engines back-
ing. *Black Dragon*, more a home to him than anything had been since he'd returned to the South
China Sea.

The engines of the sleek gunboat died and *Black
Dragon* slid the last few dozen yards silently. A
seaman appeared on deck, barefoot, picking up
the forward line. The boat bumped gently against
the floating dock directly below the *rumah*, and the
seaman jumped down and secured the line to a
wooden cleat. A short, squat figure stepped out
of the wheelhouse, crossed the deck, and stepped
down onto the dock. He reached the heavy bamboo ladder at the end of the dock and climbed
easily up to the verandah. He was dressed in camouflage greens and combat boots, and there were
three official-looking stars on each one of his ep-
aulettes. His skin was dark, burned to the color
of old leather by the sun after years of exposure.
The man's hard features were Chinese. His name
was Fu Sheng and he was Khan's second in command. The two men had known each other for
almost twenty years.

Khan's old friend clambered onto the porch.

"*Apa kabar*, Dapu Sheng?" Khan asked in Tanjong, an ancient dialect spoken by fewer than a hundred people, most of them members of his own Rejang River clan. "What news?" Dapu was Fu Sheng's nickname: Big Gun.

"*Kaba baik, tuan*," replied Fu Sheng, bowing slightly. "The news is good, master." He continued. "I have spoken with our people at the shipping company. They have confirmed the situation. The ship is some way south of us still."

"And the business in London?"

"It proceeds," said Fu Sheng. He shrugged. London was only a place he'd heard of, never seen, and matters there did not really concern him.

"Follow the ship but do nothing yet. As to London, keep me informed."

"Yes, *tuan*. Will you remain here?"

"Three days, only, then come for me. Those clowns from the Maritime Enforcement Agency are due for one of their patrols. Let them find nothing."

"I don't know why you go to such lengths to hide, *tuan*," said Fu Sheng. "Their pencil has no point," he scoffed. "We have more ships than they do, and more guns."

"I don't want to make war, Dapu Sheng. I want to make money. We pay bribes for that reason— to keep their pencil dull."

"It isn't the honorable thing, *tuan*," growled Fu Sheng, refusing to give in, his voice tinged with anger and regret.

"Perhaps not, old friend, but it is the prudent thing. We live in a world that holds honor in no esteem. It is extinct, just like the words we speak." He reached out and laid his hand on Fu Sheng's broad shoulder. "It is not the time."

"Will the time ever come?"

"Perhaps sooner than you think, Fu Sheng. Our ancestors are calling. If we heed them we shall have our day."

"You speak in riddles, *tuan*."

"Perhaps." Khan smiled. "But then again, what are riddles except mysteries waiting to be solved?"

6

"Very mysterious," said Billy Pilgrim, staring at the painting on its tabletop easel. He and Finn Ryan were standing with James Tulkinghorn in his small, book-lined conference room. The table the easel sat on was oak, dark and very old. It looked as though it belonged in a monastery, and Finn could just imagine silent hooded monks eating their simple meals around it.

The painting itself was small, no more than a foot square. It showed an almost comical little ship, full sailed and high decked, running through stormy seas. In the background was a clearly defined reef with crashing surf and behind that a jungle landscape. The sky was painted in vivid sunset colors. The famous signature appeared in thick, almost italic letters in the lower right-hand corner: *Rembrandt.*

"According to information given to me by the

Boegart archives, the painting is a commissioned portrait of the *Vleigende Draeack,* or *Flying Dragon*—the ship with which Willem Van Boegart made his original fortune in the East Indies. It was painted in 1671. The painting disappeared just after the beginning of World War Two and was recently discovered in a Swiss bank vault."

"It's a 'jacht,' the first of the types of ship used by the Dutch East India Company. It's where we get the term 'yacht,' " Billy supplied.

Tulkinghorn nodded. "Quite so."

"It might be a yacht," said Finn, "but it isn't a Rembrandt."

"I beg your pardon?" Tulkinghorn said, sounding a little offended. "It's signed."

"That doesn't mean very much," responded Finn. "Rembrandt had a workshop and employed dozens of apprentices, all of whom were authorized to sign his name. It's almost like a rubber stamp. On top of that Rembrandt was well known for signing his own name to paintings that he never put a brush to."

"But you can't be sure of that."

"Sure I can," said Finn with a smile. "If it was painted in 1671."

"Why is the date so important?" Billy asked.

"Because Rembrandt died in 1669," she answered. "I'm no expert in the subject, but I remember that much from my art history classes." She reached out and tentatively ran her fingers along the ornate gilded frame. "Interesting, though," she said quietly.

"What is?" Billy asked.

"The frame. I'm almost sure it's by Foggini."

"Who?" Tulkinghorn asked.

"He was a Florentine during the seventeenth century," said Finn. "I spent a year in Florence before going for my master's. I got interested in him then. He was an artist in his own right, a sculptor, but he's most famous now for his picture frames. Frames like this one. Gold, ornate, a lot of decoration."

"I'm not sure I see the point. Why is the frame important?"

"If the painting is a forgery, or a copy, why would you put such a valuable frame around it?"

"Maybe to make people believe in the authenticity of the painting," said Billy.

"But if you're going to all that trouble," mused Tulkinghorn thoughtfully, "why would you ascribe a date to the painting that was incorrect, nay, impossible, and, I would think, extremely easy to prove that it was so?"

It really was amazing, thought Finn; the man spoke like Sherlock Holmes come to life. But the old lawyer was right.

"Can I take a closer look?" Finn asked.

Sir James nodded. "Of course. The painting after all now belongs to you and His Grace."

Finn picked up the little painting. Given the

weight of the ornate frame, the picture itself was quite heavy for its size, which meant that it had been painted on a wood panel, almost certainly oak. One of her night classes at the Courtauld Institute had been about dating wood panels used in painting by dendochronological analysis—counting tree rings. She looked closely at the surface of the painting and immediately saw the weave of canvas in several worn spots near the edges. Canvas over wood? She'd never heard of a painting done that way, and certainly not in the seventeenth century. Frowning, she flipped the painting over. The back of the painting was covered in old, very brittle-looking kraft paper.

"Anyone have a penknife?"

Sir James nodded and reached into the watch pocket of his waistcoat. He took out an old pearl-handled jackknife and snapped it open. The old man gave it to her. She took the little knife and carefully cut along the kraft paper, keeping well away from the edges of the inner frame, or stretcher. She lifted the paper away, revealing the back of the panel. Dark wood. There were several scratched initials, what appeared to be the chalked number 273 , the 7 struck through in the European fashion, and two labels, one, clearly from the Nazi era, the other a simple paper rectangle reading *Kunsthandel J. Goudstikker NV.*

"Goudstikker was the preeminent gallery in Amsterdam," said Finn. "The Nazis cheated him out of everything in 1940. The Dutch government only resolved the whole thing a little while ago. It was big news in the art world."

"This Goudstikker was a person?" Billy asked.

Finn nodded. "Jacques Goudstikker. If I remember the story right, he inherited the gallery from his father."

"What happened to him?"

"He fled Holland on a refugee ship for England, but they wouldn't let him into the country because he was a Jew. He would have been interned. The ship went on to South America with him still aboard. Apparently he had an accident on the ship and died." She stared at the upper edge of the painting. Frayed edges of canvas could be seen, almost glued to the wood with age. "But Goudstikker's not the point."

"What do you mean?" Billy asked.

She pointed to the canvas edging barely visible at the inner edge of the frame. "Most paintings this old get relined every fifty years or so—the original canvas is bonded to a newer blank canvas to give it strength. It's usually done with wax or resin. This is different. The canvas with the ship painting is a mask, a ghost image put over the original wood panel."

"You think there's something underneath?" Sir James said.

"The Nazi label probably dates from 1940. The Goudstikker label is much older. I think somebody took an old Rembrandt copy and stuck it on the wood panel to hide the identity of the original painting from Goering's people."

"How can you be sure?" Billy asked.

"I know a man at the Courtauld who can help us."

"Today?" queried Tulkinghorn.

"Why the sudden urgency?"

"The Amsterdam house," explained Tulkinghorn.

"What about it?" asked Billy.

"Mr. Boegart's instructions are quite clear, I'm afraid," the old man replied. "The house, like the other bequests, must be taken into possession personally and by both of you within fifteen days or the items will revert to the estate."

"The boat as well?" said Finn. "That means we have to go to Amsterdam and then Malaysia? All within two weeks?"

"Precisely, Miss Ryan." Sir James cleared his throat. "And the *Batavia Queen* is a ship, not a boat."

"What's the difference?" Finn asked, suddenly irritated with Tulkinghorn's old-fashioned nitpicking.

"The usual definition is that a ship is big enough to carry its own boat," said Billy. "But this is all madness. Why on earth is Boegart doing it?"

"At a guess, I should venture to say that he is trying to tell you something," offered Tulkinghorn.

"He's trying to get us to follow in his footsteps," Finn said.

"But why?" Billy asked.

Finn looked at the ornately framed object on the table in front of them, still bearing the ugly emblem of its violent past and the name of a man long dead. "I think it starts with the painting," she answered. "And that means a trip to the Courtauld."

7

Somerset House is a gigantic neoclassical building a quarter mile long. Its original function in 1775 was to be larger, more imposing, and more important than any other so-called national building in the world. Its secondary function was to provide office space for every government bureaucracy in England anyone could think of, from the tax department and the Naval Office down to the office of the King's Bargekeeper, the Public Lottery, and the office of Peddlers and Hawkers. Over the years the bureaucracies have come and gone, but the huge building always remains. It occupies a single enormous block of London real estate bounded by the Strand, Lancaster Place, Surrey Street, and the Victoria Embankment.

When it moved from its old quarters in Portman Square to the Somerset House North Wing on the Strand in 1989, the Courtauld Institute of Art, with all its galleries, laboratories, lecture theaters, and libraries, barely made a ripple at its new home. Few people outside the rarified world of art history would have known the Courtauld even existed if it hadn't been for the less than illustrious tenure of its onetime director and Surveyor of the Queen's Pictures, the infamous and disgraced KGB spy, Sir Anthony Blunt. The Courtauld, however, managed to survive the revelations about its former director's seedy past, and over the years it became one of the world's great postgraduate institutions concerned with art in all its aspects.

Dr. Alpheus Duff Shneegarten, professor emeritus in the Department of Conservation at the Courtauld, was a very short, very round man in his eighties who might well have been the model for Tolkien's Hobbit. He had a large head that was ten percent snow-white hair, forty percent hooked patrician nose, and the rest of it jutting chin with an ancient curved briar stuck between large, nicotine-stained teeth and a pair of smiling lips. His intelligent eyes were sparkling blue, and he looked as though he was always on the verge of delivering the punch line of a particularly dirty joke. Shneegarten was invariably dressed in a decades-out-of-date gray Harris tweed three-piece suit no matter what the weather. On his overlarge feet, he wore ancient Birkenstock sandals. He had been born in Germany or Argentina, no one knew for sure which. According to Shneegarten he still lived in England using a student's visa.

He was, as he'd once told Finn: "Entirely unique. Search for Shneegarten on your Giggle or whatever you call it and you will find nothing. Nothing, I tell you! I am unique among men! There is only one Shneegarten and he is me!" The old man had been at the institute since before the war and had been friend and adviser to all three founders, industrialist Samuel Courtauld, diplomat and collector Lord Lee of Fareham, and the art historian Sir Robert Witt.

Shneegarten had been a pioneer in the field of X-ray fluorescence and infrared analysis of paintings. Using these methods he had conceived of and created a database of artists' fingerprints that had saved more than one museum's curator from being fooled by clever forgeries.

Retired from active teaching long ago, Shneegarten now occupied a rabbit warren of lofty attic rooms on the top floor of the institute, which was only accessible by climbing several sets of dusty staircases and one extremely rickety spiral one made out of cast iron that shivered and clanged as Finn Ryan and Billy Pilgrim climbed it. In one of these attic rooms they found the professor bent over an immense canvas that looked like some kind of Turkish or Moroccan street scene. Shneegarten was examining a tiny square of the painting with a jeweler's loupe screwed into the socket of his right eye and he was rubbing a cotton swab delicately over the area. There was a faint odor of ordinary soap.

It was late afternoon now and it had started raining again; drops pattering lightly on the large, soot-grimy skylight overhead. The illumination on the room was an almost magical silver that seemed to fill the atmosphere with a foreshadowing intensity. He stood up as Finn and Billy stepped into the workroom and popped the jeweler's loupe out of his eye.

"Ah," he said with a smile. "My American girlfriend!" He winked at Billy. "Believe me, sir, if I was only seventy years younger, I would sweep her off her feet and have my way with her! Depend on it!"

"And I'd probably let you," said Finn, smiling as she poked the man lightly in his round, protruding belly. He laughed uproariously and poked her back. She introduced Billy.

"Ah yes, the impoverished lord you mentioned. I'm honored, Your Grace."

"William, or Billy if you'd like. Your Grace makes me sound like the Archbishop of Canterbury."

Shneegarten smiled.

"What are you working on?" Finn asked.

"A dirty Delacroix," the old man grunted wearily. "Another one of those dreadful things he painted in Tangier, people rioting, women with improbable breasts being raped in improbable positions, horses underfoot dying awful deaths. A terrible lot of meaningless activity and violence. The Quentin Tarantino of his day!" He nodded toward the package under Billy's arm. They'd wrapped it in Tulkinghorn's salmon-pink copy of the *Financial Times* and tied it up with twine. "That is for me?" said Shneegarten.

"Yes," said Finn. Billy handed the package to the professor. He sliced the string with a scalpel, neatly took off the newspaper, laying it aside on the worktable, and looked at the painting.

He nodded. "The frame is almost certainly Foggini as you said on the telephone." He screwed the loupe into his eye socket again and bent down. "Brushstrokes are appropriate for Rembrandt's studio, although I would say the subject matter looks more like Jan van Leiden or Willem van der Velde. Just look at that sky! Those Dutch, they always painted the sky as though the world was about to end." He flipped the painting over and, using a small, stainless steel tool like a stiff putty knife, he popped the painting easily out of the frame. "Very odd," he muttered, his white eyebrows rising. "Canvas over a wood panel. I would say that the canvas is from the correct period, perhaps 1660 or so, but the tacks are much newer, definitely twentieth century."

"Contemporary with the Goudstikker Gallery label?" Finn asked.

"Undoubtedly. And also the Nazi one. That label is from the *Einsatzstab Reichsleiter Rosenberg*, the ERR."

"What are you saying?" Billy asked.

"Look," Shneegarten said, pointing with one bony finger. "The tacks are brass, but in between you can see the small holes and stains from the original nails. You can also still see the marks where the original stretchers were placed. What it means is that this painting of the ship was probably painted sometime in the mid-seventeenth century, contemporary with Rembrandt certainly, but was taken out of its own frame in modern times and used to cover the wood panel beneath, which bears the ERR label and the Goudstikker label. You can even see that the original painting was larger. This section has been cut to fit and the Rembrandt signature applied."

"Who would do a thing like that?" asked Billy.

"Presumably it is as Finn suggested—to cover that which lies beneath from prying eyes."

"Can you remove the canvas?" Finn asked.

"Certainly," said Shneegarten. "The canvas wasn't glued. It was simply tacked onto the panel. Give me a moment." He picked up another tool, shaped like a flat-nosed pair of small pliers, and began easing out the tacks. When he was done he gently pulled back the canvas.

As Finn had expected there was another image on the board beneath the canvas. It showed a man in his middle years dressed as a Dutch burgher wearing a red velvet blouse and a plumed hat. He was standing beside a draped area that had a table set out in front of it covered with various exotic-looking seashells and several equally exotic brass nautical instruments including something that looked like an early version of a sextant. In one gloved hand he held a pale, calfskin-covered book and in the other an ornate, basket-hilt rapier. Light came in strongly through a very narrow stained-glass window on the far left. The image on the stained glass was a heraldic shield. The coat of arms showed a complex plumed helmet seated on a shield divided into a checked field of opposing black and yellow stripes on one set of opposed squares with Turkish crescents and French fleurs-de-lis on the other set.

"That's the Boegart crest," said Billy, excited.

There was a signature in the lower right-hand corner, done lightly in black. It was entirely different from the one on the canvas.

"The real signature of Rembrandt Van Rjin," announced the old man with a theatrical flourish of his hand.

"Is the painting genuine?" asked Finn.

"Let me check," said Shneegarten. He shuffled across the room to a computer terminal on a very cluttered desk and began hitting keys. He talked while he tapped.

"Back in 1968 I was part of the Rembrandt Research Project, which was established through the Dutch government to assess the number of actual Rembrandts in existence. We were a team of experts from all over the world. As well as establishing the authenticity of the pictures we also, by definition, assembled a database of the paintings themselves." He hit a few more keys. "When you cross-index that data with the information in the Courtauld's own Provenance Research department of Holocaust-related works, you wind up with an exceptional fund of information." He paused, squinted, and tapped a final key. "Ah," he said finally, pleased with himself.

"Ah what?" Finn asked.

"The painting, very mysterious I think," murmured the old man, staring at his computer screen. "According to this, it is a portrait of Willem Van Boegart painted by Rembrandt in 1659, roughly in midcareer. The commission appears both in Rembrandt's records and those of Van Boegart, held in the family archive. Willem Van Boegart would have been thirty-seven at the time it was painted. It was never sold and remained with the original Van Boegart collection in Amsterdam until 1938 when it was stolen along with half a dozen other paintings. None of those paintings was ever recovered. The only reason we know of its existence at all is through a photograph for archival purposes taken by Jacques

Goudstikker in 1937 at the request of the Boegart family."

"Where is the photograph now?"

"There are two copies, one in the U.S. National Archives Holocaust Provenance and Documentation Office in Washington, D.C. The other is in the Rijksmuseum Archives in Amsterdam."

"Jacques Goudstikker takes a photograph in 1937, the painting is stolen in 1938, and the picture, with another painting overtop, appears in Goudstikker's inventory in 1940?" Billy Pilgrim shook his head. "It's obviously no coincidence, but it doesn't make any sense, either."

"It does if they were all in on it—Goudstikker, the thieves, the Boegart family," said Finn.

Shneegarten nodded. "A plausible theory. Both men were Jews. Both knew Hitler was coming and that his path would inevitably take him through the Netherlands. They all conspired to make the painting disappear before he got there."

Billy scowled. "I still don't see it. Why that particular painting? And if it was meant to disappear, why does it have the Nazi label?"

"That bears some investigation, I should think," said the old man, stroking his large chin with the stem of his old pipe. "You can leave the painting with me for a few days, yes?"

Finn looked across at her new friend. "Billy?"

"I suppose so."

"Good!" Shneegarten said and jammed the pipe back in his mouth. He clapped Billy on the back. "I'll get you some answers, my lord. Rest assured! I am like the Canadian Mountie in his bright red jacket—the man I always get!"

8

Finn and Billy left the old professor muttering over the painting and found their way down to the Strand entrance to Somerset House. It was raining even harder now and it was already dark. They stood under the great stone portico and stared bleakly out at the street. Like every other thoroughfare in London at that time of day, the Strand was jammed with traffic, the lights on the rooftops of lumbering, beetlelike black cabs winking like fireflies in the rain. Almost nobody was honking. This was England after all. A line of people, most of them with umbrellas, stood drearily by the taxi stand at the curb.

"It'll take us an hour at this time of day," groaned Billy.

"What about the Tube?"

"The closest station is Temple, on the Embankment," said Billy. "We'll be soaked by the time we get there. On a night like this, it'll smell of old socks.''

"I don't think we've got much choice," answered Finn.

"You have no choice at all, Miss Ryan," a strange voice said behind her. Something hard prodded her in the small of the back. Startled she glanced back over her shoulder. She caught a brief glimpse of a well-dressed man, Asian, not Chinese, maybe one of the small East Asian countries. He held an umbrella in one hand and had a folded newspaper over his other arm. There might have been a roll of quarters in his hidden hand, but she didn't think so. With the brief look she saw there were two of them, one behind her, one behind Billy. The hands holding the umbrellas were encased in surgical gloves. Professionals.

"There is an automobile parked around the corner. A blue Audi. You will get into the car without any muss or fuss. If you give us any muss or fuss we will kill both of you. Jolly good?" The hard thing, presumably the barrel of a gun, prodded her in the back. She gave Billy a quick glance. He looked appropriately nervous but still in control. Together they went down the steps and turned right. The two men behind them made no polite allowance for the pedestrian traffic—they simply moved straight ahead using Finn and Billy like the prow of a ship. The people on the sidewalk moved obediently aside, heads bent, blinded by their umbrellas, concentrating on their own feet. Kidnapped in the middle of a crowd. If Billy and she got into the car, it was all over. This wasn't a simple mugging—this was something much worse. If the kidnappers had been waiting for Billy and Finn, it meant that they'd been followed, from Tulkinghorn's or maybe even before that.

Tumble. The word came to her out of nowhere. Miss Turner, her phys ed teacher at Northland, had called it that. Miss Turner, inventor of Turner's Torture Exercises. Miss Turner, who had fought a faint mustache and too much testosterone. Miss Turner, with more than a hint of Marine drill sergeant in her background. Never something sexy like "gymnastics." Tumbling. Jackie Chan and how to take a fall.

There was another prod. Finn kept on walking. It was now or never because Finn knew without a doubt that if they climbed into the blue Audi, they were dead. Something grabbed at her—a coldness and anger. It was more than the fact that she'd been in this position once or twice before in her life: under the streets of New York, a hundred feet down in the Caribbean, in the jungles of the Yucatán with her mother when she was a kid. This was different. This was something innate, something Miss Turner could never teach, only perhaps encourage. Something you were born with. Something diamond hard in her mind—a deadly preternatural calm.

"Jolly good," she said quietly, hoping Billy would understand. They were past the island in the middle of the road on their left that held the church of St. Mary Le Strand. A number 52 Waterloo bus went by, tires hissing on the slick gleaming asphalt of the roadway. There was a steel barrier between them and the street now, a line of newspaper boxes chained to it along with several bicycles. To their right was the closed and abandoned entrance to the Strand Underground Station, out of use for more than a decade.

They turned the corner on to Surrey Street. The traffic sounds abruptly faded. A few yards away, she saw the dark blue Audi pulled up onto the wide sidewalk beside the old Strand Station exit, a shadowy figure behind the wheel. The lights were off but the engine was running, exhaust wisping in the rain. Three against two. Twenty, perhaps thirty seconds and it would be too late. Her roving eyes found a low wrought-iron gate beside a door, a pair of neglected rubbish bins, and a little pile of builder's junk. God bless you, Miss Turner from Northland High School, wherever you are. Tumble.

"Jolly good!" yelled Finn at the top of her lungs. She went into a simple tuck and roll, her hand reaching out blindly, fumbling, grabbing the length of old narrow plumbing pipe. She came out of the somersault, facing back the way she'd come, and swept the pipe around as hard as she could, aiming for the knees. The pipe connected and she felt the shivering, wet crunch of impact run up her arm. The man screamed and dropped his newspaper and his umbrella. She saw that there really was a gun in the man's hand, a flat, chunky-looking automatic. Then chaos.

"Is do nach bhfuil seans ar bith ann!" screamed Billy, turning on his heel and bringing his booted foot up into the crotch of the man behind him. *"Perite! Irrumator Mentula! Spaculatum Tauri!"* Finn was vaguely aware of the man in the Audi getting out of the car.

"This way!" she yelled, grabbing Billy by the arm. She took a few short steps, jammed the lead pipe into the chain around the steel grate covering the old station exit, and pulled hard. The corroded, rust-caked links snapped. She pulled the grate aside and raced into the station, Billy on her heels.

Amazingly there was light to see by; every second fluorescent bar in the ceiling of the old ticket hall was lit. There was a white-tiled entrance archway on the right and a sign: THIS WAY TO TRAINS. Once upon a time, there had been two large passenger elevators, but all that was left now was the emergency exit, a pirouette of iron steps fitted in a descending spiral, filling one of the paired elevator shafts. Oddly the lights were on here as well.

They clattered downward, footsteps clanging loudly, echoing off the old brick. The air was thick and musty.

"Where the hell are we going?" yelled Billy, a few steps above Finn.

"How should I know?" she yelled back.

There was another sound. High above them; steps on the staircase and then a whining roar. The stairwell–elevator shaft was suddenly filled with an earsplitting, roaring echo.

"They're firing at us!" Billy yelled. Another shot rang out, whirring and banging off the metal steps as it ricocheted past.

"Come on!" Finn hurtled down the seemingly endless steps, finally reaching the bottom. There was a narrow sloping tunnel, brightly lit, and then she erupted onto the old platform. She stopped dead in her tracks and felt Billy stumble to a stop, barging into her, pushing her farther out onto the platform and into a waiting crowd. Directly in front of them was a waiting train, doors open.

"Bloody hell," Billy whispered. There was a poster on the curving wall beside them. Three soldiers with rifles marching left to right and the message below:

TAG DER WEHRMACHT
17 MARZ 1942
KREIGSWINTERHILFSWERK

There was also a large metal sign on the wall giving the station's name: PICCADILLY CIRCUS.

The crowd on the platform was made up of an assortment of men and women, all dressed in vintage clothing, some carrying rolled umbrellas, others with newspapers or parcels. There was also a sprinkling of men in uniform. German uniforms. A whistle blew loudly, answered by a second whistle from the head of the train. The crowd surged forward and a distinctly British voice called out:

"Mind the gap, ladies and gents. Please, mind the gap! Mind the gap, *mein herren*! *Auflachen der kluft bitte*!"

"Definitely not Kansas," muttered Finn. She could hear echoing footsteps coming from the passage behind them.

"What do we do?" said Billy.

"Get on the train."

They joined the crowd surging onto the train and found themselves pushed through the open doorway. There was a pause and then the doors slid closed and they began to move.

"This is insane," whispered Billy. Directly in front of them, hanging on to a strap, was a man wearing the soft cap and gray uniform of a sergeant in the Nazi Landspoliezei, the regular police. He had a copy of *Signal*, the German version of *Life* magazine, under his arm. Above him was an advertisement for Dr. Carrot, guaranteed to bring you good health if you ate a lot of him. The Landspoliezei sergeant had a holstered Luger pistol on his hip. He looked bored.

"Did they get on?" asked Finn.

"I didn't see."

"Do you know where this train goes?"

"No, except that wasn't bloody Piccadilly back there." The German cop was definitely staring at them now, a worried expression on his face. He started to say something, then turned away. "This is giving me the collywobbles," Billy muttered. He looked away from the cop. There was another poster beside the Dr. Carrot advertisment. It was a stern black-and-white illustration of a strong man with shirtsleeves rolled up, a cap on his head, and a serious expression on his face. There was a massive sledgehammer over his shoulder. He had muscles like a stevedore's. The message said something about helping the soldier on the front lines, which didn't make much sense because a man with muscles like that would have been on the front lines himself, unless he had some kind of heart condition, in which case he wouldn't have the sledgehammer over his shoulder. . . . He stopped himself; he was on the edge of losing it. Finn squeezed his hand. The train began to slow.

"We're not going far," said Finn.

"We're in trouble," Billy answered, nudging her. There was a crash as the door opened at the far end of the coach. The two Asians, minus their umbrellas, had turned into three. One of them was limping, pushing his way through the crowd of people. He looked extremely angry.

"Crap," said Finn. She threw herself forward into the arms of the Nazi sergeant, reaching for his holstered Luger and pushing him out of the way in a single motion. The gun was far too light. It wasn't the real thing. She waved it in the general direction of their pursuers anyway and instinctively half the people in the car screamed and everyone ducked, including the three Asians. The train pulled into a brightly lit station. The sign said: LEICESTER SQUARE.

"No, it's not!" said Billy.

Finn threw the Luger down the length of the car as the doors slid open. She turned, put both hands on Billy's back, and pushed him out onto the platform.

"What the hell!" A man wearing headphones jumped back, barely avoiding being run down. "Who let you on! Wardrobe! Shit! They've ruined the shot! Sean! Who the bloody hell . . . ?"

Finn still pushing Billy from behind, they skirted the camera setup, jumped over a set of narrow rails waiting for a dolly shot, and battered their way through a regulation swarm of camera people, lighting crew, grips, first, second, and third ADs, sound men, set dec, props, and assorted need-to-bes, want-to-bes, and think-they-already-ares that make up a location shoot for a major motion picture. Predictably someone shouted out the classic angry comment heard by anyone who has ever interfered with the making of a film, even if only for a moment, destroying their expensive and very fragile illusion.

"Hey! Can't you see we're making a movie here?" As though creating cinematic fantasy was more important than any possible reality that might stand in its silly way.

Billy knocked over a light stand and there was a sharp bang as a hot bulb exploded. Finn caught a glimpse of a placard announcing that they were on the set of the DreamWorks production of Len Deighton's novel *SSGB*, and then they were gone, sidestepping through a wide-open set of doors leading onto the actual Holborn Station platform and reaching the escalator. They took the moving steps two at a time, pushing past people riding to the surface, and finally found their way up to High Holborn. They were almost back to Tulkinghorn's and the British Museum. The rain had stopped. There was no sign of the men behind them. Without a pause Billy stepped off the curb and waved. A black cab came to a jarring halt. They climbed in and Finn slammed the door. As the cab moved off into traffic she looked back and saw their limping enemy and his friends come out of the station entrance. A moment longer and it would have been too late.

"Where we going, if you don't mind me askin'?" said the cabbie without turning around.

"Canvey Island," said Billy, settling back in the wide, comfortable seat.

"That's in bleeding Essex, mate!" the driver said, startled.

"I'll pay."

"Too right you'll pay," said the taxi driver. "Quite the distance. At least twenty miles."

"More like thirty," said Billy, sighing. The cabbie shrugged and slid the big car back into the stream of traffic. Ten minutes later they were on their way out of London, heading East along the Thames, making for the Channel.

"What was that before you started saying dirty things in Latin?"

"Something rude in Cornish as I recall," Billy said. "Something to do with goats and his mother's sexual habits."

"What's on Canvey Island?" Finn asked.

"Home," answered Billy. "The *Busted Flush*."

9

Ask the average person in Wichita Falls where Mariveles is, and you'll most likely get nothing but a blank stare, and for good reason: Mariveles has always been either in the middle of nowhere or at the gates of hell, depending on your point of view. The small coastal town lies at the entrance to Manila Bay on the northwestern arm of a jungle peninsula. The harbor is a deep-water anchorage clinging to the base of an immense, forest-covered volcanic cone. This mountain is usually wreathed in flirtatious mists, occasionally giving a glimpse of the summit as it waits patiently for better times to come again, as they had a few years previously for the mountain's fiery brother, Mount Pinatubo, less than fifty miles away.

Historically Mariveles was once a resting point for ships entering the bay and the famous Chinese pirate Li Ma Hong reportedly stopped there for food and water before attacking Manila in 1575. Under Ferdinand Marcos the town became the center of something called an "economic zone," and the original fishing town was swept aside to make way for factories, docks, and official-looking government offices, most of which were now empty, and even a nuclear reactor, which they could never get to run. The grain terminal didn't quite work out and neither did the "plastic city" manufacturing polyethylene sheets. Given Imelda Marcos's infamous fetish, there was a certain irony in the fact that one of the few surviving factories manufactured Nike knockoffs. At the end of the day, if Mariveles was known for anything, it was as the place where the Bataan Death March began in 1942 and also as the place where the tennis balls for Wimbledon are manufactured. Though it's supposedly a "first-class" city of seventy-five thousand or so, the real population is almost twice that, mostly unemployed and mostly living in slums on the far western side of the harbor and well outside the boundaries of the "economic zone." It is a mixed-culture port town of immigrants fleeing even poorer places in the world and a place where hope is a commodity in shorter supply than jobs. The favorite recreation in Mariveles is the consumption of *shabu*, the Philippine version of methamphetamine, cooked up in enormous quantities in illegal, and violently explosive, drug microbreweries all over the hillside squatters' ghettoes.

From where he sat in the open-air beachside snack bar, Briney Hanson could see the old-fashioned cranes loading the *Batavia Queen* at the old Mariveles docks a little farther along the harbor. With berthing charges being what they were, Manila itself was far too rich for the old *Queen*'s blood and she was lucky to be picking up any cargo at all in Mariveles: banana chips and processed cassava meal for animal feed, which meant the *Queen* was going to stink all the way back down to Singapore.

They'd off-load the banana chips there, pick up a load of electronics stuff, and then make a run up to Rangoon with the cassava meal. The last leg would involve taking the electronics stuff on to Madras, or Chennai as it was now called, for assembly into everything from car radios to talking teddy bears. After that, it was anyone's guess. But right now Hanson and the *Queen* were still in Bataan.

He took a swallow from his longneck liter bottle of Red Horse beer and swabbed a piece of "chicharon" pork crackling into the hot sauce on his plate. He forked up a mouthful of crunchy squid heads in rice and washed it all down with another hit of the strong, amber pilsner. Mariveles might have had the most corrupt municipal government in the

Philippines—and that was saying something—but it had unbelievably good snacks.

Hanson had spent the entire morning with his old friend Dr. Nemesio Zobel-Ayala, the local abortionist, Pratique officer for the docks, brother-in-law of the mayor, and all-round *mordida* man. Without kicking back to Ayala, you could be quarantined for a month, not allowed to off-load or on-load cargo, and even wind up getting beaten to a pulp if you even tried to step onshore.

Hanson had swallowed his disgust and played the Good Buddy game just like always, sitting with the little weasel in his stifling dockside office above the customs warehouse for hours, watching him drinking shots of Napoleon Quince and listening to endless stories about his conquests in La Zona, the local brothel area where women and girls, most of them native and some no more than ten or twelve years old, plied their age-old profession in little blanket-divided cubicles, serving the seagoing trade and foreign workers from the few remaining factories in Mariveles.

Zobel-Ayala had all the bases covered. Not only was he a pimp to half the girls in La Zona, but he was also the public health officer for Mariveles and made a bit extra on the side by selling off government-supplied antibiotics to the highest bidder.

The doctor had big plans, most of which involved setting himself up in America one day, but Hanson thought it more likely that the slimy son of a bitch would probably wind up floating upside down under one of the Mariveles piers with his throat cut, either by his rivals in the Kuratong Baleleng or the Pentagon, both of which had big money in *shabu* labs and smuggling all through the islands.

Hanson ate the last of the food on his plate, finished off the Red Horse, and dropped a few crumpled bills onto the counter. He climbed down off the old-fashioned, chrome diner stool, gave a satisfied belch, and headed back along the crushed coral path to the dock road. It was blisteringly hot and he could feel the beer leaching out of him, sweat dripping down the back of his neck from underneath the band of his old captain's cap and down his sides.

Even though he was wearing sunglasses, the light was enough to make Hanson squint, as it glinted off the small broken waves in the harbor and hammered down like a ringing gong from the cloudless sky. Like everywhere else in this part of the world, he knew it could change into black monsoon within a single tick of time, turning the harbor into a witch's cauldron and bouncing the *Queen* around like a beach ball at her moorings, but for the moment he was trapped inside a furnace with its thermostat on the blink.

The meal at the snack bar and the few minutes

by himself had been a nice break after a morning with the sleazy doctor, but making his way past the tumbledown warehouses and the junk-fronted chandlers' shops along the quay brought Hanson back to reality with a hard knock; the oppressive heat, the stink of rot and old rope, of tarred pilings and the dead fish along the bilge-filthy waterfront was the stink of his own future, and he knew it. Endless runs through dangerous seas taking things to one place and other things back again. It was no way for anyone to live. If something didn't change soon . . .

Hanson could see the jib cranes at the dockside working, swinging over big, two-hundred-pound bags of cassava meal in rope slings. On deck Elisha Santoro, his first mate, was overseeing Kong and a few hired Filipino day-hands. The day-hands were dressed in *bahag* loincloths and Eli wore jeans and a Grateful Dead T-shirt. The closest thing to a uniform on the *Batavia Queen* was the dull strip of gold braid on Hanson's battered cap.

He frowned, staring down along the pier. The banana chips wouldn't arrive until the next day, but there was a pile of wooden crates on the dock next to the *Queen* and a four-ton Mitsubishi Fighter Mignon truck parked beside them. Bulk banana chips were shipped in jute bags, like the cassava meal, not wooden crates. Stranger still, Zobel-Ayala hadn't said a word about any new cargo, and he would have been the first to know since every clearance certificate issued on the docks had to go through him.

As Hanson came closer, a man climbed out from the passenger side of the truck cab and stood waiting beside the pile of crates. Hanson saw that all of the crates were stamped with the familiar Slazenger pouncing tiger logo. The man from the truck stepped forward. He was fortyish, flabby, and wore a perfectly cut and blindingly white suit that almost made his pot belly disappear. He had small feet and small hands. The feet were encased in gleaming black patent leather shoes and he wore one too many rings on his pink fingers.

The costume was topped off by a Borsalino Panama as white as the suit. The man wore the formal straw hat with the forced casualness of a bald man, tilted just so, but somehow you knew there was nothing underneath. The eyes were shaded by a slightly feminine-looking pair of leather-covered Fendi Sellerias. There was no facial hair and the faint smell of expensive cologne shimmered in the overheated air. Fat lips smiled. The man had teeth like perfect polished pearls. At five foot five, he should have been almost dainty looking. But he didn't look dainty at all; he looked dangerous.

"Captain Hanson?" he asked. There was a faint, aristocratic Spanish accent.

"Yes?"

"My name is Lazlo Aragas." The smile got wider. "My good friends call me Lazzy."

Hanson nodded. Call this one Lazzy and he'd shove a knitting needle through your eye socket. "Mr. Aragas. What can I do for you?"

"It is what we can do for each other, Captain Hanson."

"Then what can we do for each other, Mr. Aragas?"

"I have a shipment that needs to go to Singapore," he said. "I understand that you are going in that direction."

"A shipment of what?" Hanson asked.

Aragas waved a jeweled hand in the general direction of the crates. "Balls, Captain. I am shipping balls to Singapore."

"Tennis balls."

"Quite so. Specifically Wimbledon Ultra Vis."

Three things were wrong with that. One, the Wimbledon balls were made in the Mariveles factory, but they were shipped out of the superterminal at Pier 15 in Manila. Two, the balls were shipped in six-dozen-can cardboard boxes plastic-strapped in dozen box cubes and loaded into containers, not wooden crates. And three, there wasn't a chance in the world that Slazenger would ever ship anything at all on the *Batavia Queen* or any tramp steamer like her.

Hanson nodded. "I see."

"Do you, Captain?"

"I think I do," he answered slowly.

"What exactly do you see?"

"I see some wooden crates with Slazenger pussycats all over them."

"Full of tennis balls," said the man in the white suit, smiling.

"If you say so."

"I do." Still smiling.

"Does Dr. Zobel-Ayala know about your tennis balls?" Hanson asked flatly.

Aragas laughed. He sounded like a particularly vicious dog barking. "*Zobel-Ayala tiene el famban barretoso,*" he said pleasantly. "If he doesn't do as he's told, I'll put my foot to it, or something more painful perhaps."

"So what does all this really have to with me?" Hanson asked carefully. If Aragas was sidestepping *El Abortista*, he was putting them both into dangerous territory.

"I need a shipper. You are here."

"You and your tennis balls aren't on my bill of lading."

"This will be a separate shipment. Just between you and me, Captain."

"Zobel-Ayala isn't going to like it."

"He'll do as he's told."

"Maybe so, Mr. Aragas, but I have to come back here. You may get to kick him in his fat juicy ass, but I'm not in the same position . . . so to speak."

"It is not your concern, Captain. Your concern

is in loading my shipment as quickly as possible."
There was ice in the words.

"And how do I explain this shipment to the
agent in Singapore?"

"You don't."

"How's that?"

"You will develop engine trouble just off Sentosa. An hour or two at most. A fast boat will take
my tennis balls off your hands." Sentosa Island
was a redeveloped fishing village turned high-end
resort just outside Singapore Harbor.

"Customs, the Checkpoint Authority?"

"Taken care of." *Mordida* again. The Philippines
had made a fine art out of it over the last four
hundred years.

"And what do I get out of all of this trouble?"
Hanson asked.

"This," said Aragas. He pulled the inevitable
envelope out of his inside jacket pocket. It was
about a half inch thick. "Euros, if that is conve-
nient." Once upon a time it had been American
dollars, but things were changing. "Twenty-five
thousand."

Roughly thirty-three thousand dollars depending
on the day rate. It didn't matter. What really mattered was that with the envelope there was no
more pretense. You didn't pay somebody that
much money for carting around a couple of hundred crates of tennis balls.

It was a distinctly nasty spot to be in because

if Aragas was in a position to sidestep Zobel-Ayala, that meant he was heavily connected. Turn Aragas down and he'd get somebody's nose out of joint. Or he could take the envelope and go along with Aragas and if things screwed up he could easily land in Changi Prison for the rest of his life—not a pleasant thought at all.

So he was trapped—damned if he did, damned if he didn't. Standing here baking in the hot sun he didn't see any way out. So he stopped looking, at least for the moment. He took the envelope from Aragas, folded it in half, and stuck it into his back pocket.

"Very good," said Aragas as though he were speaking to a dog he was training to roll over and play dead. "It would be appreciated if you could have the crates loaded as quickly as possible. As you know, there is a great deal of petty theft in this area." Anything that wasn't nailed down was considered fair game, but Hanson had an idea: Aragas could leave his crates just where they were for as long as he wanted and the locals would avoid them like the plague.

"Not a problem," said Hanson. He glanced up and saw Elisha Santoro casually leaning on the forward rail and looking down at him. Eli wasn't going to like this at all.

"Good," said Aragas. "I am very pleased that we have reached an accord on this matter. When you load the crates please make them as available as possible for quick unloading. I shall return at seven this evening."

"Return?" asked Hanson, startled.

"Didn't I tell you?" said Aragas. "I will be accompanying the shipment to Singapore." With that, he put two fingers to the brim of his hat, tipped Hanson a brief salute, and climbed back into the truck. The Mitsubishi's engine chugged to life and it lumbered off down the docks and disappeared. Hanson watched it go, feeling the lump of the envelope in his pocket pressing into him like a tumor.

Eli Santoro came down the gangway and onto the pier. He inspected the crates for a moment, then turned to Hanson. "What was that all about? New cargo?" It wasn't really a question; Eli had seen Aragas and he'd seen the envelope. He was young but he was no fool.

"Something like that," said Hanson.

"We in trouble, boss?"

"Maybe." Hanson looked at his first mate. Elisha Santoro, like everyone else on the *Batavia Queen*, was an outcast. At twenty-eight he was the youngest man on the ship with three years in the U.S. Navy, a First Officer rating from the U.S. Merchant Marine Academy, and two more years in the Coast Guard, stationed in Guam. Then an accident with a backyard barbecue at a base picnic left him blind in one eye—enough for his career to come to a crashing halt with the revoking of his mate's ticket and no chance of ever becoming a master on his own. At twenty-five Santoro was adrift, broke, and unemployed, wedded to the sea with all his hopes and dreams in tatters.

Hanson had found him bumming around the islands doing yacht charters out of Hong Kong, and after two bottles of Dragon's Back and a look at the young man's record he'd snapped him up, eye patch or not. That had been almost three years ago and Hanson hadn't regretted the decision once.

"What are we going to do?" Eli asked.

"We're screwed either way." Hanson sighed. "Load up the tennis balls. Figure it so we can dump the cases quickly if we have to."

"What do you think is in them?"

"I don't want to know and neither do you," the captain warned. "And the man in the ice cream suit is shipping out with us, so be careful."

"We've got another problem."

"What now?" Hanson groaned; as if the day wasn't bad enough already. Eli handed over a piece of yellow paper he pulled out of his T-shirt pocket. A cable flimsy. Like everyone aboard the *Queen* the young man did double duty; as well as being the *Batavia Queen*'s first officer, first mate, and quartermaster, Eli was also the radio officer. "Message from the company. The *Queen*'s been sold. We'll find out who the new owners are when we get to Singapore."

10

The *Busted Flush* made the North Sea crossing to Holland in three and a half days, running up the Channel north of Goodwin Sands in fine weather, then beating north beyond the Broad Fourteens to Den Helder. On the third night, they made their way through the tricky currents of the rushing tidal rip of the Marsdeip, finally making landfall at the locks leading into the inland sea once known as the Zuider Zee and now called the Ijsselmeer. They spent the night resting up in the calm waters on the inland side of the immense dike and on the following morning made a swift, sail-cracking run in the bright sunshine down to the little seaside village of Durgerdam. The town had everything they needed including a full-service marina and a bus stop for the ride into Amsterdam itself, only a few miles to the south, its low, dusty skyline faint on the horizon.

For Finn, tense and exhausted after the events in London, sailing on the *Flush* had been a joy. The *Flush* was a William Garden sixty-foot gaff-rigged schooner, powered by a six-cylinder Sealord North Sea diesel and capable of making twelve knots under full sail. Inside she was as cozy as a log cabin in the woods, complete with two comfortable cabins, a small salon, and a well-equipped and well-stored galley. According to Billy, she'd been built as *Sitkin* in Oregon almost fifty years before, meant for cruising the Alaska coast, and had spent time in Chile and South Africa after that as the *San Lourenco*. She'd wound up in England taking tourist charters up the coast of Scotland. At that time she was known as *Sandpiper*. Billy had owned her now for almost eight years.

"A present to myself after all those years at school," he'd told her. "Perhaps I should have named her the *Graduate*." According to him they were the best of friends, and from the way Billy handled her as he guided her Nantucket green hull into the sheltered little bay Finn could easily see that his affection for the slightly tubby-looking boat was more like love.

They'd already gone through immigration at Den Helder, and the formalities of berthing at the marina involved no more than registering at the office with the harbormaster and paying the minimum three-day berthing fee. With that done they walked along the dike road that appeared to be the only street in town. Once upon a time it had been a fishing village with small trawlers lined up along the clay and earth dike, but the fishing fleet had disappeared long ago with the creation of the huge dams that had changed the Zuider Zee's water from salt to fresh. Now the boats along the *Durgerdammerdjik* were mostly pleasure craft and the charming fishermen's modest homes were either summer homes or bed-and-breakfasts.

"I'm a little wobbly," said Finn as they walked in the bright morning air. After less than four days she'd developed proper sea legs and heading along the dike was making her feel a little dizzy, the horizon bobbing up and down ahead of her.

"Not a bit seasick, though." Billy grinned. "Make a sailor out of you yet."

Finn smiled. Physically she felt wonderful; her skin was softly bronzed and her long hair smelled like salt air. For the first time in months she was enjoying the simple act of breathing. Living in London was worse than New York; it felt as though you were smoking a dozen cigars every day and sometimes she could even feel the particulate pollution on her teeth. She breathed in deeply. The little town smelled like new-mown hay and the sea. The inland sails of a real Dutch windmill whirled slowly in the fields behind the houses. She suddenly felt ravenously hungry.

"I'm starved," she said.

They found a small hotel called the *Oude Ta-*

veerne halfway along the dike. The plain white clapboard structure stood out from the rest, much larger than the little houses flanking it. There was a patio on one side and a few tables with Heineken umbrellas out front on the pattern brick sidewalk. On the water side of the dike it appeared to have its own dock with a few picnic tables on the grass at the near end. The *Oude Taveerne* looked as though it might have been some commercial enterprise in the past, a chandlery, or perhaps a wealthy merchant's place of business as well as his home. The only building larger was the seventeenth-century town hall down the way with its domed tower.

"I smell pancakes," said Billy.

"Sausages," said Finn.

"Both," said Billy.

They went inside.

It was knickknack heaven. Things hung from the dark beams of the low ceilings, objects were hung on the walls, mugs, paintings, photographs, half models of boats, ships in bottles, shelves full of preserves, children's drawings, examples of needlepoint behind glass, a set of ceramic thimbles . . . it was endless.

The tables were crammed neatly together, each one with its own taffeta tablecloth, each tablecloth set with place mats and bright red folded linen napkins. Sun shone brightly through the windows on a dozen different patterns of wallpaper, all of it busy and ornate. An old mural of fishing boats took up half the far wall.

A couple of locals were sitting at a long, empty table reading newspapers they'd taken from a large basket between them, but other than that the dining room was empty. A plump, apple-cheeked woman in a printed apron introduced herself as Velden in perfectly good English, offered them menus, and then took their orders. She informed them that the *Oude Taveerne* had stood there since 1760 and had originally been called the *Prins te Paard*, which, she explained, meant the Prince on Horseback.

A few minutes later, she returned with the food arranged on a huge platter, which she balanced easily on one beefy arm. Something called *uit-smijter* for Finn, which turned out to be fried ham and eggs with mustard cheese, and *gevulde pannekoek* for Billy, which turned out to be two huge pancakes put together like cake layers with fried sausage as a filling. The calories and choles-terol in each meal would have given any self-respecting cardiologist a heart attack. In other words, both meals were just what the doctor ordered.

"Good Lord," said Billy, sitting back in his chair with a sigh. "Bless me, for I have sinned." He grinned. "Take me two years on a treadmill to work that off."

"Better than the alternative," said Finn. She

took a sip of the excellent coffee Velden had pro-vided. "We're lucky to be alive at this point."

"I'd almost forgotten," said Billy, his expres-sion darkening.

Finn nodded. "Me too. That's when you get careless."

"I suppose you're right," said Billy. "Those peo-ple we ran into aren't just going to go away." He shook his head. "I know we talked this whole subject to death during the crossing, but I still don't know what they expected to accomplish."

"Murder springs to mind," Finn answered. "Somebody wants us out of the way."

"Why?"

"Unless there's something in your past you haven't told me about it must have to do with the painting."

Billy snorted. "I admit it. I've led a double life all these years. Secretly I'm an Estonian spy op-erating undercover as an impecunious English lord with a silly pedigree that dates back to Boadecia, queen of the bloody Iceni."

"Then it's the painting."

"But we didn't even have it with us." Billy shrugged.

"I can't think of anything else."

"What about this . . . situation with Pieter Boegart, my dear departed cousin, and your . . . um, dad?"

Finn spoke stiffly. "He's not my dad and I'm

not sure that the 'situation,' as you call it, has any relevance."

"Maybe they were after you, not the painting."

"If they wanted to kill me, they didn't have to do it in front of the Courtauld Institute. Knocking me off in Crouch End would have been a little more discreet, don't you think?"

"And they could have done the same to me on dear old *Flush* any time they wanted," agreed Billy.

Finn nodded. "Which brings me back to the beginning. The painting. The last time a small Rembrandt was auctioned it went for nineteen million pounds. Thirty-six million U.S. That's enough to kill for."

"A thought occurs to me," said Billy, leaning forward and pushing his plate out of the way. He lined up the saltshaker, the pepper grinder, and the sugar bowl. "Pieter Boegart's instructions to Sir James. The letter had two objectives—to bring us together and to give us three items: the painting, the house, and the *Batavia Queen*. They're all tied together."

"Clues?"

"No, more like a game of hare and hounds. Do you have that in America?"

"A paper chase," said Finn.

"Exactly."

"So Pieter Boegart is the hare and we're the hounds, is that it?"

"The painting is a lure, and so is the house."

"To what end?"

"Catching the hare."

"In other words, finding Pieter Boegart," said Finn.

Billy nodded. "Or whatever he was looking for."

11

They made two telephone calls from the *Oude Taveerne*: one to the lawyer in Amsterdam who Tulkinghorn had told them was handling the house, and the other to Dr. Shneegarten at the Courtauld. The strange old man from Somerset House was apparently off doing research at the Reading Room of the British Museum, but the lawyer, a man named Guido Derlagen, was in his office and could see them immediately.

Derlagen's office turned out be in a modern block on the Rokin, a wide, boulevarded avenue just off the Dam, Amsterdam's town square, about ten minutes from the main train station and the docks. The addresses on the Rokin that weren't shops and cafés were banks, stockbrokers, and lawyers. This was Amsterdam's Wall Street. The sidewalks were crammed with tourists and both sides of the boulevard thick with traffic when they arrived. The whole city gave off a sense of healthy bustle.

Middle-aged and well-dressed, Derlagen had a somewhat lumpy but perfectly shaved head. He spoke excellent English. He was, it seemed, one of a score of lawyers who worked for the Boegart shipping business in the Netherlands. Derlagen was one of the team of *advocaats* who handled an assortment of personal trusts held by individual Boegart family members, in this case Pieter Boegart. Derlagen had a moderate-sized office with a window that looked down into the busy street. Finn could see a yellow tram-train squeaking down the tracks embedded in the old brick. Through the fluttering leaves of the trees that ran down the boulevard she could see the garish yellow and red sign of a Chinese restaurant.

The furniture in Derlagen's office was sparse and modern. His desk was a heavy slab of tempered glass on chrome legs. The desk had a flat-screen computer angled to one side on it and nothing else. There was a striped rug, a row of filing cabinets, and a pair of chairs across from the desk. The chairs were black leather. The walls were blank and art gallery white with no decoration at all.

Finn and Billy sat down.

"You're here about the house on the *Herengracht*," said the lawyer. His accent in English sounded heavily South African, which wasn't surprising since the first Boer settlers were from Holland. He tapped some keys and glanced at his computer screen. "We here at the firm were surprised when we heard of this transaction, yes? Because, you see, the house has been owned by members of the Van Boegart family since it was built in 1685."

"I'm a member of the family," said Billy. "Pieter Boegart is my cousin or something."

"Yes, or something, that is correct, Lord Pilgrim."

"Just Billy if you don't mind, or Mr. Pilgrim if you like."

"Certainly, Lord Pilgrim." The man turned to Finn. "Your relationship to *Meneer* Boegart, however, is less clear."

"Yes, it is." She didn't like the man's officious and slightly condescending manner of speech. "But from what we understood from Sir James everything is in order, isn't it?"

"Yes, it appears to be," the man murmured, checking his screen again.

"So if that's the case," continued Finn, "why don't we just get on with it unless you've got some objection . . . Guido?" She pronounced his name with a heavy Italian accent.

The man reddened. "It is not pronounced that way. It is more the way you would pronounce 'van Gogh,' the artist."

"Van Hhok," Finn said with the proper guttural

effect. It made it sound as though you were getting ready to spit on the sidewalk.

"Yes," the lawyer said primly.

"Which would make your name *Hogweedo*, yes?" Billy added, overdoing it with an innocent smile.

Derlagen reddened even more as he realized they were teasing him. "The pronouncing of my name is of no importance," he said a little angrily.

"That's right. It's not important at all, any more than my relationship to Pieter Boegart, so why don't you just go and fetch whatever papers we have to sign and we'll get out of your hair, okay?" Finn said.

"Quite so," said Derlagen. He got up from behind the desk and left the office.

"Pinched," said Billy. "I used to have professors at Oxford like that. Always with that pinched look one gets when one's bowels aren't moving as they should."

"In other words, he's got a pickle up his ass," said Finn.

"Exactly," said Billy.

Derlagen returned with a file folder full of documents and a small leather-covered box. They signed the documents, which made them the only two stockholders of an already formed Dutch royalty conduit nonresident corporation called *Vleigende Draeack* LLC—the Flying Dragon Company. The only assets of Flying Dragon were the painting, which they had already received; the Amsterdam house on the *Herengracht*; a very elderly freighter due to be scrapped; and a tract of utterly unapproachable snake-infested jungle somewhere in the middle of an unnamed island in the Sulu Sea at approximately 7 degrees north by 118 degrees south. By signing the documents, Finn and Billy were legally agreeing to physically take possession of these assets within a limited period of time. Failure to do so would result in the forfeiture of all the assets, including those already taken into their possession.

"So we have to actually go to this so-called snake-infested unapproachable tract of land on the unnamed island or we lose everything. Is that what you're saying?" Finn asked.

"Precisely," said Derlagen, smiling for the first time. It was not a friendly smile.

"Well," said Billy airily, "I'm not doing anything else at the moment, Miss Ryan, how about you?"

"I'm game if you are, Billy."

The lawyer's lips pursed as though he'd just sucked a lemon. "As you wish," he said.

They signed. Derlagen went away again to get copies of the signed agreements and their stock certificates.

"Can't be very high up the food chain," Finn commented. "He doesn't even have a secretary."

"I'm feeling very much the CEO. Perhaps I'll buy lunch," said Billy.

"We just had breakfast, and how come you're the CEO?"

"All right, you be the CEO, and I'll be the stuffy old chairman of the board hired on merely for my escutcheon on the creamy linen letterhead and my portrait in the boardroom."

"You," said Finn, "are a very silly man."

Derlagen came back with the papers. He placed them in a manila envelope, which he handed to Billy, who in turn handed it on to Finn. "She's the CEO," he explained blandly. "I'm just chairman of the board."

Derlagen looked a little perplexed. He frowned and opened up the box. Inside was a key, something that looked like a fat guitar pick, and a delicate, half-inch-high figure of a man mounted on a horse. It was obviously very old. Just as obviously, it was made of solid gold.

"It is from Mali," explained Derlagen. "Experts at the Rijksmuseum say it is from the reign of Mansa Musa, who was apparently the king of Timbuktu."

"It's beautiful," said Finn, turning it over in her hand. "But what does this have to do with us?"

"*Meneer* Boegart left it in our vault for safekeeping. It was purchased from an antiquities dealer named Osterman in Labuan, just off the coast from the sultanate of Brunei, which was the last place *Meneer* Boegart was seen. According to this man Osterman the gold figure was to be given to you in the event that he . . . disappeared. The figurine is for you specifically, *Vrouwe* Ryan. The other two items are the key to the front door of the house and the device used to disarm the security system. The panel is on the right as you enter. Simply place the narrow end of the device in the appropriate spot and squeeze. The light should turn green. Everything else is automatic. There is a cleaning service we have hired, which comes every Wednesday morning for three hours. If there is anything else you need to know, I am, of course, at your service, day or night." It didn't sound like much of an invitation. Derlagen went on, voice droning and uninflected. "As the documents describe you are not allowed to sell either the house or any of its contents for at least twelve months, and if you do the Boegart Family Trust has the right of first refusal, that is to say—"

"We know what it means," said Billy.

"Then if that is all . . . ?" answered Derlagen. He pushed away from his chair. They were being dismissed. Finn carefully put the little gold figure back into the box. She put the box into her bag.

"How do we find the house?" Finn asked.

"Nothing could be simpler," said Derlagen. "Walk back up to the *Dam*, turn left on the *Raadhuistraat*, cross one bridge, and turn right onto the *Herengracht*. It is the first block, before *Driekonigenstraat*, number 188. It cannot be missed. It is dark stone with a green door."

"Thanks," said Finn, holding out her hand. Derlagen ignored it.

"*Geen dank,*" he responded, giving her a little bow.

A moment later, when they were back on the street, Billy said, "Not the friendliest type in the world, was he?"

"What did you expect?" said Finn. "He's a lawyer, and I don't think he understands any of this any more than we do."

"And there's nothing that makes a solicitor more unhappy than not knowing what's going on." Billy nodded. "I see one of those brown cafés or what do you call them? Let's gird our loins with some coffee and then go see the house."

"Fine by me."

The coffee was excellent once again, and the walk was pleasant and just about as simple as Derlagen had described it. The weather was perfect and the streets were full of tourists, bicycles, and bright yellow tram cars. There was an enthusiasm in the air Finn hadn't felt in London, and after a few blocks, she thought she knew what it was. The people here, the ones in the sidewalk cafés, or walking by, seemed less interested in business and money than they did in just enjoying themselves. Instead of being on cell phones or busily tapping away at laptops, they were actually reading books and talking to one another face-to-face. The overall surroundings were less intrusive too; there was neon enough certainly, but even it was fairly restrained, and there wasn't much in the way of giant billboards or screaming mega-screen TVs either. She knew a lot of her of friends back at NYU would call it retro or old-fashioned, but Finn thought it was refreshing.

The *Herengracht* was a canal side street of small trees and large houses. Cars were angle parked next to the canal and there were large houseboats lined up in the dark water. As usual there were more bicycles than automobiles on the street. In the air, there was a faint, heavy smell that Finn couldn't quite place—a hint of the sea but something else and slightly unpleasant, like old garbage gone sour.

"It's the sewage system," Billy offered, seeing her nose wrinkle. "Amsterdam's probably the last major city that dumps its raw sewage directly into the water table."

"Into the canals?" Finn said, astounded. "Untreated?"

"They depend on the tide to wash the effluent away."

"I guess you learn something new every day," she said, slightly depressed by the information; walking the few short blocks from Derlagen's office, she'd begun to fall in love with the gentle, unpretentious city with its trams and its politically correct bicycles. Love might be blind, but it still had a sense of smell. She sighed.

"Here we go," said Billy. They were standing in front of number 188.

The house was three stories plus a ground floor that looked as though it might have once been for servants. It was a big place without being grandiose, absolutely symmetrical. There were four tall windows and a door on the main floor, and five windows on each of the next two floors with a pair of evenly spaced single window dormers set into the steep roof angle and two identical chimneys jutting upward. There was a massive stone portico and the Boegart crest with a "1685" carved beneath it.

"Honey, I'm home," said Finn. She took the key out of her bag and they climbed a short flight of steps to the imposing front door. She fitted the key into the lock, pushed the door open, and they stepped inside.

12

There was a Chubb keypad on the wall just as Derlagen had described it. Finn fitted the guitar pick's narrow end into a little slot, and the red pulsing light turned green. A message appeared in an LED panel: REPEAT TO ARM.

"Close the door," she said to Billy. He did and she squeezed the guitar pick again. The panel light pulsed red and the LED said: ARMED. "Okay, let's look around."

"I feel like I'm trespassing," said Billy.

Finn nodded. Billy was right; there was something a little unsettling about wandering around in a stranger's house, even if she did now own it. There was a mustiness in the air. No one had been here in quite a while. She had an urge to run around opening windows.

Directly in front of them was a long hallway with rooms on either side. The hallway walls were hung with a number of paintings, all modern. The walls were painted flat white. The overall effect was a kind of studied blankness as though Pieter Boegart didn't want to reveal anything about himself through his taste in decor.

There were two front rooms, like large parlors, flooded with light. The one on the right was laid out like an office. Behind the parlors were a large rectangular living room with an ornate fireplace and an equally large dining room on the right. A narrow staircase led upstairs and an even narrower one led down. At the far end of the hallway was a moderate-sized room that looked out onto a tiny garden. It might have served as a breakfast room or an old-fashioned music room.

"No kitchen," said Finn.

"If it's anything like England, in a house this old the kitchen would be in the basement," answered Billy.

"Somehow this isn't what I expected," said Finn.

"Nor I," agreed Billy. "I thought it would be all stuffy and Victorian. Uncomfortable couches filled with horsehair. Pictures of the ancestors lining the walls, that sort of thing."

It was quite the opposite. There wasn't a scrap of wallpaper to be seen. Like the hallway, the rooms were painted a uniform white and hung with large framed photographs from exotic locales and modern, nonfigurative paintings in splashy primary colors. The furniture looked as though it came from some sort of upscale Dutch version of Ikea. The floors were narrow, pegged, highly polished rosewood.

They went back to the stairs and up to the second floor. There were four bedrooms and a single bathroom with a separate toilet cubicle. Only one of the bedrooms, the one above the front parlor, appeared to be in use. More white, more modern furniture. There was a freestanding wardrobe filled with expensive suits and a second wardrobe full of more casual clothes. A pile of books on the bedside table, most in Dutch, mostly history from the look of the covers. One in English: *The Land Below the Wind* by a woman named Agnes Newton Keith. Finn picked up the book and flipped it open. A British edition published by Michael Joseph Ltd. in 1939.

"Adventures in Sandakan." She flipped to a map just after the title page. "Looks like a province in North Borneo."

"Do I begin to see a pattern here?" Billy asked.

Finn flipped through the pages. "It looks like cousin Pieter underlined a lot of things and made notes in the margins," she said.

"Hang on to it," replied Billy. Finn slipped the book into her bag. They went up to the third floor. There were a half dozen small rooms, empty except for the dust on the windowsills. "Servants' quarters," said Billy. There were two large storerooms in the dormer garret, also bare except for pieces of furniture, most of it old but not antique. They poked through it, but the only thing of interest was the fact that there was absolutely nothing in the way of personal material—no old scrapbooks, papers, letters, pictures, or memorabilia.

"It's as though he never lived here at all," said Finn.

"Now there's a thought," said Billy. "What if this is just some sort of, how would you describe it?" He paused and then went on. "A pied-à-terre where he hung his hat while he was in Amsterdam? Maybe he actually lived somewhere else."

"We never checked his flat in London," agreed Finn. They wound their way back downstairs, even inspecting the basement kitchen. Fully stocked, but the big refrigerator was completely empty except for a six-pack of something called NALU. It was a faint green color and came in a screw-top bottle. Finn opened one and took a sip.

"Not bad, mango . . . sort of," she said.

They took their bottles of NALU and went back up to the main floor. Billy looked around, frowning. "What's the matter?" asked Finn.

"Just figuring the angles." Billy went to the front rooms, then came back to the hall. He stood with Finn at the bottom of the stairs leading to the second floor. "It's not here," he said finally.

"What's not here?"

"The painting we uncovered with your friend

Dr. Shneegarten at the Courtauld Institute . . . describe it."

"It's a portrait of Willem Van Boegart dressed up as some sort of burgher. There's a table with some nautical instruments and some velvet drapery behind it." She thought for a moment. "He is standing on a rosewood floor." She looked down at her feet. "Just like this one."

"Where is the light in the picture coming from?"

"The left," said Finn, squeezing her eyes shut, remembering her first sight of the painting in Shneegarten's workshop. "A narrow stained-glass window on the left." She stopped. "What's wrong with that? Eighty percent of Dutch Master portraiture has the light coming from the left . . . Vermeer, Frans Hals, Gerrit Dou, Van Dyck, Rembrandt—just about all of them."

"The window was stained glass. It had the Van Boegart crest. The same crest carved into stone over the front door of this house. The floors were rosewood."

"The portrait was painted here," said Finn.

"Exactly," said Billy. He made a sweeping gesture. "But where? Figure it out. . . . If Willem Van Boegart is standing on the right side of the painting and the window is on the left, then where in the house is he standing? There are two possibilities on each floor: front left room, back right room. And none of those windows is stained glass.

They're old dormers that don't look as though they've been opened in three hundred years, let alone been replacements, not to mention the fact that they're far too wide."

"Then we're wrong," said Finn, shrugging. "It wasn't painted here after all. Maybe it's a figment of the artist's imagination. Rembrandt's studio had a huge window on the left. Virtually every one of his commissioned portraits was painted there."

"Then why the stained-glass window?"

"Because Willem Van Boegart asked for it."

"And why would he ask for it even if it was painted somewhere else?"

"Slow down," said Finn. "You're losing me."

"The painting was done here, or at least the idea came from this house. Nobody imagined that stained-glass window. It existed."

"Then where is it?" Finn asked.

"Not here."

"But you say it has to be."

"We're going around in circles."

"Which means we're missing something," said Finn. "So let's look again."

They moved slowly through the house a second time, silently, pausing in each room and turning carefully. No stained glass anywhere or any sign that it had ever existed. Finn checked Billy's theory and saw that he was right. Standing in the position of Rembrandt painting Willem Van Boegart's portrait three centuries before left very few alternatives. It had to represent one of the rooms Billy had described—left front, right rear, going up the three stories.

On the other hand, if the painting had been a "tronie," a fantasy portrait done from memory or his imagination, then Rembrandt could have painted it anywhere. She tried to remember the Rembrandts she studied in the university over the years.

Rembrandt had painted hundreds of portraits during his career, many of them self-portraits, and in most he hadn't made very much representation of the backgrounds at all. He'd been interested in the human figure, not the props involved, with the possible exclusion of his studies like *Bathsheba at Her Bath* or *Aristotle Contemplating the Bust of Homer*.

In the portrait uncovered by Shneegarten, the coat of arms had been specific, and so were the floorboards at Willem Van Boegart's feet—expensive, narrow, pegged rosewood. She'd seen lots of photographs of Rembrandt's studio, and even in the famous painting he'd done called *The Artist in His Studio* the floors were honey-colored and very wide, either pine or oak. Certainly not the deep red hardwood she was standing on now.

They went back to the main floor. "This is nuts," said Finn. "It has to be here."

"The room in the painting doesn't exist," answered Billy, frustrated.

"When is a room not a room?" said Finn quietly, turning the problem into a riddle. She turned and looked up and down the hall. Something niggled and then fell into place. "The room that looks out onto the garden," she said.

They walked down to the small, brightly lit chamber. A table and four chairs. A small side table with a plain blue vase full of wilted, dried-out flowers. Brown-eyed Susans. Windows left and right and a French door in the middle giving access to the outdoors.

The little patch of garden had turned into an overgrown jungle. The grass needed cutting and the rosebushes were in need of work as well. The high wall separating Pieter Boegart's property from the one behind it was overgrown with vines. There were weeds everywhere and the few pieces of cast-iron furniture were spotted with rust.

Finn handed the guitar pick security key to Billy. "Disable the alarm, would you?" she asked. Billy nodded. He returned a moment later.

"Done," he said. Finn pushed down on the handles of the glass and wood doors. They opened and she and Billy stepped outside. It was a perfect spring day. The air smelled of damp earth and dew-wet grass. There was a cricket somewhere, scraping out its tinny little song. Bees buzzed among the red and yellow roses and the sun shone down into the shafts created by the tall houses.

"Pretty," said Finn.

"What are we looking for?" asked Billy.

Finn went to the wall at the end of the garden, turned, and looked back at the house. She pointed upward. "There," she said.

"Bloody hell," whispered Billy, seeing what she saw.

Seen from outside, the structure of the house was easily identifiable. The house itself was a tall rectangle with the little garden room at the back sticking out, connected to the main house by a short span of stonework. Directly above the garden room on the second floor the stone extension was a set of tall, narrow windows. There were heavy curtains drawn over the panes. They moved slightly to the right. Between the back of the house and the jutting room on the second floor, they could see a tall, narrow window of stained glass.

"There," said Finn. "The way the windows are laid out on the second floor, that stained glass is in a blind spot. You'd only see it if you were looking for it. The chimney must be a dummy," she added. "There's no connecting fireplace down here."

"And the windows below the chimney piece on the second floor?"

"A hidden room," said Finn.

"Brilliant," said Billy.

They went back through the doors into the garden room, and before they went upstairs, Finn carefully paced out the distance between the door and the foot of the stairs.

"Twenty-five feet."

They went up to the second floor and Finn paced off the distance in reverse. Twenty-five feet took them to a monumental carved wardrobe fitted flush against the end wall of the corridor.

"Did you ever read any C. S. Lewis when you were a little girl?" Billy asked.

"You mean *The Lion, the Witch, and the Wardrobe*?" said Finn. "Of course."

Billy opened the door of the wardrobe. Like the one in the book, the cupboard was filled with heavy winter coats. He pushed them aside and felt around on the back wall of the wardrobe.

"There has to be some kind of catch." His fingers touched a small protuberance in the upper right-hand corner. He pressed firmly and there was an audible *click*. The back of the wardrobe gave under the pressure of his hand. "Got it." He pushed through the coats, Finn right behind him. The back of the cupboard swung open and they ducked into a narrow, dusty chamber.

Finn felt a sudden chill, aware of what she was seeing. To the left was the tall, narrow stained-glass window with the now familiar Boegart crest. Sun shone through, picking up the tiny motes of dust in a golden haze that struck the old rosewood floor in a puddle of golden light. The chill turned into a shiver that ran up her spine. She was standing exactly where Rembrandt Van Rjin had set up his easel three hundred years before to paint the handsome figure of the wealthy merchant and adventurer Willem Van Boegart. The sense of the master and his subject was so strong she could almost see the scene: Rembrandt, with his brushes and palette, poised; the merchant, tall and arrogant, standing proudly against the far wall; the wonderful honeyed light filtered through the stained glass falling across their shoulders like a benediction. It was almost as if she was standing inside Rembrandt's ghost, his pale shadow, still shimmering there.

"Look at the door," said Billy softly.

Ten feet away, at the far end of the little chamber, was a heavy, dark oak door fitted with massive hinges and an ornate lock and latch.

"It was hidden behind the drapery in the painting," said Finn. "Van Boegart didn't want anyone to know it was there." She stepped across the little room and tried the latch. It squeaked noisily and the door opened. Finn stepped through the doorway and into the secret room beyond. She stared.

"My God!" she whispered.

13

"It's a cabinet of curiosities," said Billy. The small room was jammed with shelves, niches, little tables, and glass display cases, all overflowing with a museum of artifacts arranged in no particular order. Hardwood boxes filled with seashells sat next to a case containing a butterfly or moth with jade and crimson wings as wide as a man's hand.

On a shelf they saw a bell jar containing a dried and mummified head that might have been a man's or a great ape's. There was also a collection of glass eyes. An alligator hung by wires from the ceiling. Immense twisted narwhal tusks were leaned in a corner together with a half dozen rusted harpoons. They saw an Indian headdress, a lump of rock with one brightly shining facet, a dozen kinds of skeletons, dried bats in flight, a dusty-looking cat with a missing eye, an impossible mixture of a huge carplike fish and a monkey's body joined together.

Animal, vegetable, and mineral—everything was represented, even abstracts, like a half dozen wooden models of geometric designs. There was no surface left uncluttered. Even the walls and the ceiling of the little chamber were a wonder, a masterpiece of the plasterer's art, intricate designs of flowers, fruit, animals, and birds, a carved, stark white jungle setting for the glorious insanity of the relics on display.

Billy cleared his throat, then quoted: " 'A goodly, huge cabinet, wherein whatsoever the hand of man by exquisite art or engine has made rare in stuff, form, or motion; whatsoever singularity, chance, and the shuffle of things hath produced; whatsoever Nature has wrought in things that want life and may be kept; shall be sorted and included.' Sir Francis Bacon, 1594."

"You're kidding. You memorized that?"

Billy nodded. "Benefits of a classical education again. Part of Bacon's well-known monologues from the *Gesta Grayorum*, the Gray's Inn guest book."

"Sure, very well known," laughed Finn.

"Look," said Billy, his finger outstretched.

At the point where the walls met the ceiling above the door, a Latin motto had been carved into the plaster:

"Fugio ab insula opes usus venti carmeni," said

Finn. "Escape from my island of treasure . . . and something about wind . . . 'venti.'"

"More like, 'Escape to my hidden island of treasure on winds of music,'" said Billy promptly. "He must mean this room. His hidden island."

In the center of it all was a table covered in ancient, dusty fabric and set out with a scattering of large seashells, as well as a half dozen brass maritime instruments including an astrolabe, precursor to the sextant. Among the instruments was a calfskin-covered book, the same one that had been in Willem Van Boegart's hand in the Rembrandt portrait. Leaning casually on the table, almost as though it had been left there only moments before, was the basket-hilt rapier that had been in the Dutchman's other hand. Finn felt the cold chill run down her spine again; the ghostly presence of the man in the painting was so strong that she almost expected him to step into the room and introduce himself. Without thinking she looked back over her shoulder at the open doorway.

"Collections of all the things he saw on his travels," said Billy. He stepped forward and carefully picked up the calfskin book from the table. He opened it gently. "It's a *rutter*," he said. He turned another page. "And it's in English."

"What's a *rutter* and why is it in English?" Finn asked.

"A *rutter* is a book of dead reckoning—point-to-point navigation," explained Billy. "You go from one physical landmark to the next. Rather like hares and hounds again. It's where the word 'route' comes from. The French called it a *routier*. It's what they used to navigate before they had proper charts."

"And the English?"

"Part of the Boegart tradition. They sent all their children to Sherborne School in Dorset and then Cambridge. Me as well." He smiled. "Except I was a black sheep and went to Oxford afterward instead of Cambridge. That's how the English side of the family came about."

"Cambridge again," said Finn.

"It made sense in those days to write in English," Billy went on. "*Rutters* were worth their weight in gold. You didn't want other people to know how to get where you were going, so writing in English would have been like writing in code. Not many people could write at all, let alone in another language." He eased over a page in the book and read a little more. "Good Lord," he whispered. "This is Van Boegart's *rutter* for the first voyage of *Vleigende Draeack*, the Flying Dragon." He read aloud from the opening page: "'*Being a Journey in Search of the Hidden Islands and the Secret of Bao Tse Tu, the Leopard King.*'"

"*Vleigende Draeack*," said Finn. "The ship in the painting."

"This book is a treasure map," said Billy, excitement rising in his voice. He flipped through page after page. "Unbelievable!"

"What are the Hidden Islands?" Finn asked. "Do they actually exist?"

"According to this they do," said Billy, holding up the book. "They're a myth, like Neverland in *Peter Pan*. Islands somewhere in the China Seas populated by lions and tigers and elephants and all sorts of other creatures."

"And this Leopard King with the Chinese name?"

"Bao Tse Tu. A Chinese Marco Polo who found the Fountain of Youth on one of the Hidden Islands and who stole an Emperor's treasure for himself."

"And Willem Van Boegart found it, right?"

"Part of it, or so the legend says," Billy said with a shrug.

"Do you believe it?" Finn said.

Billy reached out and plucked a roughly shaped, bloodred crystal from one of the display cases. It was the size of a hen's egg. "If this is a ruby, maybe he really did after all."

"So now what do we do, or need I ask?"

"I think there's a pretty good chance Pieter Boegart disappeared looking for the treasure his ancestor was after. That's what this ship, the *Batavia Queen*, is all about."

"We're supposed to follow him?"

Billy nodded. "I think that's the idea."

"You'd think he would have taken the *rutter*

along with him," said Finn, nodding at the book in Billy's hand.

"He had to leave us something. He probably made a copy."

"And what if we're wrong about all of this?" Finn said. "What if we're overestimating Pieter Boegart? It could be it's all a coincidence: the painting, the room, the book. Maybe they're not connected. Maybe this is all a fantasy."

Billy gave her a long look. "I'm not like some detective on a cop show who doesn't believe in coincidences. I think they happen all the time, but this . . . ?" He held up the book. "I don't care if it's coincidence or if it's some kind of warning from the heavens. Willem Van Boegart's blood runs in my veins, and yours as well by the sound of things." His voice was almost pleading in its intensity. "This is the kind of adventure I've been waiting for all my life." He paused and Finn could see the muscles in his jaw working as he tried to keep his emotions in check. "What do you say?"

"What about those people in London?" Finn asked. "This is no adventure to them. This is serious business. They were out to kill us. They may still be on our tail."

"Then they'll still be on our tail whether we run away or not," argued Billy.

Finn thought about it for a long moment. "All right," she said at last. "Let's go find out what happened to cousin Pieter and his lost treasure."

"Put this in your bag," said Billy, handing her the *rutter*. "Then let's get out of here."

They found a Kinko's a few canals away and spent an hour carefully photocopying the old logbook, then shipped it to Tulkinghorn in London for safekeeping. They spent the rest of the day organizing their trip to Singapore, getting the appropriate shots, and shopping for tropical clothes. That done they headed back to Durgerdam to arrange for longterm berthing of the *Busted Flush*. They got off the bus in front of the Oude Taveerne, then stopped for a bite to eat. After sleeping in the *Flush*'s narrow bunks for the better part of a week they decided to treat themselves to a pair of rooms above the restaurant for the night. They dropped off their purchases in the rooms, then went down the narrow street along the dike, heading for the marina.

The setting sun had turned the windows of the little houses on the inland side of the dike into sheets of liquid gold, and the sky over their heads was deepening through purple into the black silk of night. Finn could just make out the turning vanes of an old windmill in the fields behind the village. A faint breeze riffled the water on their left. It was the perfect image of peace and for the first time in days she felt herself truly relaxing. Even Billy fit perfectly into the scene, and watching the wind blowing through his thick blond hair she could easily see his clear-eyed Dutch ancestors as they set sail for distant lands.

"I've never owned a tramp steamer before," she said as they walked, almost laughing out loud at the thought of it. She'd never even owned a car, let alone a nine-hundred-fifty-ton anything. "What does nine-hundred-fifty-ton displacement mean?" she asked.

"It's not the weight of the vessel. It's the amount of water she displaces when you put her in the water. Then there's gross tonnage, which is calculated in multiples of a hundred cubic feet and doesn't have anything to do with weight, net tonnage, which is useful space for cargo and passengers, and deadweight tonnage, which is the actual weight of the cargo, fuel, passengers, and stores a ship is capable of carrying. The *QE2*, if memory serves, is about forty-five thousand tons of displacement and seventy thousand gross tonnage. Does that help?"

"Vaguely. Relative to the *QE2* the *Batavia Queen* is pretty small, right?"

"Relative to the Pacific Ocean, it's tiny," answered Billy. "But, according to the information Tulkinghorn gave us, she's got a shallow draft, only eleven feet, which makes it ideal for us. It means she can go almost anywhere, even up a lot of rivers." They reached the yacht basin and went down a short flight of wooden steps to the floating pier. "Did you ever watch Jacques Cousteau on the telly?"

"Sure. That horrible John Denver song and all those guys in red wool hats."

"*Calypso*, his research ship, was a converted minesweeper, almost the same as the *Batavia Queen* but smaller."

There was almost no activity in the marina; there was a note on the door of the little hut at the foot of the stairs. Lights burned in the big clubhouse farther along the yacht basin. "Probably having his dinner," said Billy. "Let's go check out the *Flush* and then see if we can find the harbormaster." They turned left along the dock that floated parallel to the dike. It was almost fully dark and the only noise was the lapping of the water against the pier footings and the dull thumping of yacht fenders as they banged against the moorings.

They reached the berth where they'd tied off the *Flush* that morning. Billy stepped onto the boat first and Finn followed close behind. The ship rocked slightly as they boarded. Finn heard a sharp clicking sound. Directly in front of her Billy was silhouetted against the mast.

Suddenly he spun around. "Do you smell that?"

Finn sniffed the air. Faint but there.

Gasoline.

Billy threw himself toward Finn, knocking her backward.

The *Busted Flush* exploded. The sun rose all around them. There was a terrible noise with a pummeling life of its own. Heat blossomed like a huge bright flower and then there was nothing at all.

Finn came to less than a minute later, coughing, soaking wet, and terrified. She sat up and realized that she'd been thrown into the tall grass and shallow water between the floating pier and the dike. She could see the burning remains of the *Flush* fifty feet away, settling into the water on the other side of the pier. She climbed to her knees, muddy sand clinging to her hair. She stood and then staggered toward the dike. "Billy?"

"Here."

She heard coughing and splashing water. A shadow rose up in front of her, hand extended. She reached out and grabbed it. Together she and Billy made it to the dike and pulled themselves up. They turned and stared. The *Busted Flush* was a torch on the water. The pier where it had been berthed was on fire as well. They could see people running along the dock from the direction of the clubhouse. Suddenly there was another thunderous roar and a blast of heat as the gas tank on the forty footer that had been berthed two slips down from the *Flush* exploded. A lurid bright green flare arced crazily out across the water.

"What happened?" said Finn.

"Bomb," answered Billy.

"I heard a sound, just before."

"So did I. A trembler switch, I think it's called. Some kind of motion sensor anyway."

"I smelled gas."

"They cut the fuel line."

"Make it look like an accident?"

"Maybe," said Billy. He ran his hand through his hair. There was a look of anguish on his face. "They blew up my boat. The bastards. They blew up my boat." There were tears in his eyes.

Finn grabbed his arm. The people from the clubhouse were getting close. Finn could hear the screaming of a siren. "We have to get out of here. There'll be questions. Questions we can't answer. We could be held up for days."

"How could they do that? Blow up the *Flush*?"

"It could have been worse," said Finn. "It could have been us. If you hadn't pushed me off the boat when you did, I'd be dead." She kissed him on the cheek. "You saved my life, my lord."

"Don't be an idiot," he said, but he was smiling now. The light from the burning boats flickered across his face.

"We'll get them for what they did," promised Finn, pulling him away. "But now we've got to get away from here, fast."

They vanished into the night.

14

The flight to Singapore was a grueling fifteen hours in a brand-new Airbus-A380. The double-decker monster had taken off from Schipol Airport in Amsterdam with air-conditioning problems and all the twelve-wheeled grace of a flying sperm whale. There was supposed to be a gym somewhere on the enormous airliner as well as a coffee shop, but Finn never found either.

As they flew over all of Europe and most of Southeast Asia, she dozed, swaddled in the sounds of five hundred people chattering in a dozen different languages. She woke up for reheated meals and brief inconsequential conversations with Billy and gave in to the dubious pleasures of watching three John Travolta movies in a row on her little seat-back video screen. After a while being thirty-eight thousand feet in the air and going six hundred miles an hour began to feel almost normal.

After seven and a half time zones, one rubber omelet, two glasses of second-rate Riesling, and a Hainan chicken snack in puff pastry that looked like a McDonald's fruit pie, they arrived at Changi Airport in the middle of the night. According to Finn's and Billy's body clocks, it was early morning and time for breakfast, but all Finn saw on the way in from the airport was a forest of brightly lit skyscrapers and about ten thousand redbrick apartment buildings. They went down some streets with low-rise buildings containing small shops, but they were few and far between; the entire island of Singapore appeared to be one massive downtown.

They climbed out of the cab in front of an aristocratic nineteenth-century building surrounded by floodlit palm trees. It looked like something out of a story by Somerset Maugham, which was exactly what it turned out to be. The name in gold written on the stark white portico above the entrance said it all.

"Raffles?" Finn asked. The most famous hotel in the old British Empire.

"The very one." Billy nodded, grabbing their bags. "Noel Coward, Rudyard Kipling—all that. The last tiger in Malaya was shot under the Raffles bar."

"I didn't know that," said Finn, cocking an eyebrow.

Billy smiled. "Neither did I until I read the brochure on the flight."

"Isn't this going to be a little expensive?" Finn asked as they stepped into the soaring, ornately decorated mid-Victorian lobby. It was no Motel 6. There were silk carpets on marble floors and silver buckets filled with exotic flowers wherever they looked.

"Yes," said Billy. "But it doesn't matter. It's just for one night. I called Tulkinghorn on the plane and told him about the *Flush*. She was well insured and I have other resources as well." He grinned broadly. "Including a bank manager who loves extending my overdraft just to have an overextended duke on his list of clients."

"That kind of thing really goes on?"

"You bet your patootie it does sweetheart," Billy answered, doing an awful James Cagney imitation. "Watch this." She followed him to the front desk and stood by as he introduced himself to the night manager of the hotel, a man in his sixties wearing a turban and what appeared to be an Armani suit. The first clue seemed to be Billy's aristocratic English accent. The second clue was the first mention of the word "lord." Finn never even saw a credit card produced for identification or money change hands. The night manager stiffened, rang a bell, and started snapping orders to subordinates. Within thirty seconds someone had taken the bags from Billy's hand, and thirty seconds after that they were on one of the old-fashioned elevators being shepherded up to their Palm Court suite. Ten minutes later, with the smell of orange blossoms and jacaranda all around her, a suddenly exhausted Finn Ryan slid between silk sheets and was instantly asleep.

The next thing she knew, it was morning and Billy was standing beside her bed wearing a fluffy white bathrobe and drying his hair. "Wake up," he said. "The shower awaits. Breakfast on the verandah in fifteen minutes. Eggs. Bacon. Orange juice. Coffee. Scones. Jam. Hurry up."

The shower was like a piece of heaven and the breakfast was even better. The suite had its own porch that overlooked the broad rectangular courtyard of the hotel, jammed, as advertised, with scores of palm trees. A crystal bowl the size of a volleyball stood in the center of the table, overflowing with every kind of fruit imaginable. Everything was served on silver. The toast came in a rack, the butter was chilled but not hard, and the scrambled eggs were perfect. The bacon was ambrosia; the coffee was dark, pungent, and delicious.

"This is the kind of breakfast movie stars eat," Finn said.

"Then that would make you Julia Roberts," said Billy. "Have some juice."

Finn happily followed orders and finished up her breakfast. After the food was eaten, they stayed on the balcony enjoying the last of the coffee and the exotic view.

"Okay," said Finn after a few long moments staring down at the crushed stone paths, the flowers, and the palms. "Enough Rudyard Kipling for one day. What's on tap?"

"On tap? In the Writers Bar? Tiger draft, I expect."

Finn launched a piece of cold toast across the table at him. "You know what I mean."

"The hotel has a computer I can use. I want to research that gold piece Derlagen the skinhead attorney gave you, and I thought we should check that book you picked up against the rutter. The author was a diplomat's wife or something."

"I'd forgotten all about it," she said. She got up, went back into the suite, and rummaged around in her overnight bag. She found the book and the box with the figurine in it and brought both back to the table.

"Agnes Newton Keith," said Finn, reading the flyleaf blurb. *The Land Below the Wind.* Her husband was with the Colonial Service as Conservator of Forests. She'd been a reporter for the *San Francisco Examiner*. It's all about their adventures in Sandakan, a remote province of North Borneo. I thought all of Borneo was remote."

"Some places more than others, I expect," answered Billy. "It's a gigantic place. Third-largest island in the world. A quarter million square miles and almost all of it jungle. That's as big as Holland, France, and Belgium combined. About the same size as the Saudi Arabian Desert."

"You've been reading brochures again." Finn smiled.

"It was a long flight."

Finn took the gleaming figurine out of the box and set it down on the pure white linen tablecloth. "So what does North Borneo have to do with a gold pendant from Central Africa?"

"It could be anything," said Billy. "As I understand it gold is very hard to age. It looks the same if it's a thousand years old or if it's been smelted yesterday. Eternal gold and all that."

"Mansa, or King Musa, went on a pilgrimage to Mecca in the thirteen hundreds," said Finn, "but that only gets us as far as Saudi Arabia."

"Who traded with Saudi Arabia back then?"

"There was no such thing. It was a bunch of separate sultanates. There are theories about Chinese treasure fleets getting to Oman and Jeddah around the same time as Mansa Musa. It's a stretch, but it's a possibility."

"Of course there's also the possibility that cousin Pieter is just a rich, eccentric lunatic who's gone and got himself bunged up in the rain forest somewhere, and none of this lot means anything." Billy laughed. "My family's actually rather famous for being eccentric, myself being a prime example."

Finn picked up the little figure, letting her thumb gently run over the soft, buttery metal. "Willem Van Boegart went away on the *Flying Dragon* in the late seventeenth century and came back to Amsterdam a wealthy man. That much we know is true, the *rutter* proves it. Our little gold horseman here may be proof of where that wealth actually originated."

"A Chinese treasure ship?"

"Admiral Zheng. He made seven great treasure voyages, the last one in 1433. There were hundreds of ships involved. They took porcelain and silks with them on the outward voyage and returned with gold, gems, ivory, and spices. There were reports of several hurricanes and wrecks. Maybe our little gold friend came from a wreck that Willem Van Boegart discovered on the voyage of the *Flying Dragon*."

"Wouldn't that be bloody marvelous?" said Billy. "Picking up where old Willem and Pieter left off. Now *that* would be an adventure."

"In my experience danger and adventure are often the same word," cautioned Finn. "Remember what happened to the *Busted Flush*."

"I haven't forgotten," said Billy. "In fact I hope we run into those fellows again."

"It makes for a nice movie plot but reality is something else again, believe me." She didn't have to dig very deeply in her memory to see the body of the man who'd died on a railway line in Italy, or a young boy slaughtered beside a tomb in Cairo's City of the Dead. In her short life, she'd seen enough violent death to last her forever; there was no bravado or courage in it, only brutality, pain, and the hot copper smell of spilled blood. Suddenly the coffee tasted bitter and the heat of the bright sun became oppressive. "What about the ship?"

"I've already talked to the shipping agent. She's due to dock in Jurong Harbor at midnight. I think we should be there to meet her."

At just after eleven p.m., the *Batavia Queen* waited in the eastern approaches of Singapore Strait, a mile or so off Sentosa Island, prudently staying just outside the main shipping lane to the container port at Keppel Harbor. Keppel was one of half a dozen docking facilities that made up the Port of Singapore from Jurong in the west to Marina Bay in the east. Once upon a time it had even been possible for break-bulk ships like the *Queen* to navigate through the Johor Strait between Singapore Island and the Malaysian mainland, but the construction of the Johor-Singapore Causeway in the 1920s closed the strait to navigation.

"I can't stay out here much longer," said Briney Hanson, standing by the starboard rail of the ship. "We'll have the Harbor Police sniffing around if we don't watch out." He scanned the night. The darkness was absolute. The sea was a gently undulating pool of inky blackness and the stars were blotted out by a layer of overcast. There was no moon. The only light came from the condos and hotels on Sentosa Island and the garish lights of Singapore beyond.

"Patience, Captain," said Lazlo Aragas, standing at his side. He was dressed as he had been when they met: white suit, glistening shoes, and the Borsalino Panama set squarely on his head. The only thing missing was the sunglasses. They had been replaced by an antiquated pair of horn-rims that were somehow even more sinister. A pair of Russian-made night-vision binoculars hung from a leather strap around his neck. Beside the two men the Slazenger crates had been hoisted onto the deck. Above them, on the bridge, Eli Santoro stood watch, ready to call on McSeveney to give them full steam ahead if necessary.

"Easy enough to say," responded Hanson. "But I'm not sure I like the idea of going to Changi Prison for trying to smuggle your tennis balls."

"You won't be going to Changi," said Aragas. "At least not yet, and not because of me." He lifted the night-vision glasses and peered into the darkness. "Ah," he said softly. "They're coming." Aragas turned to Hanson and smiled. "Would you like to have a look?"

Hanson nodded. Aragas lifted the binoculars,

careful not to disturb the Panama as he brought the strap over his head. In the six days since sailing from Mariveles he'd never seen Aragas without it. He took his meals in his cabin, and according to Bazooki, the Samoan steward and cook's assistant, the Borsalino was in place even there.

Hanson lifted the night glasses. The world turned a lurid green. Three hundred yards off the starboard bow he could see the shape of a fast boat, its sharp bow leaving a broad green slash in its wake. Even in the night glasses the boat's lines were distinctive and so was the broad dark stripe down the side: Singapore Police Coast Guard, one of their half dozen Rodman 55 Jet boats. There was no point in getting on the blower to McSeveney; the Rodman could do thirty-five knots in a calm sea and the *Queen* would be lucky to make half that. They'd been screwed.

He lowered the glasses and turned to Aragas. "Bastard."

"Betrayal is a wonderful thing, no?" Aragas said.

Hanson felt his insides knot. It was all over. "I could toss your sorry little ass overboard right now." He pulled the Curry Lockspike out of his pocket and snapped the blade open. "But first I'd open up an artery for the sharks to work on."

"Don't be silly, Captain. That boat has a fifty-caliber machine gun mounted on the deck and my men are all armed as well. The boat is also equipped with four medium Whitehead acoustic torpedoes. Your ship would be turned to scrap metal within a minute and a half. You'd be dead before the first shark took a bite."

The patrol boat was getting closer. A searchlight on the bow flashed on, bathing the entire flank of the *Queen* in brilliant light. Eli came out onto the flying bridge and called anxiously down to Hanson.

"We get a problem, boss?"

"I'll let you know," yelled Hanson. Eli went back into the deckhouse. Hanson turned to Aragas. "So you're some kind of cop?"

"Indeed, Captain, I am some kind of cop. Have you ever heard of CISCO?"

"Private spooks," answered Hanson. CISCO stood for Commercial and Industrial Security Corporation, a privatized sector of the Singapore Police Force, usually dealing in industrial crime and intelligence.

"A specialist. Antiterrorism."

"Isn't everyone these days?" Hanson snorted. "You'd think there was no other crime."

"In my case there isn't," replied Aragas. "Terrorism is an expensive business for all concerned. Drugs are generally what finances it."

"So what are we doing here?" Hanson asked.

"Just as I told you in the first place," said the dapper little man.

"Shipping tennis balls," said Hanson, jerking his chin toward the pile of crates with the leaping leopard logo on the side.

"That's right." Aragas smiled. The patrol boat came alongside, searchlight blazing, and within a few seconds, uniformed men were swarming up the companionway ladder Hanson had ordered to be lowered to accommodate whoever came out from Sentosa Island. The men all carried CIS drum-fed machine guns and Sphinx 3000 nine-millimeter automatic pistols. They looked extremely efficient.

Aragas nodded to the lead officer, a three-striper with a face that looked like it had been dragged along a dirt road, and gestured toward the stack of crates. *"Membuka dia!"* he ordered. The man with the jackhammered face stepped forward and smashed the butt of his weapon into one of the crates. The wood splintered and he tore the box open. Aragas went to the box and removed one of the familiar dark blue Slazenger tubes. He brought it back to where Hanson stood at the rail and pulled open the vacuum-sealed top. There was a slight hiss and four bright yellow tennis balls dropped out of the tube and hit the deck of the *Batavia Queen*. As the ship rolled slightly they drifted off toward the bilges.

"Tennis balls," said Aragas. "Slazenger Ultra Vis."

"What's the story?" Hanson asked, staring.

"The story is the oldest one in the world, Captain Hanson," said Aragas. "We have established precisely what you will do for a price. In this case you proved yourself both corruptible and intelligent. These are two assets I expect to find very useful in the future."

"Isn't this all entrapment?"

"Entrapment is an American word from their police movies, Captain Hanson. It doesn't apply in the real world. We have a half dozen official witnesses who will swear that you have been caught illegally bringing items into the sovereign state of Singapore. The fact that it is tennis balls is irrelevant. The crime is the same: cocaine or coconuts, heroin or handguns, *shabu* or Shetland ponies. You can be convicted of smuggling anytime I see fit—do you understand?"

Hanson understood that the slimy little bastard had him by the short hairs and that he was in no position to negotiate; his livelihood, his very life, hung in the balance. Somewhere in the distance a ship's horn sounded. Water lapped against the hull in a flat, unending rhythm. "What do you want?"

"Your cooperation."

"Which means?"

"Your vessel has been sold to new owners. Two young people—an American woman and her companion, a British subject of some aristocratic rank—have inherited this ship as part of one of Boegart Shipping Lines trust agreements."

Hanson nodded. "They're supposed to be meeting us in Singapore."

"Yes," said Aragas. "I am also informed that a man named Khan has shown a decided interest in these two people. You know the name?"

"Of course, everyone in this line of business does. You're talking about the pirate."

"He does not think of himself as a pirate. Pirates are easy to deal with. They are motivated only by greed and greed is an easy thing to feed. Our Khan fashions himself a revolutionary, an idealist, a zealot. Like our friend Mr. bin Laden, Jackson Abang Abdul Rauf thinks he has God on his side. There is nothing more dangerous than a true believer, Captain Hanson, take it from me. Such men cannot be dealt with simply by giving them an envelope filled with cash." Aragas paused and turned toward the three-striper. He snapped his fingers and the sergeant started barking orders to the other men who had boarded the *Batavia Queen*. They began taking the crates down the companionway ladder to the patrol boat alongside.

"What are you saying?"

"Khan is the leader of an organization with a very long reach, Captain Hanson. He tried to have your new owners kidnapped in London and then tried to eliminate them again in Holland. No doubt he will try again now that these two people have arrived in Singapore."

"Why?"

"Indeed. That is the question I would like answered myself."

"So I'm supposed to find out for you?"

"If you'd be so kind, Captain Hanson. It would be of interest to me to know why these two people are important enough to pose a threat to a man like Khan."

"And if I find out anything?"

"Report back to me."

"How? You want me to send it out on the radio? Khan monitors all the maritime frequencies. That's how he knows what ships to go after. He's also got spies in every one of the major shipping agency offices." He gestured at the men loading the crates. "I'll bet he's got people in your operation as well."

"The Coast Guard Police aren't my operation as you call it, Captain Hanson. You might say I am my own operation." He turned and snapped his fingers again. The gravel-faced sergeant stepped forward and stood to attention in front of Aragas. He held out his hand. The sergeant reached into the pocket of his jacket and took out a palm-sized telephone unit with a slightly larger than usual antenna wand. He handed the phone to Aragas, who in turn held it out to Hanson. "This is a Hughes 9505A iridium satellite telephone. It has a restricted memory, which means the only person it will call is me. Switch it on, press the number one, and you will be connected automatically. Is that too difficult for you, Captain?"

The men in the Police Coast Guard uniforms removed the last crate of tennis balls and manhandled it down the companionway stairs.

"No, I suppose I can manage that," said Hanson, taking the phone. It was extremely heavy for its small size. There was no use in trying to bluster his way out of the situation he was in; Aragas had played him perfectly. "Do you have any idea what Khan is looking for? Drugs? Weapons? What?"

"There is a rumor . . ." Aragas glanced across the deck. The last crate was gone along with the police. The sergeant stood alone at the head of the companionway leading down to the waiting patrol boat. Aragas made a small gesture with his hand and the sergeant turned away and went down the stairway. "There is a rumor that Khan searches for a great treasure from the war."

"There's a lot of those rumors going about," said Hanson. "There's been rumors like that for years. Japanese loot from the occupation of the Philippines, gold coins dumped in Singapore Harbor just before the invasion. Then there's that rumor about the Brooklyn Bridge being for sale."

Aragas ignored the comment. "Have you ever heard of a Japanese submarine, *I-52*?"

"I read *National Geographic*. It was supposed to be filled with gold and opium. The Brits sank her in mid-Atlantic. Three miles down."

"There is some question about the submarine's actual identity. The Japanese are many things, Captain, but they are not stupid. Some people would call them devious, in fact. Khan has discovered information that might lead one to believe that there were two *I-52* transport submarines."

"I'm not sure I see the point."

"One was a decoy. It was the one that sunk. The second one, the real *I-52*, vanished before it even left the China Seas."

"Where?"

"They were under strict radio silence, but according to the information Khan has received she was last seen by a fishing boat on January first, 1944, off the northeast coast of Palawan."

"Is there some significance to that date?"

"It's two months earlier than the official date for *I-52*'s departure from Japan. It is also the beginning of what came to be called the New Year Typhoon. The official name was Typhoon Amy. Japanese and Allied operations were shut down for the better part of ten days. The fishing boat said it appeared to them that *I-52* was running for safety."

"Why didn't she just submerge?"

"Who knows? She was a C-3 transport, one of only three ever built. A new design. Perhaps they were having problems. Maybe the fishing boat was right. The captain was seeking shelter."

"Where?"

"Perhaps that is what Khan has discovered," said Aragas softly. "And perhaps it is what your new owners have discovered as well."

"And I'm caught in the middle."

"So it would seem, Captain Hanson. So it would seem." Aragas patted Hanson on the shoulder and smiled. "Sometimes being in the middle can have its advantages. It's much harder for people to sneak up on you." He patted Hanson's shoulder again, then headed for the companionway. He turned and paused just before stepping down toward the waiting patrol boat. "Do keep in touch," he said. "I'll be expecting your call." He gave a little wave and disappeared.

There was a dull, decelerating roar from overhead and Hanson looked up. The lights from a big wide-body flashed above him as it descended toward Changi International.

He looked up at the bridge and saw the glow of Eli's cigarette in the darkness. He held up his hand and gave a thumbs-up. A few moments later, he heard the dull, strained rumblings of the engines taking hold as McSeveney put the *Batavia Queen* to half ahead and Eli turned them toward the distant lights of Singapore. Hanson looked down at his watch. It was getting on toward midnight.

15

The *Black Dragon* rested easily in a narrow inlet at the mouth of the little river estuary. The ghostly gunship was almost invisible in the night and fog. Khan stood on the bow of the *Black Dragon*, listening. He was wearing lightweight jungle camouflage gear stolen from a shipment meant for the Philippine Army. It came with a floppy Tilly hat, which he chose not to wear, preferring the simple black beret of the police commando units. He had a pair of U.S. Navy night-vision binoculars around his neck, but he ignored them. He much preferred his own senses. In the distance he could hear the surf breaking on the narrow line of reefs and closer, the slap of waves against the hull of the *Black Dragon*. He could smell the sick-sweet odor of the mangroves a few yards away and the rotting vegetation swirling among their roots, the stink of dead fish, and faintly the thin scent of gasoline.

"You're sure?" Khan said to Fu Sheng, standing just behind him on the deck.

"Yes. She draws almost eight feet. They need deep water to moor."

"Why here?"

"There is a spring half a mile or so upriver. They use their skiff to fetch fresh water."

"How many?"

"Four. Three men and a woman. Young."

"Strange that they would be joined by a girl. This kind of thing is hardly woman's work."

"They are Americans," said Fu Sheng with a shrug, as though their nationality explained everything. "The girl is proof, I think."

"Proof?" Khan queried.

"Their victims think as anyone might. They put her in a bikini, sunbathing on deck. She waves and smiles. What could be wrong? You think."

"And then they spring their trap and we are blamed."

Fu Sheng nodded. "That is their method." A new sound rose above the rhythmic thunder of the surf breaking on the reef. The burbling of an engine. It became louder as it approached. The two men waited, listening. "It is them," said Fu Sheng quietly. "What is your order, *tuan*?"

"Wait until they drop anchor and set off in the skiff." Khan paused. "How many will fetch water?"

"Two. The girl remains and one other. We have watched them several times now."

"Kill the two in the skiff as they approach the shore. We will take *Dragon* and board them before they have a chance to escape."

"Yes, *tuan*," said Fu Sheng. He turned away, crossed the deck to the wheelhouse, and went below.

Khan stood in the bow and waited for the boat to sail into the trap that had been laid for it. The boat had been in the area for more than two years now, but he had never seen it. Originally the boat, then named *Quicksilver*, had belonged to a wealthy real estate agent from Vancouver traveling around the world with his wife and eleven-year-old daughter. The husband and wife were both experienced sailors and should have known better, but human nature being what it is, they hadn't checked the backgrounds of the two young people they picked up hitchhiking through Asia by part-time crewing on pleasure boats. The husband had his throat slit in the middle of the night several days out of Manila, while the daughter and the wife had been kept alive for more than a week and raped repeatedly during that time. Sometime in that week, the *Quicksilver* had rendezvoused with a second boat, the *Artemesia*, piloted by the other two members of the gang. After another gang-rape session lasting two days, the mother and daughter had been set adrift without food or water in the *Artemesia*, which was the smaller of the two vessels. Before being set adrift, the *Artemesia*'s engine was disabled and an ax had been used to hack a gaping hole in her side. The sailboat had foundered but remained afloat and eventually was spotted by a dive boat from the resort at Pulau Tiga, the original *Survivor* island. By the time the dive boat reached *Artemesia*, the child was dead of exposure and internal injuries, but the mother lived long enough to tell the story of what had happened. *Quicksilver*, under several different names, had been sighted as far north as Hawaii and as far south as New Zealand and was thought to be responsible for a number of disappearances. So far there had been no absolute identification of the brutal "pirates," but one of them was thought to be the "Surfer Dude Bandit," wanted for several counts of armed robbery in Los Angeles.

The sound of the boat engine grew even louder and Khan lifted the night glasses. The world turned a bilious green and he spotted their quarry almost immediately. The boat was a forty-two-foot Sabre, built in Maine and only five years old. Her mainsail was down and furled. The fifty-horsepower diesel was capable of pushing her along at eight knots, but she was probably doing no more than four against the sweeping, almost invisible current of the muddy river. She wasn't showing any running lights. A man with long hair was standing at the wheel, guiding the sailboat upriver. There was a second man, this one in shorts and a baseball cap, standing in the bow. He appeared to have a rifle slung over his shoulder. There was a large parang machete hanging from his belt and a holstered sidearm. Some sort of large revolver.

As Khan watched through the night glasses, the boat slowed and the engine sound faded. The man in the bow knelt, then rose, holding a Fortress claw anchor by its nylon rope. He slid the anchor over the side without a splash, setting it on a short line. He went to the stern, set a second anchor, and then began to haul up the skiff that had been trailing along behind. The skiff was an eight-foot inflatable in jungle camouflage. It looked hard-worn and much older than the Sabre, probably taken from another boat along the way. Pirated from some other poor American fool playing at sailing in monsoon seas. Khan sent up a brief and silent prayer for the soul of the little girl who had died so foully at these men's hands and watched as they climbed down into the dingy carrying a half dozen five-gallon plastic jugs. The man with the rifle sat in the stern of the little boat and switched on the three-horsepower Briggs and Stratton outboard. A faint whirring sound rose into the still air and the dingy moved off. Out of the corner of his eye Khan caught the small movement of one of his own men. He waited until the dingy was well away from the Sabre before he gave the order.

"*Sekarang*," he said quietly. *Now.* His man triggered a short burst from the bare-bones Type-64 Chinese submachine gun. The weapon had an integral silencer and barely made a sound as it ripped through its thirty-round clip in less than a second. The shells tore the dingy to shreds and a half dozen thumped into the two men. A few banged loudly into the outboard motor housing. The two men, screaming, toppled into the swirling brown water. Still watching through the night glasses, Khan saw a pair of heavy, dark shapes launch themselves out of the mangrove shallows on the far bank and slide toward the thrashing bodies of the wounded men. One of the long-nosed saltwater crocodiles reared up and caught the long-haired man's head between its jaws. There was a small crunching noise as the skull was crushed and the pale wet brain popped out in several pieces like chunks of rotted fruit. The second man, arms windmilling, tried to get ashore, but the second armor-plated reptile caught him at the belt line and carried him under the surface.

"*Lekas!*" *Quickly.* There was a sudden thunder as the *Black Dragon*'s huge engines burst into life. The throttle was engaged and the fast-attack craft roared out of its narrow hiding place between the mangroves and powered across the river to where the sailboat was anchored. Less than thirty seconds had passed since the first shots were fired. A figure appeared in the cockpit, naked except for a pair of boxer shorts. The figure was carrying a handgun.

"Lampu cari," ordered Khan, dropping the night-vision goggles away from his eyes. The searchlight in the cockpit snapped on, bathing the sailboat in a blue-tinged glow. The half-naked man raised a hand to shield his eyes. He was well muscled, tanned, and blond.

"Drop the weapon!" Khan called out loudly.

"Who the hell are you?" shouted the blond man in the sailboat.

"Ke dalam sungai," said Khan to the man standing behind him with the Type 64. The man snapped another clip into the submachine gun and aimed into the river beside the boat. He let off a burst of fire and the water by the stern of the sailboat jumped and spattered. "Drop the weapon," repeated Khan. This time the man in the sailboat did as he was told. The pistol dropped into the water. Fu Sheng reappeared at Khan's side. He had another Type 64 slung over his shoulder and a twenty-inch bolo in a canvas sheath at his waist.

The *Black Dragon* thumped against the hull of the sailboat. Fu Sheng and the man who had fired on the inflatable took lines from the deck of the gunboat and boarded the other vessel. They used the lines to lash the two boats together. The man in the boxer shorts remained in the cockpit of the sailboat, hands in the air. Khan noticed that the man had a thick, ropy scar that ran from one shoulder halfway across his chest. A knife fight long ago. The kind of raw wound you got in prison. The man's eyes were hard in the glare from the spotlight. No fear, only anger.

Fu Sheng and the man with the gun moved into the cockpit. The man with the gun stayed on deck while Fu Sheng went below. Fu Sheng reappeared a few moments later, pushing the naked figure of a young woman up on deck ahead of him. She tried to cover herself with her hands. She was pale skinned and dark haired, not very pretty but with large breasts and long legs. Tears were streaming down her cheeks. She was very frightened. In the harsh light Khan could see the slight puckering of the flesh of her thighs. The tears had made her makeup run. She was older than she had first appeared. In a bikini, from a distance, it wouldn't matter. He wondered what kind of woman wore makeup in the middle of the ocean. The kind of woman who would make herself naked for a man like the one with the scar. The man and the woman reminded him of the flat-headed water snakes he sometimes saw in the swamps. People without souls.

"Awak boleh berbahasa Inggeris?" the man with the scar asked. His pronunciation was terrible.

"Yes," said Khan. "I speak English."

"Why are you doing this? We've done nothing to harm you."

"This is my territory," answered Khan. "You have no business here."

"Then let us go."

"Perhaps. Not yet."

"You killed Hank and Jimmy!" This from the naked girl. "You bastards!"

"What is her name?" Khan asked the man with the scar.

"Her name's Bonnie."

"Tell Bonnie that if she doesn't keep quiet I will cut out her tongue and throw it to the *buaya* she saw eat her friends in the river."

"Don't you dare touch me!" screamed Bonnie, jerking in Fu Sheng's grip. "I'm an American citizen, goddamn you!" She jerked again. Fu Sheng used his free hand to punch her directly in the face as hard as he could. Several teeth broke and so did her nose. Blood spurted and streamed, covering her chin. Screaming wetly she fell to her knees. Fu Sheng let her go. She curled up in a ball on the deck of the cockpit and moaned loudly. The man with the scar never took his eyes off Khan.

The pirate turned, handing his night glasses to

the man standing at the wheel of the *Black Dragon*. He stepped to the gunwale and dropped down onto the deck of the sailboat. He went to the cockpit, stepped over the bleeding woman, and ducked his head, going down three steps into the main salon.

"*Membawa mereka*," said Khan, without turning. *Bring them.*

He looked around the salon. It was quite luxurious, although it had clearly not been cleaned in a long time. The headliner was cork inset with pot lights in strategic points. Everything else was done in some pale exotic wood. There was an efficient-looking galley on the right complete with gas stove, refrigerator, and an inset microwave. Opposite the galley was an impressively equipped navigation station. A narrow passage led back from the navigation station into what was presumably the master cabin, below the cockpit. Ahead of the galley and the navigation station was the salon proper. There was a settee on the right that looked as though it converted into a single berth and an eating nook on the left in a boothlike configuration. The upholstery of the settee and the benches in the booth were done in a rich sea green. There were several lozenge-shaped portholes on either side. In the morning light, it would be bright and inviting. There was another narrow passage leading forward to a bulkhead door. Probably a pair of berths set into the bow.

The galley was filthy and there were dirty dishes on the table in the booth. The whole below-decks area smelled of body odor and alcohol. Khan knelt and pulled open a drawer built in below the settee. It was neatly packed with expensive-looking foul-weather gear. Gill Ocean Racer in bright blues and red and yellow. Expensive. The previous owner had been careful and meticulous. The people who came after had been pigs. But that was over now. There would be balance.

Fu Sheng brought the half-naked man stumbling down the short companionway into the salon. The other soldier brought the girl. The girl dropped down onto the settee and curled up, sniveling through the blood bubbling out of her torn mouth and the crushed remains of her nose. Fu Sheng pushed the man in the boxer shorts onto the bench in the breakfast nook. Khan sat down across from him. The man looked frightened now, something scurrying behind the small blue eyes.

"You know who I am, don't you?" Khan said.

"You're Khan, the pirate *bokap*."

"And you're the Surfer Dude Bandit."

"Is that what they call me?" The man gave a sour little smile.

"You robbed convenience stores."

"Yeah, I did that."

"And then you came here."

"It seemed like a good idea at the time."

"You think you're a funny man."

"Sometimes."

"But not now," said Khan. "This is not a joke."

"No, I guess not."

Khan reached into the pocket of his combat blouse and took out a small, gleaming wafer of metal. He placed it on the Formica surface of the table between them. It was a gold bar, approximately one inch by two inches, the corners gently rounded. There was a circular, sixteen-petaled imperial chrysanthemum stamp at one end and below it the numbers 777.

"You recognize this?"

"No," said the man in the boxer shorts.

"You're lying." Khan looked up at Fu Sheng, who stood beside the table. *"Nia tangan,"* he said. Fu Sheng reached down, grabbing the half-naked man's arm. He pulled a short length of surgical tubing from the pocket of his combat blouse and wrapped it tightly around the wrist.

"What are you doing?"

"It's to stop the bleeding," said Khan.

"What bleeding?"

In a single smooth motion Fu Sheng swept the long bolo knife out of its sheath and brought the razor-sharp blade down onto the man's hand, cutting through the fingers at the first joint. The little stubs of flesh bounced with the blade and dropped down onto the deck of the salon. White-faced, the man in the boxers stared down at the blood and the remains of his hand. Fu Sheng re-sheathed the bolo and pulled the surgical tubing even tighter. The bleeding from the stubs of the fingers slowed. The blond-haired man looked as though he was going to faint. On the settee the naked woman stared at the ruined hand and the chunks of flesh on the deck and vomited.

"It's a one-ounce gold bar from the Nippon Ginko Bank. Japanese. World War Two vintage. Do you recognize it?"

"Yes," answered the man, teeth clenched.

"You sold it to a Malay bullion dealer on Labuan named Wei Yang." Labuan was a freeport island a few kilometers off the coast of Brunei.

"Yes."

"Where did you get it?"

"A guy I met . . . in a brothel. Chinese."

"What was his name?"

"I didn't ask."

"Where did he get it?"

"He took it from a boat."

"What boat?"

"A smuggler. Tried to take him. This guy took them instead."

"He killed them?"

"Yes. Killed all of them."

"How many?"

"Five."

"What kind of boat?"

"Looked like an old pearling lugger. Could have been an old trawler. Hundred tons maybe. Some American turned it into a live-aboard years ago. The smuggler killed him, took it. Fast, big engines. Not enough guns, though." The man with the ruined hand made a deep moaning sound. His face was the color of ash. Shock. He'd pass out in a few minutes.

"Did the boat have a name?"

"*Pedang Emas.*"

Gold Sword.

"Out of what port?"

"He didn't say."

"Zamboanga?"

"Maybe. Maybe it's a gypsy. No port."

"Why did he tell you all this?"

"He wanted to sell me the gold bar. He was drunk. Full of himself. Boasting."

"Where did this happen and when?"

"Two months ago. Kampong Sugut."

A village off the coast in Kudat Province. The east coast on the Sulu Sea. Three nights' journey in the *Black Dragon*. The *Gold Sword* had probably made the lucrative run from Zamboanga carrying anything from drugs to weapons from the Chinese mainland.

"Did the Chinaman question the smuggler about the gold bar?"

"I don't know."

Khan looked up and nodded at Fu Sheng. He

unsheathed the bolo and raised it. The man with
the mutilated hand winced and jerked away.

"Did he ask about the gold bar?" Khan repeated.

"Yes."

"What did the smuggler say?"

"Some story. Stupid story."

"What story?"

"A man on a raft."

"What about him?"

"He was wearing a uniform. What was left of
one."

"What kind of uniform?"

"He said Japanese."

"Japanese?"

"World War Two."

"And the gold?"

"He offered it to the smuggler if he would take
him aboard their boat. He said he had more. The
smuggler tortured him. He died before he could
tell him where it was from."

"A crazy story."

"Yeah, crazy."

"Kampong Sugut."

"I told you already."

Khan thought about the currents and the winds,
imagining the raft and its occupant. He reached
out and picked up the little gold wafer, rubbing
the soft metal between his thumb and forefinger.

"The little girl," said Khan.

"What?"

"The little girl who was on this boat."

"What about her?"

"You raped her, left her and her mother for dead."

"Yeah, so?"

"What was her name?"

"What are you talking about?"

"Do you even know her name? You rape a child and you have no idea who she was?"

"Screw you."

"Dia leher," said Khan to Fu Sheng. He grabbed the man and forced his head back, exposing the throat. Khan curled his hand into a fist and punched the man as hard as he could, crushing the small bones and muscles in the larynx and rupturing the thyroid cartilage or Adam's apple. The man's throat immediately swelled and closed directly above the trachea, effectively stopping his breathing. His face began to turn blue and he started to struggle as he began suffocating. The girl looked on, horrified.

"What's happening?" she screamed. "What are you doing?"

Khan punched the man a second time, breaking his nose and teeth and sending blood flooding down his sinus passages and his throat, drowning him now as well as suffocating him.

"Bring him on deck," he said to Fu Sheng in Malay. Khan slid out of the narrow booth and went out into the fresh air again, breathing in the heavy, ripe scent of the river and the jungle. Behind him Fu Sheng dragged the choking, dying man, whose eyes were bulging with terror now, his lungs desperately trying to suck in oxygen through his ruined throat. "Throw him over the side," said Khan. He reached into the left pocket of his uniform blouse and took out a thin, hand-rolled kerak cigarette, lighting it with a kitchen match. He watched as Fu Sheng pushed the dying man over the side and into the muddy water. The man went under and then rose up again, arms splashing the surface of the water. The man's face was very dark now and his long hair was plastered wetly across his features. He jerked hard as the first of the huge crocodiles struck him invisibly from below. He made a strangled, screaming noise as the second reptile tore into his midsection, ripping away his legs and groin. The first croc surged upward out on the water, waggling the man's torso in the air, his intestines squirting out around the immense, gleaming teeth. The man was still alive, head thrown back, his hands flapping weakly as the crocodile twisted away and brought its jaws together, crushing the man's ribs and chest, then carrying him below the surface.

"The story about the Japanese sailor again," said Fu Sheng.

"You believe it?" Khan asked.

"It is the third time we have heard it now."

"There have been rumors of it for years."

"He had a place. Kampong Sugut."

"What do you think, old friend?"

"I think rumors are rumors and facts are facts."

Khan smiled. "What of old wives' tales and children's stories?"

"You mean *Naga Pulau?*"

"Yes." *Naga Pulau*, Dragon Island, the Isle of Storms, mythological home of *Kinabalu* and *Yamato ne Orochi*. The Three Treasures and *Kusanagi*, the Sacred Sword. The legendary island, wreathed in mist, surrounded by reefs and a thousand wrecks, somewhere lurking in the South China Seas like every sailor's nightmare nemesis. Perhaps even the origin of the King Kong story or even Jurassic Park.

Fu Sheng made a snorting sound. "I think dragons are for video games and white women pretending that they know something of feng shui. I think old wives' tales are for old wives and children's stories are for children. I have sailed these seas since I was a boy and have never seen it. There is no such place as *Naga Pulau*."

Khan laughed, puffing on his clove cigarette. "You are a sour old man."

"True, but at least I am alive to be that way, unlike our Surfer Dude Bandit friend." Fu Sheng shook his head. "He was really called that?"

"Apparently so."

"The Americans are truly a strange race. They are very much like their cartoons on Saturday mornings." Fu Sheng was a long-standing fan of the *Animaniacs*. He looked down at the fast-flowing muddy river. "What are we going to do now?"

"We will proceed. I will take *Black Dragon* to Kampong Sugut. You follow with the sailboat. We will meet there in five days."

"What about our friends from Amsterdam?"

"We missed our chance once. We will not miss again. Find me the *Batavia Queen*."

16

The wardroom of the *Batavia Queen* was a large, low-ceilinged room, forward of the engine covering and directly below the bridge. Originally intended as the officers' mess when it was a minesweeper, it had been paneled somewhere along the way in cheap plywood and fitted out with a tuck shop for the whole crew. The deck was painted a bilious green. There were a few booths against the bulkheads and three tables bolted down. Shelves had been placed here and there over the years, some fitted with small appliances like a toaster oven, a microwave, and a giant boom box, others stacked with dry goods and ratty-looking paperbacks or magazines.

Supposedly overseen by Bazooki, the steward, the cleaning and operation of the wardroom were actually done on a catch-as-catch-can basis divided among everyone on the twelve-man crew, including Briney Hanson, the captain. Given that fact, it was surprisingly clean and tidy, with an overpowering scent of some sort of industrial-strength cleaner that made Finn Ryan almost gag with the wafting odor of a synthetic pine forest.

The *Queen*'s engines droned in a dull, idling hum barely turning over while the ship stood against the fueling wharf in the Jurong Docks area of Singapore Harbor. Through the portholes on the port side, Finn could see across the dark roof-tops of the Jurong warehouses to the neon strip of Pioneer Road and beyond it to the Ayer Rajah Expressway. New York might have been the city that never slept, but Singapore was the city that never stopped. It was almost three in the morning and the flow of traffic on the expressway was a never diminishing thunder of engines and blur of headlights. She tried to concentrate on Briney Hanson's story about the chubby police officer, this Lazlo Aragas, who sounded like something out of an old Humphrey Bogart movie, but her eyes kept drooping with the need for sleep. Hanson had been talking since they'd arrived on board the rusty old freighter and she was still confused.

It was obvious that Billy was still confused as well, Finn thought. "So Aragas is after this pirate—this Malay you claim was the one who blew up my boat?" he said.

"From what I hear, Khan is more of a revolutionary than a pirate, and if he is a pirate, he's the Robin Hood sort."

"Steals from the rich, gives to the poor, you mean?" Billy asked.

Hanson nodded. "Something like that."

"Yet he's got the connections to blow up a boat in Amsterdam and have us kidnapped in London?"

Hanson shrugged. "Apparently," he said. "And I'm not surprised. If a man in a cave in Afghanistan can blow up the World Trade Center in New York, why not Khan? It's a small world these days. Paris for lunch, Fiji for the weekend."

"I suppose you're right," grunted Billy.

"But you think this has more to do with money?" Finn asked.

"I don't believe Aragas is simply interested in bringing a pirate to justice."

"So you believe this story about the Japanese submarine?" Billy said, his skepticism obvious in his tone.

"I believe that Aragas believes it. Everything about the man smells of greed. If he thinks Khan has found some kind of treasure, he wants his cut, if not the whole thing."

"What about this CISCO bunch he works for?"

"A private sector of the Singapore Police Force, affiliated with the Singapore Armed Forces and the Coast Guard."

"Corrupt?"

"Does the pope still eat fish on Fridays?"

"Then you think Aragas is using CISCO to get the treasure for himself?"

"Yes. There might be others in it with him, but he's the boss."

"And we're in the middle."

"I never should have left Columbus," said Finn, yawning. "Okay, then where do we go from here?"

"Away from Singapore for one thing. It's one of the most expensive port facilities in the world. I'd like to be out of here as soon as we're finished fueling. That's the last time I'll be able to fill her bunkers on the Boegart Shipping line of credit." Hanson looked across the wardroom table at Finn and Billy. "As their new masters, you'll have that responsibility now. The *Queen* is still willing and able to work, but freighters run on bunker C and hauling contracts, not pipe dreams and buried treasure."

Billy reached into his jacket, took out his billfold, and withdrew a credit card. He dropped it on the table with a metallic clicking sound. It was anodized black with titanium letters and numbers on it.

Hanson picked up the card and examined it. He tapped it against the table. Definitely not plastic. "I thought those were just urban legends," he said.

"That particular urban legend will pay for your

bunker C from now on," said Billy. "The last place Pieter Boegart was seen was the island of Labuan. Can you get us there?"

"I'll lay in a course now." Hanson grinned, dropping the card back onto the table.

The journey took them a little more than three days, moving through the Singapore Straits and the Api Passage, then following the mangrove line of Borneo's west coast northward on a track that would eventually have taken them back to Bataan and Manila. The weather was clear and fine, the hot sun burning down on the old ship, making the rusty deck plates and the bulkheads too hot to touch with a bare hand or foot. The air-conditioning units were set into a constant roaring symphony that played in concert with the throbbing engines, the gentle pounding of the sea against the hull, and the dissonant clanging of Run-Run McSeveney's monkey wrench against some stubborn piece of machinery as well as the constant, inventive, and multinational cadence of his swearing.

Finn used the time to roam the ship, looking into every corner from the steering gear platform in the stern to the paint and lamp room in the bow and everything in between, all of it strangely intoxicating and exciting as though she'd been born to live in an environment of the smells of the sea, hot oil, and old rope. She got to know the crew, helping McSeveney lubricate his precious engines, catching fish on a long line over the side with Toshi Minimoto, the Japanese cook, which she then helped him prepare in the cramped little galley behind the deckhouse and listened to Elisha Santoro describing the geography of the places they could see no more than a mile or two away along the coast.

Billy spent most of his time on the bridge with Hanson, trying to get a feel for the complexities of what it was like skippering an old-fashioned tramp steamer like the *Batavia Queen*. He quickly learned that it wasn't like sailing in the Thames or even across the English Channel. Here there were a dozen different kinds of channel markers and danger buoys in colors that came in stripes, diamonds, and quarters and shapes like cones, circles, spars dolphins, and spindles—each shape, color, and combination having a different meaning.

"It's worse than driving a bloody car or piloting an airplane."

"And it's different wherever you go. There's supposed to be a unified system but the Malays, the Brunei, the Vietnamese. and the Chinese all have their own little variations."

Worse than the buoys and ocean signals were the unseen dangers of reef shoals and what Hanson called "foul ground," visible only at low tide. Between Singapore and Labuan, there were almost a thousand islands, twice that many almost invisible atolls, and ten times as many shoals. To make matters worse, the Palawan Passage, as it was called, was one of the most heavily used in the world. Given the size and inertia of the ships involved, it was roughly equivalent to driving in Los Angeles rush-hour traffic and doing it without traffic lights or exit ramps.

The physical dangers ranged from the hidden rocks at *Badas Kepulauan* to the widespread shoals beyond *Telok Tambelan*. Even the terminology was strange and confusing. A *malang* was a reef, or a shoal, but so was a *napu*. A cape was a *tandjong*; a smooth sea was *tenang*. *Sawang* was a narrows, *selatan* was south, and *sungai* was a river. A *tukoh* was a sunken rock; a *trumbu* was a reef that dried. *Tjeck* was a shallows and *terumbu* was a connecting channel.

"And most of the time, you need to know the words in Dutch as well, because some of the best charts are the old Dutch ones," laughed Hanson. "Keeps you on your toes, believe me."

Labuan, derived from the Malay word for "anchorage," is a thirty-square-mile island of low jungle that looks like the ponderous three-toed footprint of some giant Godzilla-like dinosaur with all three toes pointing to the tiny kingdom of Brunei on the mainland. In between the second and third toes is a deepwater harbor and a town of seventy thousand that was once called Victoria back in the days of the white rajahs but was now

called, somewhat less romantically, Bandar Labuan, or Labuan City. Originally used as a naval
base against pirates and then as a location for the
Singapore–Hong Kong Telegraph cable, Labuan
was never much more than a colonial backwater.

When it joined the Malay Federation in the
eighties, some attempt was made to encourage Labuan as a center for offshore banking, a freeport,
and a petroleum center, but nothing really worked
and by and large the small population seems to
prefer it that way. Qualified technical personnel
working in the petroleum refinery and at the huge
government shipyards live in neat, subsidized
high-rise accommodation in the center of the town
along with a scattering of tourist hotels, while the
unskilled laborers and their families live in the
shacks on stilts of the *kampung ayer*, or water villages, on the far side of the harbor on the shore
of the island's middle "toe."

There are two of these sprawling semislums in
Labuan, *Kampung Bebuloh* and *Kampung Patau-
Patau*. Both of these are tourist showplaces, full of
stores and small craft-ware factories, the tin-
roofed, open-walled structures connected by a
maze of wooden plank walkways and accessible
by water taxi. A much larger *kampong ayer* is occupied by several thousand Filipino squatters on the
near side of the harbor.

These are Labuan's true poor, the majority of
them indentured sex industry workers employed

in floating brothels in the *kampong ayer* as well as in bars, discothèques, karaoke lounges, hair salons, and massage parlors in the resort and hotel district. Among the knowledgeable Labuan is as important a sex trade tourist destination as Bangkok with every imaginable vice available to whoever has the money to pay.

The *Batavia Queen* arrived in Labuan shortly after noon, docking at the Merdeka Pier close to the ultramodern ferry terminal. From the wheelhouse Finn and Billy could see across the length and breadth of the island; according to Briney Hanson, it was flat as a pancake with its highest point no more than a hundred fifty feet above sea level. From where they stood, there was nothing but the gleaming white structures of the beach hotels and small, modern cityscape to the east and a sea of jungle green stretching off to the north. In the far distance, beyond the hotels and the gold and white onion dome of the central mosque, they could see the belching stacks of the petroleum refinery and the huge sheds of the government shipyards.

While Elisha went to the Customs House to clear their arrival and arrange for the bunkers to be topped up, McSeveney and Toshi Minimoto headed for the supermarket on *Tun Mustapha* Road for supplies, including several cases of Orangeboom Dutch Lager, the *Batavia Queen*'s beer of choice. Hanson went with Finn and Pilgrim to

look for Osterman, the mysterious antiquities
dealer who'd sold Pieter Boegart the little gold
statue.

They took an oddly modern Panga twenty-six-
foot water taxi across the bay at a breezy forty-five
miles an hour and arrived at *Kampung Patau-Patau*
ten minutes later after deftly skirting a fleet of
dive boats on their way out to the "resort wrecks"
sunk along the shoal lines of the sprinkling of
atolls and small islands that stood between Labuan and the Brunei mainland. There were four
wrecks that Hanson knew of: the *Tung Huang*, a
Chinese freighter with a load of cement once des-
tined for the sultan's palace in Brunei; the SS *De
Klerke* commandeered by the Japanese during
World War Two and sunk by the Australian Air
Force; the USS *Salute*, a minesweeper much like
the original *Batavia Queen*; and a Philippine fishing
trawler, the *Mapine Padre*, which caught fire and
sank sometime in the eighties. The four wrecks
and the sex trade were the real basis for Labuan's
day-to-day economy.

The taxi dropped them at a rickety-looking
wooden pier without guardrails and they climbed
up a bamboo ladder. "How are we supposed to
find this man Osterman?" Billy asked, staring
down the narrow plank-surfaced wharf. Facing
them was a patchwork of buildings made out of
everything from flattened oil drums to heavy plastic sheeting. It seemed as though every house had

its own small boat anchored close by and every window opening was festooned with overflowing flower boxes. The tin roofs and the walls of a lot of the houses were painted in bright blues, yellows, and greens.

Finn shrugged. "We just ask, I guess."

A group of young children was playing farther along the pier, happily flinging themselves off the planks and into the sea, then climbing out again, swarming up the bamboo supports, and repeating the whole process. They were wearing an assortment of clothes ranging from nothing at all through bright white underpants to colorful sarongs. There didn't seem to be any adult supervision, the oldest of the children clearly keeping an eye on their younger companions. Suddenly Finn found herself transported back to her childhood and her uncle Danny's farm that backed up to Big Darby Creek just outside Maryville. She'd gone swimming just like this with no fear of drowning or being swept away and with not a worrying adult anywhere in sight. It seemed to her that the world had been a safer place then, but at least a little of it seemed to have remained in this strange, out-of-the-way place. She smiled and laughed at the kids' antics, which were clearly accelerating and becoming noisier because the children had an audience.

Finn looked down into the water. It seemed

clear and unpolluted, perhaps ten or fifteen feet deep down to a sandy bottom. The surface was remarkably clear of domestic garbage; she couldn't see a single piece of floating plastic or anything else. The local occupants were obviously very house-proud. The boats tied up at each dwelling's private pier were nothing more than old rowboats fitted with small outboards, but they were all freshly painted in gaudy colors like the roughly built homes, and each had a name neatly written on the prow.

As Finn and the others approached, the kids stopped playing and stood watching them silently, their eyes wide and curious. No calling out, no begging, just a silent careful assessment: friend or foe.

"Di mana Osterman tuan?" Hanson asked. One of the kids, the tallest, who wore raggedy red shorts, pointed solemnly to a large shack with a bright blue tin roof and a window box full of blazing rhododendrons.

"Tuan Osterman kedai," said the boy solemnly.

"That's Osterman's store," explained Hanson.

"Terima kasih," said Finn, using a bit of Malay she'd picked up from Bazooki, the steward. It meant "thank you."

"Sama-sama!" replied the boy, surprised and pleased.

"Should I give him some money?" Billy asked.

"Why?" Hanson answered. "He was just giving you directions. He doesn't expect anything. These people aren't beggars. They're just poor."

They followed the child's pointing finger, taking a series of ever narrowing walkways, and eventually reached Osterman's store. The whole front of the building was open, the front wall made up of rolled bamboo blinds that could be lowered at night. The store was one big room, lined with shelves that held a bizarre assortment of items ranging from ornately framed pictures from Victorian times to a set of Asian-styled Barbie Doll knockoffs arranged in gaudy cardboard display boxes with clear plastic tops that looked like coffins. It was a junk store: Osterman was hardly what you would call an antiquities dealer, Finn thought. For a moment she wondered if the little boy outside had steered them wrong.

A man appeared from behind a bamboo curtain that sectioned off the rear of the shop. He was tall, stooped, and in his sixties or seventies. His hair was very long and stringy, and his very pale belly hung over the waist band of a soiled native sarong. He wore very out-of-date black plastic-framed glasses and he was carrying a plastic bowl and chopsticks.

"Mr. Osterman?" Finn asked.

"Call me Bernard, dear," said the man. He used the chopsticks to guide a slurry of noodles into his mouth, watching his guests over the rim of the

bowl. "Not browsing tourists by the look of you."
He smiled. The accent was German or Austrian,
but the English was excellent.

Finn reached into the pocket of her shirt and
took out the little gold amulet. She held it out in
the palm of her hand. Bernard Osterman looked
down at it but made no move to take it from her.

"I was wondering if that little trinket would
come back to haunt me," he sighed.

"You sold it to a relative of mine. Pieter Boegart," said Billy.

"That's not what he told me his name was. I knew
he was Dutch. He said his name was Derlagen."

"That's his lawyer.

"One of *the* Boegarts?"

"The black sheep," said Billy.

"I know that feeling myself," Osterman said,
smiling.

"He must have come here for a reason," said
Finn. "I don't think he was a browsing tourist any
more than we were."

"Quite right, dear." He paused. "I'm not sure I
see your part in all this."

"Pieter Boegart is my relative, as well," she answered, realizing that she was admitting to her
mother's infidelity at last and perhaps even to her
own paternity. Somehow it didn't seem to matter
so much now.

"I see . . . I suppose," murmured Osterman,
looking back and forth between Billy and Finn.

"How did Pieter Boegart find you?" asked Billy.

Osterman smiled again and slurped up some more noodles. He put the bowl and chopsticks down on a nearby table and gave a small contented belch. "I learned my trade in Berlin as a very young boy, six or seven or so, too young then even for the *Deutsches Jungvolk*. To survive in Berlin after 1945, you learned a great many things, but above all you learned to trade one thing or another until you found what you wanted. You also learned to do whatever was neccessary along that path to find what you wanted or to stop others from finding it first. Whatever was necessary, no matter how unpleasant. Most important you traded in information. You, as they say, kept your ear to the ground. Later, when it became necessary for me to leave Berlin and to come eventually to this godforsaken place, I simply applied the same principles, you see?"

"Not really," said Finn. "But you still haven't told us how you got the little gold figure."

"Do you know what it is?"

"It's from Mali," answered Finn. "Fourteenth century."

"From the reign of Mansa Musa, the king of Mali and Timbuktu, the first of his race to make Haj to Mecca. Yes, yes, all the old stories about King Solomon's mines and your Rider Haggard, but that is not the real answer."

"Why don't you tell us, then?" said Hanson.

"The real answer is where the figure was found and how it came to be there."

"So where was it found?" Finn asked.

"Such information should be worth something, don't you think?"

"How much did Pieter Boegart pay?" Billy asked.

"You are not he. This is another transaction."

"You sent Pieter Boegart somewhere, perhaps to his death," said Finn. "Pieter may well have been the black sheep of his family, but he was a Boegart and I'm sure the police would be interested in the fact that you were the last person known to have seen him. I wonder how you'd like a bunch of policemen crowding around in here, making a mess of things."

"You are far too pretty a woman to be making such threats."

"I'm not pretty," said Billy. "Would it make any difference if it was me making the threats?"

"Not in the slightest," sighed Osterman. "But I think it is a very unpleasant way to treat an old man."

"What about the figure?"

"It was in the hands of a rather unscrupulous fellow named Wei Yang. He knew I liked such things so he traded it to me."

"Where do we find this Wei Yang?" Hanson asked.

"He had a shop on Dewan Street, but he is no longer there."

"Where is he?"

"Perhaps the morgue? In an ornamental urn somewhere? With his ancestors at any rate. He was found floating under the barter trade jetty by the fish factory with his belly slit and his eyes gouged out. He was also missing several fingers on one hand and it was not from the fish nibbling at them."

"Who did it?"

"Who knows?" Osterman shrugged. "This is Borneo. Kalimantan—call it what you want. The world's last mystery. They still have tribes who collect human heads and shrink them. They sew the teeth back in and hang them from the rafters of their longhouses. You can hear the teeth rattling like wind chimes in the night. I've heard it myself. Wei Yang was a bullion dealer among other things, and a smuggler. He dealt with the Dyak gold prospectors from the interior, from the *hutan*, the deep jungle, and he dealt with the *penyeludup*, the smugglers, as well. It could have been any one of them, because he cheated them all at one time or another and everyone knew it."

"And you knew where he got the gold figurine, don't you?" Hanson asked.

"A smuggler named Lo Chang. Part Chinese, part God only knows what."

"Where did Lo Chang get it?" Finn asked.

"According to Wei Yang he didn't say."

"Or wouldn't."

"Or wouldn't," agreed Osterman.

"So where do we find this Lo Chang fellow?" Hanson asked.

"He operates a boat called the *Pedang Emas* out of Kampong Sugut. Makes the run to Zamboanga. Does a bit of piracy, as well. He'll be somewhere between the two, I'd think."

"Where's Kampong Sugut?" Finn asked.

"Just north of Labuk Bay on the Sulu Sea," said Hanson. "Below the Tegepil Shoals at the mouth of the Sugut River. Chang lives there with a woman named Cai Quin Ma. She runs one of his brothels. Looks like a goat in a dress. Can't miss her."

They found another water taxi and returned across the broad expanse of the bay to Labuan City. Everyone was back on board; Labuan didn't have too much to offer if you weren't interested in illegal sex or offshore banking. Toshi was in the galley rustling up an aromatic lunch and Elisha Santoro was in the wheelhouse waiting for them with a set of charts spread out in front of him.

"I hope we're not going north," he said, a worried expression on his young, handsome face. He scratched his eyebrow above the patch.

"Why's that?" Hanson asked.

"I was just at the meteorology office in town. There's a typhoon brewing in the Sulu Sea. A big one. They're saying it might go to plus ten. Super-

typhoon. The barometer's dropping like a rock."
He looked at Finn and Billy. "Why, where are
we heading?"

"North," said Hanson. "Into the Sulu Sea."

17

Pedang Emas was a hundred-foot-long, hundred-ton wood-and-iron whaling ship with a history that predated the *Titanic*. She'd begun life in 1907 as a small-scale Swedish factory ship built by Nyland Versted in Oslo with the designation *Hull133*. She was sold to an Icelandic company and given the name *Haraldur Kristjánsson*.

In 1921 she was transferred to a New Zealand whaling company and renamed *Rangitoto*. Nine years after that, she was returned to Scandinavian waters and sold to the Stavanger Sardine Company, maker of the Royal Brisling brand, ostensibly as a fishing vessel but actually outfitted as a yacht for the chairman of the company. A lavish owner's cabin was built over the main hatch, and the hold was used for small cargo and an oversized fuel tank.

Her name was changed to *Kristianiafjord*, but a

few years after her extensive refit, with war beginning to loom, she was leased to the Royal Norwegian Navy as a watch boat and was renamed *King Haakon VII* in honor of the aging monarch of the country.

Inevitably the German Navy took the little ship over in April of 1940 and didn't call it anything; they simply painted over the name on the bow and painted an identification number on the funnel. Her engines were removed and she was refitted with two-thousand-horsepower diesels for use as a patrol boat with a top speed of eighteen knots and a Nazi *Kreigsmarine* pennant where the sardine company's flag used to fly.

After the war she had a long career as a coastal steamer under the name *Hammerfest*, her far northern home port, but by the late nineties regulatory changes in the crewing of Norwegian ships made her too costly to run, especially with those big deisels. She was sold back and forth half a dozen times until she was finally bought and refurbished by a retired Canadian dentist with a cocaine habit renamed her the *Atropos* after Horatio Hornblower's first ship in the immensely popular series of books about a young officer in the Royal Navy during the Napoleonic Wars.

It was just about as much as the dentist knew about the sea. He hired the wrong crew in Singapore who accidentally discovered his stash of coke and waited until they were deep in the Palawan

Passage before they slit his throat and belly and fed him to the sharks. Lo Chang had not been quite truthful to the Surfer Dude Bandit about events following the death of the foolish dentist.

In fact it was Lo Chang himself who fed the dentist to the sharks, and later did exactly the same thing to his partner and the rest of the crew after getting them smashingly drunk. This was shortly following their meeting with the mad little Japanese sailor on the raft. Lo Chang, being illiterate and not very bright, had no idea of the significance of the stamp on the ten-tola bar of gold. He only knew that it was gold and he wanted whatever there was for himself alone. Besides, he didn't really need much of a crew to pilot the *Atropos*, or *Pedang Emas* as she was now called.

Four days out of Zamboanga, after delivering another shipment of young girls to the sex clubs there, he returned with a cargo of five hundred Negros fighting cocks crammed into split bamboo cages stolen from a top breeder in the hold. At between a thousand and fifteen hundred dollars a bird, his profit was going to be enormous. In Borneo and the Philippines, it was said that there were three landmarks in every village—the market, the church, and the local cockpit. They were stinking up the little hold, making horrible noises and dirtying everything they touched, but the money would make it worthwhile.

The only thing worrying Lo Chang was the

weather. He never bothered with the expensive navigation and meteorology equipment installed by the unfortunate dentist. In the first place, he didn't know how it worked and couldn't read the results anyway, and in the second place, when he hadn't been in jail, he'd spent most of his life at sea and intuitively knew when the weather was changing. There wasn't a cloud in the sky, the sea was dead flat calm, and the air was hot, all perfectly normal for this time of year, but there were signs.

Standing in the squat little wheelhouse ahead of the Lido deck awning, Lo Chang kept both doorways open but there was no cross-draft. In fact there was no wind at all—only a strange, uncomfortable oppressive feeling along with the flat, almost surly roll of the ocean. The color was wrong too; the water had a gray, almost silver light in it, muting the green and making everything look as though it would taste like licking a doorknob. Ozone, was that what they called it? He leaned forward and blew into one of the old-fashioned speaking tubes beside the wheel.

"Cam Dao!" he called out to the Vietnamese girl whose face had been ruined by a knife-wielding patron at Cai Quin Ma's *Puki Rumah* establishment in the big house behind the fish market. The girl was no use any more for clients, but she loved to cook and almost above all other things Lo Chang liked to eat. *"Trung nguyen!"* he called. The skinny, little creature made excellent iced coffee, which he loved. If it was dark and he'd been a long time from home, he'd occasionally use her as she'd been intended and she was quite satisfactory at that as well, not a small feat when the customer for her services weighed close to four hundred pounds.

Lo Chang looked out through the port-side doorway. Over the railing he could see the coastline, a faint gray shadow several miles away. He usually steered closer to shore, navigating by well-known landmarks, but this was the area of the Torongohok Reefs and even with a draft of only seven and a half feet, going any closer to shore was a risky proposition.

Cam Dao appeared on the bridge with his special silver-chased coffee glass. She gave a little bow and handed him the coffee. He took the glass, holding it in one meaty fist with the other hand gripping the wheel. He took a long draft of the rich coffee and sweet condensed milk mixture, then sighed with pleasure.

"Bring me lunch," he snapped. "Some *pho* and a dish of that *muc xao thap cam* you make so well." His Vietnamese was curt and fluent. Although Lo Chang was ethnic Chinese, he was also Vietnamese by birth. A skinny orphan child in Hanoi during the war years, he had both prospered and fattened in the time since, becoming well known for his ability to procure anything from war surplus AK-47s and Russian RPGs for the northern bandits and drug runners to lady-boys and knock-off copies of guidebooks for the sex tourists.

He had also become known for his easy willingness to commit violence and had spent a number of years as an enforcer for Truong Van Cam's Fifth Orange Gang. After the gang boss's arrest and execution in 2004, Lo Chang had fled the country, eventually settling in Kampong Sugut and beginning his flourishing prostitution and smuggling enterprises. In the Chinese way, he was very philosophical about these changes; life offered an assortment of tragedies and opportunities. The trick was to turn one into the other and to think about the past as rarely as possible.

Jampongong Island appeared in the distance directly ahead and Lo Chang suddenly had to make a decision. He reached into the pocket of his vast white shirt, produced a tin of Neos Pacific Cigarillos, and lit one with the platinum Dunhill he'd taken from the unfortunate Canadian dentist. The steady bow wave curled up with a mustache of foam. In the distance Jampongong looked like everyone's idea of a perfect tropical paradise. Coconut palms fringing startling white sand beaches, forest, hills, and dense jungle beyond, all rising to a sultry forested mountain peak, its summit almost always shrouded in mist. A classic island in the Sulu Sea. Very romantic on a travel brochure for idiots like the Canadian dentist.

The problem was that off Jampongong was a

large fringe of reef that swept in shoals a dozen miles out to sea. Inshore, however, between the island and Kinalubatan Point on the mainland was a channel three-quarters of a mile wide and a passage through the center with at least eight fathoms, or forty-eight feet, below the keel of the *Pedang Emas*. On either side of that middle passage were rocks and shoals that stood like razor fangs just below the surface, completely hidden from view on a day like this by the sun dazzle on the water and capable of ripping the little ship's belly out like the knife that gutted the late dentist and his even later partner. Take the channel and he'd save half a day getting back to Kambong Sugut; don't take the channel and he risked putting himself far out to sea in uncertain weather, losing a half day in the process.

"*Najis*," he said in Malay, swearing. The diesel thudded beneath his feet and the wheel felt slippery with sweat under his thick hand. The island was getting closer with every passing minute. He glanced out to port at the thick green line of the mangroves overhanging the water on the mainland. He took another swig of the cool brew that the little knife-scarred whore had fetched, then put the silver-handled glass down on the narrow "dashboard" shelf that ran along beneath the windscreen of the wheelhouse.

"*Puki mak dia*," he muttered, cursing again. He swung the wheel with both hands, turning the ship toward the shore and the channel that lay between it and the island.

Half an hour later, his prodigious belly full of Cam Dao's succulent sautéed squid chased with a big bottle of Halida beer, Lo Chang was confidently swinging *Pedang Emas* around the lee side of the high volcanic island, keeping an eye out for any distinct variations in the color of the water that would signal shoals or shallows. He also made sure that the island's main landmarks, the high northern bluffs and the jutting shape of Bankoka Hill, were well away on his right; the currents at the foot of the clifflike bluffs that ran directly down into the water could spin his little ship like a top and smash him against the rough stone walls in an instant.

Even from a mile off he could hear the pounding of the sea against the rock and he shivered slightly. The thought of being crushed against the cliffs was one thing, but being thrown into the sea was something else. Lo Chang, for all his balloonlike size, could not swim a stroke. He'd tossed enough men into the ocean to know exactly the sort of predators that lurked just below the water in great abundance. Better to put a bullet in his brain than drown in the sea.

The little inlet that ran back into the center of the island appeared to starboard, and if he hadn't been watching so carefully he would have missed the prize within. A good-sized schooner stood at anchor just off the pebbled foreshore that marked the entrance to a narrow river. Lo Chang picked up the dentist's pretty blue and yellow Pro Mariner binoculars and took a look.

He focused the glasses and the boat came into view. Neatly anchored. Thirty-eight, maybe forty feet. Dark hull, bright white superstructure. A woman was sunbathing on the foredeck, topless, her big breasts lolling, her arms spread out against the cockpit to catch the sun, a big floppy sun hat shielding her eyes. She was dark-haired, tanned, and reasonably young.

Barely hesitating, Lo Chang reached out and eased back the throttles, the sound of the engines dropping. He swung the wheel, guiding the *Pedang Emas* into the inlet. He'd stopped here for fresh water in the past and knew there would be more than enough sea beneath his keel, even at low tide.

He swung the binoculars around, checking the beach and the jungle behind it, looking for anyone else. Nothing. Just the white sand, the lush jungle, and the shaded entrance to the river. He smiled, his heavy lips spreading apart to reveal a gleaming mouthful of gold teeth. In addition to the woman there might be one or two more aboard the boat. Easy to deal with. He pulled up the tail of the saillike white shirt covering his belly and took out the old Nagant revolver he'd preferred since his days in Vietnam. Its seven-round cylin-

der would be more than enough for the job at
hand.

He throttled back to dead slow and coasted forward through the flat calm, coming up on the sailboat almost silently. The girl on the cockpit cover
was obviously asleep. She hadn't moved since
he'd first spotted her. Lo Chang's smile broadened; there would probably be a supply of liquor
on board and some money as well. Maybe even
more cocaine. He'd grown a taste for it since the
dentist. There might even be a weapon, perhaps
a shotgun. Most small boats carried them in the
pirate-infested waters in the area.

Lo Chang liked the idea of being part of an
infestation. When he imagined himself in such a
way he usually saw himself as a powerful snake,
a constrictor perhaps, one who used brute strength
to kill its prey rather than stinging venom. He
hefted the World War Two–vintage pistol in his
hand. Venom, on the other hand, had its place.
He leaned forward and blew into the voice pipe.

"*Cam Dao!*" he called. "*Di voi toi!*" Within a
few seconds, the young woman appeared on the
narrow bridge, coming up from the galley directly
below. "Take the wheel," he said in Vietnamese.
"Bring her in slowly."

"*Co,*" said the woman with a nod, her expression blank. She knew exactly what her master intended to do, but nothing she could say or do

would stop him. The fate of the half-naked woman on the sailboat was sealed. The Vietnamese woman stepped forward and took the wheel. Lo Chang went out on deck and lumbered forward to the bow. Lo Chang kept the pistol half hidden behind his back. As the ship slid forward he tried to put on a pleasant expression and dredged up the small amount of English he'd learned over the years.

"Hello, you!" he called out. They were a hundred yards off now. Too late for the sailboat to start whatever auxiliary engine it carried in an attempt to escape. Not that it would have done any good. The monster diesels installed by the Germans all those years ago still gave the old ship an easy eighteen knots, enough to run down any sailboat afloat.

"Hello, you!" he called again. The woman hadn't moved an inch. If there was anyone else on board they were asleep. Fifty yards. Still the woman hadn't moved. Lo Chang squinted. The large pillowy breasts were bright red. Sunburned. She'd been sunbathing too long, it seemed. Being something of an expert when it came to nipples and their sensitivity, Lo Chang was sure she would be in great pain. Why didn't she go below?

Twenty-five yards now and still no movement. He took a small apprehensive step back from the gunwale. The woman should have moved by now.

He could almost see it, coming up on her elbows, pushing back the big hat, maybe with sunglasses underneath. The sudden look of surprise. The fear.

Cam Dao swung the wheel, bringing the ship broadside to the sailboat. The bow wave reached out and smacked against the side of the other vessel. The sailboat began to rock quite violently. The big breasts flopped back and forth like balloons filled with water, her legs slapping together and tangling with each other.

Ten yards away and Lo Chang's apprehension turned to full-blown anxiety. The woman didn't just have her arms spread across the cockpit—they were nailed there. There was no blood because the nails had been struck into the flesh earlier, shortly after she'd attacked Fu Sheng with a carving knife from the galley. He'd struck her across the face with the butt of his weapon, but she'd turned to the side at the last second and the blow had struck her temple instead of her face as he intended. It hadn't taken her very long to die, but even dead she had her uses. She could still be a decoy for a fat pig like Lo Chang.

Too late Lo Chang realized that the boat and the woman were a trap. He moved heavily back toward the bridge. Out of the corner of his eye, he saw movement in the overhanging bushes shading the mouth of the little river. He took the Nagant out from under his shirt, but he knew now it was far too late for that kind of thing.

The bushes weren't bushes at all, but camou-flaging brush piled up on the bow of some sort of old-fashioned, sharp-prowed torpedo boat almost as big as *Pedang Emas*. The boat came nosing out of the river mouth, powerful engines burbling. He could see the bell-shaped muzzle of a heavy machine gun mounted forward and a Malay in a vague jungle uniform standing behind it, grinning. The *Pedang Emas* was less than three hundred feet away from the hidden torpedo boat. At that range they could chew him to ribbons and sink him without even reloading the big-box magazine.

Lo Chang felt his stomach gurgle with fear and he belched, tasting Cam Dao's squid in his mouth again along with the sour tang of bile. He had a sudden, terrible suspicion that the tables were about to be turned and that soon he would be lunch for the squid rather than the other way around. He turned and saw the woman crucified on the deck. He found himself thinking about the dentist and his fate.

A gust of wind blew across the deck of the sail-boat and the big floppy hat came off the bare-breasted woman's face and was whisked over the gunwale and into the water. Her whole head was crushed on one side, her right eye like a white blotch in a lump of ruined, overcooked meat. The people on the torpedo boat had done that. He knew they could do, would do even worse to him and he knew why, because now he remembered the sailboat and where he'd seen it before, although the hull had been red, not blue as it was now, and he remembered the girl too and her blond boyfriend, the one with the scar who thought bringing her to a brothel was a good joke.

Most of all he remembered the old man on the raft and the gold wafers wrapped in yellowed pages from the old military edition of *Yomiuri-Hochi* from sometime during the war. The gold wafers that were still in the strongbox in his cabin.

They would question him and when they were done they'd drop what remained of him over the side. The torpedo boat was almost alongside now, rumbling between him and the sailboat. He was looking right down at the dead woman. He could hear the buzzing of flies.

Lo Chang tilted his head back and closed his eyes. His mind wandered for a moment, searching, and then he remembered sitting in the small park beside Hoan Kiem Lake on a clear, bright day, close to Tortoise Tower. He was combing Quyen's waist-length hair, using the brush with one hand and his other hand to smooth it as he brushed, letting it fall through his fingers like jet-black, shining mercury, but really, secretly caressing it, feeling her curved neck through the thick fall of it, bent to his brushing suffering agonies of young passion, knowing that it would never be more than a precocious fat boy brushing the hair of a pretty girl.

Later his friend Trung told him that she didn't really like him at all, but only liked what effect she had on him. It didn't matter. He breathed in and smelled the faint scent of the *dao phai*, the pale peach flower of his birthplace that grew everywhere around the Tortoise Tower. The smell of the girl, Quyen. So long ago. But nobody lives forever. At least he wouldn't drown. Lo Chang opened his eyes and saw the man standing in the bow of the boat, the two-foot-long bolo machete in his hand.

He felt the weight of Quyen's hair in his hand again and he brought the Nagant up to his temple and pulled the trigger quickly, never hesitating for a second.

18

In the simplest terms a typhoon is a violent tropical storm with cyclonic, or circulating, winds that usually have their origins in the western Pacific or the Indian Ocean. Above the equator these winds circulate in a counterclockwise direction, and below the equator they turn clockwise. Basically typhoons are caused by a coincidental conjunction of several basic factors, including substantially higher than normal water temperature, an upper layer of moist air, and inwardly spiraling winds caused by an area of low pressure.

As these areas begin to revolve, usually in pairs, they quickly cool the water beneath them, both by simply blocking out the sun and by drawing the heat upward to the colder masses of air in the form of evaporation. The result of all this is a rotating heat engine that begins to feed on itself, moving across the surface of the ocean, seeking and expending more and more energy, which, expressed in human scientific terms, means that a tropical cyclone can release heat energy at the rate of fifty to two hundred trillion joules per day.

For comparison, this rate of energy release is equivalent to exploding a ten-megaton nuclear bomb every twenty minutes, or two hundred times the worldwide electrical-generating capacity per day. This is no Perfect Storm, no majestic sweep of enormous rolling waves and perfectly digitized little ships upon a perfectly digitized ocean; this is hell on earth, where shattered water hammers against itself, battering to pieces everything that happens to cross its erratic and ever changing course, its "eye" or center as wide as two hundred miles across with an "eyewall" where winds can move up to two hundred miles an hour. Within the eye a lenslike uplift in the ocean itself can be created, sometimes rising in a huge dome up to forty feet high, the waters beneath it spiraling faster and faster, the giant unseen vortex as deep as three hundred feet, sometimes scouring the seabed itself. It is this "lens" or "storm surge" as it is called that holds the potential for the typhoon's greatest cruelty.

Moving toward land the storm surge follows the upward slope of the seabed, growing higher and higher and traveling at over a hundred miles an hour, scouring the land and destroying, inundating and drowning everything within its wrathful path with catastrophic effect that can utterly destroy entire coastal plains and sometimes whole countries. Thousands and sometimes tens of thousands can die within a single day.

Briney Hanson knew they were in trouble less than two hours after turning the corner at the top of Borneo's Sabah Peninsula and heading through the Malawali Strait. The barometer continued to drop and the steady chop of the sea heading up the coast had become a long oily swell moving under them like the undulations of some enormous, sluggishly moving sea monster. There was no wind, a deadly oppressive heat, and a heavy, dark line on the horizon that seemed to snatch what few clouds there were and breathe them into its maw.

"Trouble?" Billy Pilgrim asked, standing beside Hanson on the bridge with Eli at the wheel. Even within the bridge the sound of the rising wind was a sharp, electrical whistling as the rushing air thrummed over the ship's wire rigging.

"Yes," said Hanson. "North-northeast," he called out to Santoro. The young man nodded and turned the wheel. A few seconds later the helm answered and the *Batavia Queen* turned heavily across the swell and moved away from the distant coast, putting them farther out to sea. The seas broke harder against her bows and she began to heave and plunge in long steady rolls.

"Isn't this dangerous, putting farther out to sea like this?"

"Yes," said Hanson again. "But if we're running into heavy weather, I'd rather have some distance between me and the reefs. The way we're standing doesn't give us much room to maneuver." Hanson's original intention had been to slip down the coast ahead of the typhoon and put into some safe anchorage to ride it out, maybe even making it to Kampong Sugut and the wide mouth of the river there, but that was impossible now. Both the radar and his own eyes were showing him the typhoon almost dead ahead and moving too quickly to avoid. The best thing to do was meet it head-on as far out to sea as he could get. A typhoon over the ocean was bad, but a typhoon sweeping toward the land was a monster.

Down below in the galley, Finn was helping Toshi shut down the stoves and make cold sandwiches for the upcoming festivities while the rest of the crew hurried around lashing down anything loose on deck or below. To them it was a familiar story. They'd weathered plenty of storms with the *Queen* before. As the day wore on, the swells grew broader and deeper, the crests tipped with long trails of dead-white spume that spun off the tops of the waves like froth from the jaws of some terrible rabid creature—not far from the truth in this case.

Over time the water had turned from deep

green to pewter and finally to black, unfathomable with nothing of life to be seen. Porpoises and flying fish sought their pleasures elsewhere and the seabirds had fled from the storm long before it even made its presence known.

By late afternoon they were giving a wide berth to the roaring surf around the reefs of Pulau Tigaba and the sky overhead was dark as breaking dusk. Finn managed to make her way up the swaying companionway to the wheelhouse with mugs and a big thermos of steaming coffee, getting thoroughly soaked along the way even though she was tightly bundled into an old oilskin Toshi gave her.

"That's the last of anything hot for a while. Toshi says it's too dangerous to even keep the pilot lights going on the stove."

"He's right." Hanson nodded, taking a mug from her and sipping. "In weather like this the last thing you need is a fire to add to your problems."

"At least it's not raining," said Billy. He stared out at the heaving sea and the darkening sky.

"Give it time," said Eli, struggling with the wheel.

Hanson stepped to one side and looked down at the radar plot.

"That doesn't look healthy at all," he said quietly, bending over the scope.

"What are those little lines coming out of the center of the white thing?" Finn asked.

"The rain your friend was asking about," said Hanson. "Lots of it."

"And the hole in the center?"

"The eye," Hanson explained. "Very small, very tight, and very dangerous."

"I thought the eye of a hurricane was supposed to be an area of calm," said Billy, hanging on to the compass platform as the *Queen* began its long, slow climb up the face of the next oncoming wave.

"It is, relatively," explained Hanson. "But the 'eyewall,' the perimeter of the eye, has the fastest and most destructive winds of all. Going through the eyewall can tear a ship this size apart. Best to avoid it altogether."

"How do we do that?" Finn asked. "That thing looks pretty big."

"About two hundred kilometers from side to side. A hundred twenty-five miles. Still a baby."

"Can't we go around it?"

"Maybe," said Hanson. "But it's like that old story about the lady and the tiger. Which way, port or starboard?"

"Does it make a difference?"

"We're below the equator, so the winds are rotating clockwise. In this case, that means east to west, relative to our position."

"Okay, I'm with you." All of a sudden, she wasn't. The *Queen* reached the top of the crest and made a grotesque twisting motion, throwing Finn halfway across the wheelhouse and into Billy, who managed to grab her before she tumbled to the deck. He helped her upright as the *Queen* slid wretchedly across the crest and roared down into the trough like a freight train. Finn's stomach dropped as though she were on a high-speed elevator and suddenly the sky was gone, the windscreen filled from horizon to horizon with the brick-wall mass of the next wave.

"You all right?" Hanson asked.

"Fine," said Finn, glad she hadn't eaten much for lunch. "Where were we?"

"Port or starboard, left or right," said the captain, keeping a careful eye on Eli, who was struggling with the wheel as he tried to keep the old freighter sailing directly into the wind. "Think of a football player putting his shoulder forward to block an opponent. That's the starboard side, the right. The other shoulder, the trailing edge, has lower wind speeds and less rain. That's to the left, the portside."

Finn shrugged. "Sounds like a no-brainer." They reached the top of another wave and this time she grabbed the chart table for support as they went hurtling down into the trough again. She swallowed hard and regained her footing. "We should steer to port."

"Except that wind changes direction all the time," put in Billy, lurching against the bulkhead behind him. The *Queen* groaned and heaved, crashing through the crest of the next wave, a huge fountain of spray bursting over her bow.

"He's right," said Hanson grimly. "Typhoons don't follow a regular path. They have a life of their own."

"In other words it's a crap shoot," said Eli Santoro, gripping the wheel.

"Not quite," said Hanson. "That's why we're trying for sea room—give us a lot of open water to maneuver, just in case. We'll keep an eye on the storm for another couple of hours, then decide."

The *Batavia Queen* battered its way into the night, the world contracting to an endless series of twisting, lurching roller-coaster rides up the boiling, spume-topped face of one wave and down the smooth, ugly back of the next. The speed of the wind increased, the rigging snapping and whirring with a never-ending shriek that made any conversation almost impossible.

Even with everything battened down and the hatches and companionways sealed, water seemed to get into everything. Finn's cabin in the stern section of the lower deck was awash, the toilet backed up from the heaving accumulation of water in the bilges. Every seam, weld, pipe, and ventilator dripped steadily.

As the barometer dropped, so did the temperature, and even wrapped in one of Run-Run McSeveney's ancient, moth-eaten Shetland sweaters and her oilskins Finn was shivering with cold.

Worst of all was the repeated hammering shudder as the hull smashed down off each crest, a tooth-rattling, bludgeoning jar as though a giant fist were trying to pound the old ship apart and send them all to the bottom of the sea.

Finn spent most of her time in the wardroom, simply sitting gloomily, living each plunge and climb like a frightened airplane passenger experiencing every ghastly buck and thump of turbulence. She willed the ancient hull plates to stay together, almost seeing the groaning, creaking underbelly of the ship as it rose barnacle-encrusted out of the water before crashing down again.

Toshi tried to tempt her with a soggy sandwich from the galley, but the egg salad she'd chopped, whipped, and assembled in daylight set her stomach churning and heaving in the darkness. She was hungry, waterlogged, and more than a little frightened, and all she really wanted was for it to end, one way or the other. Long after midnight she made her way up the twisting, lurching companionways to the bridge again, looking for company in her misery.

Hanson had relieved Eli Santoro at the wheel, and the only other person on the bridge was Billy. If anything the rain-streaked view out the windscreen was worse than the last time. The winds were blowing with so much force that the lashing downpour was smeared into a single shimmering sheet across the glass and the top-mounted heavy-duty wipers had no effect at all. The thunder of the waves crashing into the *Queen*'s bow and flanks was like the sounding of some gigantic bell.

"We can't steer this way for much longer!" Hanson screamed, turning slightly as Finn came onto the bridge. "The waves are too big and too close together! We'll founder or break our back unless we turn!"

"You're going to put her beam on?" Billy said, horrified, his jaw dropping.

"No choice!" Hanson responded. "We can't keep on driving into it! Grab something!" He spun the wheel around to the left as hard as he could.

"What does beam on mean?" Finn yelled, startled at the suddenness of his movement.

Billy opened his mouth but before he could answer Finn was thrown halfway across the small bridge house and fell into a heap as the ship made a long slaloming turn down the side of an enormous wave that seemed to entirely fill the night sky. The great wave directly in front of them loomed like a curled fist, acres of blinding spray flying off the dark knuckles of furious water.

The *Batavia Queen* threw herself up the side of the new wave like a surfer trying to make it to deeper water. She began to turn along the crest, then fell back on herself as she pivoted across it. Before Finn could even begin to get to her feet the crest broke across the *Queen*'s deck, slamming the bridge doors open and filling the chamber with a rush of icy water. It was flushed away almost instantly, leaving Finn coughing and choking on the deck, spitting out harsh-tasting salt water.

Somehow Hanson had managed to hang on to the wheel and he took the *Queen* fully around, stern to the driving force of the wind, as they began to run away with the roaring storm, hard on her heels, but almost bearable now. The ship was flotsam on the surface of the boiling sea now, no longer fighting the direction of the raging typhoon.

"Beam on means to turn sideways. It's a little tricky sometimes!" Hanson called out, still struggling with the wheel as he finally answered her question.

Laughing wearily and still gasping for air, Finn dragged herself upright with Billy's help. "Now you tell me!"

They drove forward, letting the howling winds push them on, no longer fighting the incredible grinding power of the massive cyclone. The storm moved forward at a steadily increasing speed, gaining on the battered old ship and inevitably overtaking and swallowing it, the eyewall and the eye rushing up behind them like a surging hungry throat.

The *Batavia Queen* slid on through the darkness that was engulfing her in a whirling inferno of sound. The great swell of the waves carried her up, then sucked her down, rolling over her bows

and crushing against her sides. Finn huddled on
the bridge, watching as the sky began to lighten,
soaking wet, her mind numb, wondering how on
earth she'd managed in such a brief period of time
to go from the boring, relatively civilized environment of a London auction house to the fury of a
Pacific typhoon.

She thought about Columbus and home and
growing up and wondered if danger hadn't
haunted her every step ever since she'd left Ohio.
Most of all she wondered if she was going to die
out here, swallowed up by an unforgiving and
cruel sea.

There was a terrible sound like a shotgun going
off and Finn screamed, the sound swallowed up
by the roar of the wind. A following wave
smashed against the side of the ship, carrying
away the splintered remains of the old launch on
its davits just behind the bridge the way a fist
crushes a matchbox.

By six, with dawn coming up fast, they were
almost against the eyewall and there was no
longer any sense to the sea. Waves crashed against
each other, breaking and roaring and sending
fountains of whirling spray into the sheeted curtains of rain that surrounded them. The windscreen of the bridge gave them no visibility at all;
they were sailing blindly through the terrible
storm.

The dawn finally broke, wild and furious, sky

and sea meeting in a single rolling, terrible line. Waves rolled down on the *Queen*, and a strange, wet mist came in rags and sheets, spray and sky mixing into a wind-driven fog that roared around them at a hundred miles an hour. The radio antenna and the cables on the winches and windlasses had parted long ago like the snapped strings of a guitar. Once, staring out across the undulating sea, Finn was almost sure that she saw another ship with them, riding through the madness of the wild ocean, but before she could say anything to Hanson or to Billy, it had disappeared into the tearing fog.

Then, suddenly, the rain stopped and the silence was almost worse than the storm. They were being tossed across the waves of a frothing horror, but directly overhead were blue sky and sun.

"The eye!"

Finn stared. All around them now was the black towering mass of the eyewall. All of a sudden the doorway behind them crashed open and Eli Santoro staggered onto the bridge, his dark hair plastered across his forehead.

"What?" Hanson bellowed, struggling with the wheel.

"I've been down below in the nav room! Bottom's coming up fast!"

"How fast?"

"We're at eighty fathoms."

"Continuous soundings," Hanson ordered. "Let me know if it gets much shallower."

"Aye, aye!" Santoro turned and left the bridge.

"What was all that about?" Billy asked.

"We're supposed to be in the middle of the Sulu Sea. Limitless bottom. Eighty fathoms is crazy! A shoal or an island in the middle of nowhere."

"There's nothing on the charts?" Billy asked.

"Charts!" Hanson bellowed. "What charts? I don't have the faintest idea where we are!"

"GPS?" Billy called out.

"Try getting a satellite fix in weather like this! Not a chance!" Hanson responded, clinging to the wheel.

"I've got to get into something dry!" Finn called out. She knew she was just getting in the way by staying on the bridge. Maybe she could make herself useful, see about something to eat for everyone. She dragged herself to the doorway of the bridge, ducked her head into her already dripping oilskin, and pushed out into the storm. Hanging on for dear life, she struggled down to the main deck, waited for the *Queen* to roll down the slope of yet another wave, and then, at just the moment, when she began to rise again, she stumbled down the deck and threw herself inside the main corridor. She eventually made her way back to her tiny cabin.

She stripped off her soaking clothes and

changed yet again, cramming herself into her last pair of jeans and one of the pipe-tobacco-smelling heavy roll-neck sweaters Run-Run had let her borrow. Dry socks finished off the ensemble and after struggling back into her rubber boots she stumbled back along the corridor and into the galley.

Toshi, the cook, and Bazooki, the huge Samoan steward, were filling thermos jugs with hot soup made from dry mix and water heated with an electric kettle. Both the tiny Japanese cook and his hulking companion seemed completely at ease in the wildly tossing little galley cabin as pots and pans hanging from their spring hooks in the ceiling smashed and clanged together and six inches of water streamed back and forth across the deck at their feet.

Toshi handed Finn one of the jugs and four tin mugs on a bungee cord that he looped around her neck. He pulled an industrial-sized Hershey's Special Dark bar down from a shelf and stuffed it into the zip pocket of her slicker with a wink and grinned. She tried to smile back, pecked both men on the cheek, then stepped out into the storm again.

Squinting against the raging spray blowing up all around her, Finn made it back along the deck to the bridge companionway and started up, manhandling the jug as best she could, the tin mugs clattering around her neck in the tearing wind. As she reached the bridge itself, she heard an unimaginable sound of tearing metal like the terrible grinding of an enormous dragon's teeth. The dragon lashed its tail and an earthquake seemed to shake the ship, then grab it and shake a second time.

The horrible grinding sound came again, booming throughout the entire hull as the *Queen* lurched, groaned terribly again, then heaved up and rolled onto her side. The soup thermos flew out of Finn's hands, her booted feet slipped on the slick metal of the bridge decking, and the massive pummeling grip of the huge wave that broke over the suddenly grounded ship tossed her back and out into the air. Flailing she had a brief glimpse of the heeling rusty hull of the *Queen* and then she was in the sea, the weight of her heavy boots and the crashing surf pulling her inexorably downward into the cruel and unforgiving belly of the ocean.

19

Finn woke the following morning from a dreamless sleep as deep as death. The typhoon had passed, leaving the skies a brilliant blue, with high, pure white clouds like strips of ragged cloth and the early sun like a bright gold coin. She crawled a little farther up the wide white beach, realizing that her heavy Wellington rubber boots were gone, probably in the rogue wave that had swept her off the *Batavia Queen*. She turned her head and felt a burning pain in her neck.

She probed the spot with her fingers and felt a long splinter of wood embedded deep in the tissue just below her jaw. She pulled it with one swift movement and almost fainted with the pain as the jagged sliver came out, followed by a brief spill of blood. She felt the coppery taste of it in her mouth and realized the splinter had penetrated her throat, although the wound didn't seem terribly serious. But what was serious on an island like this? A simple cut or fever could kill you here. No drugstores just beyond the next coconut tree. She blinked hard and tried to clear her head. She couldn't remember getting the splinter wound. Didn't remember anything at all after the sudden, thunderous impact of the wave.

Finn coughed once, spit blood, and climbed slowly to her feet. She began to survey her surroundings. The storm had passed, but heavy waves still pounded, foaming onto the sand. Torn clouds raced by in the brilliant blue sky and a strong wind still shook the line of palm trees on the foreshore.

Finn turned and looked out toward the sea. The surf was rolling in angrily in hard-packed heavy waves, dark and still heavy with the passing power of the storm. There was no sign of the *Queen*, no huge wreck hanging on the teeth of whatever hidden shoal she'd hit so forcefully.

The hurricane was gone and so was the *Batavia Queen*, but the evidence of her was scattered everywhere along the beach in both directions—crates from the hold, some stove in and others intact, pieces of wood from the shattered ship's boats, the shredded remains of a rubber boat, supplies from the galley.

Finn didn't know whether to be pleased or frightened. She thought of somehow being the only survivor, like some female Tom Hanks in a twenty-first-century version of *Cast Away*. She shrugged the thought off and turned again, staggering a little on the sand. She had more important things to think about, like finding out if there was anyone else with her here. She stripped off the sodden sweater Run-Run McSeveney had given her and tossed it on the sand. Then, instinctively, she bent and picked it up again, knotting it around her waist. There might well be cold nights ahead.

She moved farther along the beach, her back to a high, rising, jungle-covered headland and the distant blur of what might be a river flowing into the sea a mile or so in front of her. A hundred yards farther, she came to a body. It was Kuan Kong, the Korean who had assisted McSeveney in the engine room. Finn had barely exchanged ten words with him, but seeing him on the beach was a horrible shock.

He lay stretched out on the sand, his short gray hair tangled with seaweed that lay around his face in long wet strings. The skin of his hands and feet was a sickly pale purple and already his limbs and belly were beginning to swell in the morning sun. He lay on his side, with his head twisted at an odd angle, both eyes already pecked away by birds. Finn felt like vomiting.

She silently told herself to calm down, then

dropped onto her knees beside the body. She forced herself to go through the pockets of his loose trousers and his shirt, but there was nothing she could use. She thought about burying him and then saw how ridiculous that was, especially when she realized that when the tide came in he'd almost certainly be swept away to sea. She had to think of herself now, and her own uncertain future. There was one other thing. Gritting her teeth she crouched down at the dead man's feet and slipped off his soaking Nikes. They were huge on her, but walking barefoot in a place like this was asking for trouble.

She continued down the beach. A hundred yards farther on, she came upon more things swept off the *Queen.* The first was a foam pillow and pillowcase. The second was an orange garbage bag Toshi the cook had used to store recyclables. She used the pillowcase and a strip of plastic from the garbage bag to make herself a makeshift head covering to ward off the effects of the hot sun that was now almost directly overhead. She stuffed one of the empty Coke cans in the zip pocket of her jacket. She tore the rest of the pillowcase into rags and stuffed them into the shoes. She laced them tightly and took a few experimental steps. Not good, but not bad, either. They'd have to do for the time being.

She started back along the beach. Next on the

list were water and some kind of shelter, even if it was only short-term. It was hot enough now, but who knew what the night would bring?

Another half hour brought Finn to the indentation in the landscape she'd seen from far down the beach. It was a mangrove swamp that went inland for quite a distance. On the far side of the swamp, she could see more sand beach stretching off to the north. To the east, out to sea, she could see the breakers that marked the hidden reef the *Queen* had struck. Finn looked across the mangrove swamp and considered trying to wade across it.

She hesitated; she'd read enough to know that swamps like that could contain any number of dangerous things, from tiny poisonous snakes and bloodsucking leeches to huge crocodiles. The swamp could wait until another time. Instead she headed inland along the narrow strip of beach that stood between her and the gnarled forest of trees, their muscular roots standing out of the brackish water almost as though they were walking toward the sea.

Another twenty minutes brought her to the apex of the cove and there she found the outlet of a narrow river, really no more than a broad creek, less than fifty feet across at its mouth. She made her way a few yards upstream, dropped down onto the low bank, and lay facedown, drinking deeply from cupped hands. The water was clear and cold, tasting just faintly of some mineral.

After drinking her fill, Finn spent a few more moments dashing more water over her face and tenderly bathing the small puncture wound in her neck. That done, she stood up and began heading deeper into the interior of the island. The land rose steadily, the creek water flashing and burbling over stones and boulders. She could see fish pointed upstream like gold and green arrows, tails beating back and forth to keep their station against the current, mouths wide to catch whatever came their way. They looked like some kind of pale catfish, tendrils around their bony mouths waving softly in the stream; not hard to catch if you knew how.

Finn paused and watched them, frowning. She wondered how she was supposed to catch them without a hook, then put the thought aside for the moment. Tom Hanks and Robinson Crusoe again, with a bit of an NYU summer internship at a neolithic dig in Alaska thrown in. If she could find the right geology here, she could easily chip herself a stone knife—a skill she'd never really thought would ever have any practical application. Like her mother once telling her you never could tell when algebra might come in handy. That at least was still in the future.

Continuing up the stream she looked around for some likely place that might offer shelter nearby. The foliage was thick and close to the bank, sometimes leaning over it. Strange-looking trees bent close to the water. Huge ferns spread over the ground with banks of broad-leafed shrubs. Long dangling vines and some heavy mosslike substance drooped from the upper limbs of trees that arched overhead like canopied umbrellas.

She continued upstream, and a few minutes later, she found what she was looking for. The bank of the waterway fell back, leaving a small crescent of sand. Above it, capped by a mass of foliage, was a large, pockmarked outcropping of pale limestone. Her view partly screened by several trees, Finn saw what she first thought was a sun-dappled shadow on the limestone but which she then quickly realized was the entrance to a cave.

Finn hesitated for a moment, remembering just about everything she'd ever heard about vampire bats and things that lived in caves, then stepped forward and ducked inside the opening. She'd just lived through a typhoon and a near drowning. What was there to be afraid of inside a cave? She stopped again and remembered the scorpions that had run over her booted foot the last time she had been in a cave. A scorpion sting would probably kill her. But so could a lot of things. She went deeper into the cave.

It was dry and well aired with a river gravel

floor and no sign of scorpions or bats or anything else. There was a skin of old lichens on the walls of the entrance. The opening was as wide as her arms held apart and a little higher than her height. Beyond the entrance it opened up into a broader room, the ceiling ten feet above her head and made of limestone rather than roofed with dirt and roots from the jungle overhead.

At the far end of the cave was another opening leading to a second chamber. It was too dark to see anything except shadows. Finn turned her cheek to the opening and felt cool air against her skin, so she knew there had to be another exit. The opening was more than wide enough for her to slip through, but to explore farther she'd need to light her way. She smiled briefly at the thought; like the stone tools, she had that covered, and a lot better than Tom Hanks in *Cast Away*.

She went back outside and spent the better part of an hour gathering together a supply of relatively dry branches from the undergrowth above the creek. She found a small piece of flat rock and used it as a scraper to gather some of the dead lichen from the head of the cave and brought it all together at the entrance. She stripped off her all-weather jacket, took out the chocolate bar Toshi had given her and the empty Coke can, and got down to work.

With an archaeologist for a father and an anthropologist for a mother, Finn knew, at least in theory, of at least a half dozen ways to make fire, from the "fire plow" method used by Tom Hanks in the movie, to the slightly more sophisticated North American Indian bow method, and even the wonderfully simple fire piston she'd discovered in an old wood lore text in her father's library called *Cache Lake Country*, a treasure trove of information about everything from snaring rabbits to pemmican recipes.

One thing she'd learned about all these fire-making methods was that none of them was guaranteed. The fact that Tom Hanks got a little bit of tinder going overlooked the fact that any wood he gathered to make his fire machine needed to be bone dry and of two distinct types: a hardwood for the pusher and a softwood for the base. The bow method also required absolute dryness, extreme patience, something to make the bowstring out of, and once again, two kinds of wood. She was never able to get the fire piston right even though the neat little drawing in *Cache Lake Country* was perfectly clear.

Without a match or a lighter or a handy-dandy magnifying glass the only way that Finn knew to make fire was the tried-and-true Coke-can-and-chocolate method she'd learned from her friend Tucker Noe in the Bahamas a year or so ago. It was the kind of thing bar bets were made of, but lo and behold the old man's idiotic method actually worked, and without too much effort at all.

Tucker had used the bottom of a can of Kalik beer and a block of baker's chocolate, but Coke and a Hershey's bar would work just fine. Using a smear of chocolate and a piece torn off the bottom of her makeshift pillowcase headpiece, Finn began to polish the slightly concave aluminum underside of the can. After five minutes of a steady circular motion, the fine marks on the base of the tin were beginning to smooth out, and after twenty minutes, the base was as bright and reflective as a mirror.

Finn found a short length of twig, split the end with her thumbnail, and inserted a dusty little wad of the old lichen in the fork. It took a minute or two to find the right angle to hold the can to catch the sun and get the distance right between the improvised "matchstick" and the can, but eventually the tinder smoked, flared, and fired. Finn pushed the flaming tinder into a larger clump of the lichen she'd arranged under a little lean-to of twigs and a few moments later she had a comfortable fire blazing in front of the cave mouth.

Pleased that she'd accomplished this basic survival feat, she spent the rest of the morning exploring the general vicinity around the cave. After a noontime siesta in the cool confines of her new home she spent the afternoon putting together a simple tool chest of a few pieces of stone splintered or "knapped" into cutting knives and axes.

She then used these minimal tools to fashion a fish spear out of a long piece of bamboo, the split end sharpened, then hardened in the fire. As the sun began to set and darkness fell over the island, Finn used the spear as a spit for the foot-long catfishlike creature she'd caught in the stream only a few feet from her new front door. The fish was delicious. She finished off with a dessert of half-melted Hershey's bar and gave a small sigh of contentment.

Fire, food, abundant fresh water, and shelter. The basics had been taken care of. Tomorrow she'd see if anyone else had been castaway on the island with her, or if she was alone. She piled some more branches on the fire, curled up close to its comforting warmth, and finally let sleep take her, trying hard not to think of her missing friends.

It was still dark when she was wrenched out of sleep by a crashing in the jungle. She barely had time to pick up the fish spear before a rushing pair of immense shadows leapt toward the flames of her hard-won fire and began scooping handfuls of the fine river sand on top of the lowering coals. She pulled herself upright and jumped forward with the spear, but one of the shadows whirled, wrenching the spear from her hands. She started to yell but a broad hand fell across her mouth and gripped hard. Somewhere close by was the foul smell of stinking, rotting meat. There was a fierce whisper in her ear.

"Not a sound or they'll hear you! We have to get you out of here, fast!" It was Billy Pilgrim.

20

They slipped into the jungle, Billy leading Finn by the hand, the other figure moving on ahead. Whoever it was had some kind of furry cape around his shoulders and an odd-looking hat. Kong's sneakers slid around on her feet and she stumbled as they raced along the dark, narrow pathway through the sleeping forest. Some kind of bird screeched loudly and a monkey chattered. The terrible smell seemed to be following them.

"Who's your new friend?" Finn whispered, struggling along behind Billy. "And why does he smell like a dead goat?"

"Because I am wearing the skin of just such an animal," said the man without pausing. "I also have acute hearing." The accent was educated Australian, perhaps even from New Zealand. "My name is Benjamin Winchester. Professor Benjamin

Winchester. I was a conservation biologist at the University of Auckland until three years ago."

"What happened three years ago?" Finn panted.

"A tsunami and a typhoon like the one you just experienced. One caused the other. It is rare but it happens." He paused, sniffing the air, and then moved forward again. "I was on a French research vessel, the *Tumamotu*. FREMER."

"Fremer? What's that?"

"French Research Institute for the Exploitation of the Seas. I was on a grant from the University of Toulon. Pteropods. I'm an expert on the subject."

"Pteropods?" Finn asked.

"It's a kind of plankton, a flagellate pseudosnail that has little tiny wings. It swims with like a sea-horse, except microscopic. You kill them to find out about the CO_2 levels in the water they live in. They're a barometer to the chemistry of entire oceans. Interesting little things. Been slaughtering them for years."

"So how's the chemistry of the ocean?" Billy asked.

"Like the air over Manchester or Los Angeles," said Winchester. "Not healthy."

Wherever they were going, it was in a steep upward direction. It was getting more and more difficult for Finn to keep her footing. The trail was muddy and seemed to be getting narrower and narrower. After a few minutes Finn was completely soaked by the water dripping from the foliage of the undergrowth on either side of the muddy track. Finally the path leveled out and Finn was vaguely aware that they were on some kind of ridge; she could see a lighter section of night sky against the deeper darkness of the jungle that lay in the bowl of a narrow valley on their right.

"Where are we going?" Finn asked as they suddenly veered downward on the three-foot-wide trail.

"Away," said the professor. "If we saw your fire, they might have as well."

"They?"

"Zangs *Shuai-chiao*," muttered Winchester. "Or maybe the Taisho's *Itto-Suihei*."

"Chinese?" Finn said, confused. "Japanese?"

"Both," answered the man in the goatskins. "In this place it really doesn't matter. They'll both hack off your head and stick it on a pole if you give them the slightest opportunity."

"I don't understand," said Finn, her brain whirling.

"You will," answered Winchester. "Believe you me, young lady, you will."

They were now walking carefully along a ledge no more than a yard or two wide with a long steep slide down a nearly vertical precipice if they slipped. On the far side of the valley, Finn thought she could see water glistening in the faint light of the stars. There was no moon. Suddenly Winchester stopped, turned, and vanished into thin air. Finn and Billy were alone on the narrow ledge.

"Where did he go?" Finn asked.

"Here," said Winchester's voice, echoing.

"Where?" Finn asked, frustrated, peering into the darkness. All she could see was jungle foliage and the steep wall beside her. Billy was right behind her.

"Turn to your left and take a step forward," the voice instructed. Finn did as she was told. The foliage parted and she suddenly found herself standing in the narrow cleft of a high-ceilinged cave.

Unlike the ledge outside, the floor of the cave was perfectly dry, made out of some kind of limestone. There was a small flare of light and suddenly Winchester was visible, a grinning apparition in the light from a flickering lamp made out of a deep bowllike shell and a cotton wick. From the smell Finn knew he was using fish oil for fuel.

"This way," he said, grinning. He turned and headed deeper into the cave. Finn followed the wavering light as it reflected off the smooth stone walls for another hundred feet or so. Suddenly the passage ended and she found herself in an immense cavern at least the length of a football field and half as wide. The roof spiraled up at least fifty feet above her head, long spikes of stalactites flowing down like hundreds of organ pipes in some incredible underground cathedral. There was just enough light from the flickering oil lamp to make out something that looked like a dark, narrow ribbon of oil at the far end of the cavern.

"A river?"

Winchester laughed, a strange, dry, rasping sound like a rusty hinge that reverberated and echoed through the giant chamber. "A stream. Pure, cold water. My own river Styx. It flows out of here and down into the valley." He led Finn and Billy across the cave and up to a small stone plateau that rose against the far wall, close to the quietly flowing stream.

Here Winchester had made himself a neat little home, although even in the huge cave the smell of rotten meat, rotten fish, and rank body odor was almost suffocating. There was a hearth made from a large flat rock and a circle of smaller stones, and something that might have been an oven made out of gray, natural clay and an assortment of tools and weapons.

Some were homemade, like the blowpipes and the bamboo spears tipped with sharpened stones that lay in a pile on the far side of the hearth, and some that looked like they'd come from a museum, including an ornate sword with a carved bone handle and a large, roughly made iron ax that had obviously been hand-forged and hammered, but still looked dangerously sharp.

There were also several entirely modern rock hammers, a few rusty screwdrivers, a pipe wrench, and hanging from a makeshift bamboo spit were at least fifty hot-water bottles in a variety of colors. Ranged on a shelflike ledge were a number of amateurishly constructed wicker storage baskets, a wooden crate with the sticker from a pineapple plantation on the side, and an economy-sized red plastic jug of Tide laundry detergent. There appeared to be a pair of brass-cased old-fashioned binoculars hanging by a leather strap from a spiky rock outcropping. Hanging above this assortment of domestic treasures was a large naval pennant, orange on white of an idealized sun with odd-looking rays.

"It's a Japanese Naval Command flag from World War Two," said Winchester, noticing the direction of Finn's gaze. He set the lamp down on the ledge, picked up a small tin box, and carried it to the hearth. There was a fire already laid.

He opened the box and took out a small sliver of dark rock and what looked like a broken piece from a carpenter's plane. He struck the flint and steel together expertly and sparks flew, igniting the wad of tinder in the center of the pile of kindling. Within seconds the tinder had caught and a moment later a small fire was going. Finn found a flat area beside the fire and sat down. Billy joined her. Finn got her first good look at Winchester in the flush of light from the fire as he busied himself with a tin can kettle and something that could have passed for tea leaves.

The marooned university professor looked like something from a nightmare. He appeared to be in his fifties or early sixties, and was on the short side, but stocky and obviously in good health. The hat on his head was made out of a roughly cured triangular piece of skin from a wild pig, bristles out, but grotesque or not it seemed to be waterproof with a large hanging flap at the back like a Foreign Legion kepi to keep water from running down his neck.

Beneath the cap, which Winchester tossed unceremoniously aside as he wedged the tin can kettle in the fire, the man's hair was a long, tangled, gray-blond mess, which he'd obviously tried to trim unsuccessfully. His skin, wherever it was exposed, was darkly tanned, burned almost black, his lips dry and cracked.

Bright blue eyes, half mad, peered startlingly above a thatch of beard that covered the lower half of his face completely. The clothes were a combination of goatskin, pieces of old nylon sail, and something that might have once been part of a rubberized tarpaulin or army surplus ground cloth—all of it held together by strips of leather, twigs twisted through roughly gouged holes, several lengths of copper wire and a heavy belt cinching the whole thing together in a horrible looking kilt and tunic combination.

The belt was the only thing that seemed solid in the entire, extraordinary patchwork ensemble. The belt buckle was brass, circular, lovingly polished, and had the same insignia as the naval pennant: a slightly eccentric version of the Japanese rising sun. What had she stumbled into?

Winchester squatted down in front of the fire and stared into the flames, a lost, yearning look in his eyes. Regardless of the state of his clothing, the professor seemed remarkably fit for a man tossed up on a desert island with nothing but a few odd tools, some bamboo spears, and amateurishly constructed blowguns to provide for his livelihood. It was an impressive feat and Finn told him so.

"I'd advise you to strip off your jeans," he replied mildly.

"I beg your pardon?" Finn said, startled.

"You've just spent half an hour walking through the jungle on an island in the Sulu Sea," he said, with that terrible, slightly maniacal laugh. "Leeches. Great big ones. You've probably been feeding a dozen of the fat buggers without noticing it."

Finn stared, wondering for an instant if he was joking, then saw that he wasn't trying to be funny at all. She struggled to her feet, unbuttoning and unzipping as she did so. Beside her Billy was going through the same routine. Winchester smiled, a bemused expression on his face.

"It suddenly occurs to me that I haven't seen a naked woman in quite some time, especially such a beautiful one. You really are remarkably pretty, my dear." He pointed to her thigh. "There's a couple," he said. "Kingdom *Animalia*, phylum *annelida*, class *clitellata*, subclass, *hirudineda*. That particularly plump group feasting on your blood are brown *Hirudo medicinalis*, standard three-jawed version. Little teeth like razors. Make Dracula proud, they would. Healthy looking."

Finn looked down at her thigh in horror. The leeches were thick, segmented, mucus-covered obscenities about four inches long. They pulsed slightly as she watched, drawing her blood painlessly. In fact she didn't feel a thing.

"Oh God," she whispered, bile rising in the back of her throat. There were more on her other thigh, and several others lower down on both the front and back of her legs. Her whole body spasmed and she pushed one hand down into her panties and then recoiled. "Get them off! Get them off!"

"What do we do?" Billy yelled.

Winchester seemed amused by their panic. "Most experts agree that it's best to do nothing at all. Just let them drop off you when they've had their fill. Hot coals or cigarette ends are no good because the creature will regurgitate its own bodily fluids into your system—good way to get all sorts of nasty infections. Salt is hard on the wound. If you really want them off, you can dig your thumbnail into the back of their heads— that's the part suckered onto you—then sort of slide them sideways and flick them away."

Billy ignored the bloated black horrors clinging to his own skin and started helping Finn frantically reach the leeches she couldn't get at, flipping them into the fire, where they sizzled and curled into desiccated ashy lumps. As Billy and Finn pulled the bloodsuckers off, Winchester kept up a running commentary on the dangers of the local florae and faunae.

"There are seventeen hundred known varieties of parasitic worms hereabouts, a hundred seventy-six species of snake, including pythons, cobras, and kraits, not to mention Russell's viper. Irritable sod, attacks with very little provocation. A strike from one of those and it's say your prayers, laddie, because you've only got a minute or so left to live, no time for antivenom. Responsible for more human fatalities than any other snake in the world.

"Then there's the diseases . . . malaria, dengue-dengue, cholera, typhoid, rabies, hepatitis. Nick yourself shaving and your jaw might drop off a few days later. Then there's the spiny little fish that's attracted to urine and swims up your privates if you give it half a chance. Bathing is not advised, I'm afraid to say." He sighed as Billy plucked the last of the shiny sluglike creatures off Finn and they began to work on himself.

"I do miss cheese, though, toasted mostly. You can live fairly well here, lots of fruits and vegetables, not to mention fish and meat, but there's nothing in the way of cheese." The man shook his head sadly. "What I wouldn't give for a bit of Barry's Bay Cheddar or some Airedale! Maybe a little sliver of Hipi Iti on a cracker. A smear of Waimata blue on some crusty bread." He glanced over as Finn pulled her jeans back on. "You'd be surprised what a man yearns for when he's castaway like I was. Surprised indeed."

"Sorry about losing it like that," Finn apologized as she sat down again. "That kind of thing gives me the creeps."

"You have to get used to 'the creeps,' as you call them, if you live here," said Winchester with a laughing snort. "There's very little here *except* the creeps. And no cheese at all."

"You mentioned that," said Billy. "A distinct lack of cheese by your account."

"Do you have any idea where 'here' is?" Finn asked.

"Somewhere north of Kagayan de Sulu," answered Winchester. "If that means anything to you." He shrugged, then took a stick and pulled the tin can kettle out of the fire and set it aside.

He went to his shelf and found several tin mugs that looked as though they might have been military issue. He wrapped a ragged piece of cloth around the kettle to insulate it, then poured steaming liquid into the three mugs and handed them around. Finn sipped at hers. It was real tea, dark and very aromatic.

"*Camellia sinensis,*" said Winchester, smiling at her surprise. "The real thing. You'd pay good money for that in a supermarket. Couldn't be much fresher. Picked it yesterday from a patch of plants I've been cultivating up the slope."

"You were saying about our position?" Billy prompted.

"Yes. North of Kagayan. I know that much because the ship was north of there when the typhoon struck. We must be pretty well off the ordinary shipping lanes as well."

"No one ever comes?" Finn asked. "Not even the locals?"

"Not in the three years since I washed up here," said Winchester. "And there are no locals." He poured himself some more tea and took a slurping sip, smacking his lips. "I'll take you up Spyglass Hill tomorrow and show you the lay of the land. Most of the coastline is made up of steep cliffs, at least on the leeward side, and the windward side is all reefs and shoals. No anchorage anywhere."

"Spyglass Hill?" Finn said.

"Treasure Island," supplied Billy.

"Quite so," said Winchester. "The place where old Captain Flint had his booty buried."

"And also the name of Long John Silver's tavern in Bristol," added Billy.

"Quite so!" said the professor, raising one very shaggy eyebrow. "You really are quite the scholar!"

"It was my favorite book as a child," said Billy. "That and *The Eagle of the Ninth* by Rosemary Sutcliff."

"The Once and Future King," murmured Winchester. "T. H. White."

"The Bull from the Sea by Mary Renault," countered Billy.

"C. S. Lewis and the Narnia tales," sighed Winchester longingly. "Not quite as good as cheese, but close. I haven't read a word in print these three long years."

"Now that you've had your little literary discussion maybe we should get down to business," said Finn. "So far I've had leeches, Japanese swords, Chinese soldiers, and cheese. I'd like to know just what the hell is going on, Professor Winchester. If you know, that is."

"Call me Ben," said the untidy man in his goatskins.

He struggled to stand, went to his shelf, and lifted the lid on one of the baskets. He came back to the fire, sat down again, and tossed two glittering objects through the flames to land at Finn's and Billy's feet. One was a small gold bar stamped with the chrysanthemum seal of the Nippon Ginko Bank. The other was a heavy gold coin two inches across with a square hole in the center and a Chinese character stamped in each of the four quadrants of the circle.

"Would you believe me if I added a mysterious giant submarine and a six-hundred-year-old Chinese galleon-junk the length of a rugby field? The bones of rhinoceroses and lions and giraffes where there couldn't possibly be? A war that's gone on for more than half a century after peace was declared? A treasure beyond compare hidden within the ancient core of a volcano? An island that eats ships and men and has been doing it for a thousand years?"

"Frankly," said Billy, "it sounds quite mad."

Winchester let out one of his crowing laughs that echoed into the farthest shadows of the enormous hidden cavern. "You think that sounds insane, young man? Listen, and I'll tell you a story."

21

"This is what we know for a fact," said Winchester, settling comfortably back on his haunches. "Once upon a time, the late fourteenth century to be precise, a man named Zheng He was born in northern China, probably Yunnan Province. He was a Muslim and his father and his grandfather were members of the governor's court. When the Ming emperor captured Yunnan, Zheng He was taken prisoner, made a slave, and castrated.

"He was made a servant in the Imperial Court in Peking. In due time he was impressed into the army and made a name for himself, rising through the ranks entirely on merit, sort of like a Chinese Richard Sharpe or Hornblower. Oddly, for a man born into the deserts of Uzbekistan, Zheng He joined the Imperial Navy and eventually became an admiral."

"I read a book about this," said Billy. "Someone wrote a book about him not too long ago. They say he even discovered America about fifty years before Columbus."

Winchester nodded. "The book was called *1421*. It's based on some controversial maps. Whether or not he discovered America may be conjecture, but Zheng He's activities in the South China Sea and the Indian Ocean are well documented. He sailed out of Nanking in enormous fleets of junks, from small eight-oared patrol boats a hundred feet long to monstrous, six-hundred-foot-long treasure junks that carried crews of a thousand men and were big enough for caged, live cargoes of everything from Egyptian dung beetles to giraffes and elephants from the African veldt."

"You seem to know a great deal about all this," said Finn.

"When you're on a research ship for several months at a time you watch whatever they have in their video libraries. The *Tumamotu* had quite a good selection. Mostly in French, mind you, but I muddled through." The man smiled. "And we do actually have our own television shows in New Zealand, you know. It's not all Peter Jackson and *The Lord of the Rings*."

"Sorry," said Finn.

"Quite all right, dear. That's what one gets for living at the bottom of the world ten thousand miles from the mother country."

"And proper cheddar," laughed Billy.

"Real Stilton," said Winchester, a wistful note in his voice.

"Enough about cheese," said Finn. "What about these fleets of yours?"

"Zheng He's career was a brief one, only twenty years. In that time he made seven of his voyages. Perhaps, as some theories say, he even circumnavigated the world. Over those twenty years and seven voyages, he lost a number of ships during typhoons. One of those ships was a full-sized treasure junk that eventually wound up here as it made its way back to China. From the evidence and the historical data we have on typhoons, it was probably in the fall of 1425. Zheng He's ships were magnificently designed, complete with watertight compartments. The ship probably survived almost intact, along with its cargo and most of its crew. The main trade route was closer to mainland Vietnam, so they were clearly blown far off course by the winds. From my own observations I'd say that close to six or seven hundred people suddenly found themselves castaway. The historical record also shows that Zheng He's ships traveled with a large number of women on board.

"Over the years and centuries here, the population seems to have stabilized at a little more than eight hundred. There was breeding stock on the ship that washed up here, cattle, goats, swine, fowl—enough to provide an agricultural base.

Most of the animals Zheng He's people were bringing back to the Ming court died off unless they managed to interbreed with the domestic faunae. There is a particularly vicious sort of wild boar that seems to have some relation to the African warthog and a few small deer, but the lions and elephants and giraffes died out for lack of habitat."

"Jurassic Park in the Sulu Sea," said Finn.

"Something of the sort. More like the Island of Dr. Moreau," replied Winchester. "It's been more than five hundred years since the ship was wrecked. In that time the locals have very little idea of the outside world. They've become like cargo cult aborigines, worshipping the remains of their past but having very little idea of the meaning of those relics."

"Cargo cult?" Billy asked.

"Native people who worship manufactured objects. It was something my mother was interested in. After World War Two, all sorts of native tribes in New Guinea started worshipping straw effigies of the airplanes that had dropped supplies by parachute. The idea was if they prayed the airplanes and their wonderful cargo would return. The idea dates back to the eighteenth- and nineteenth-century explorers who first interacted with aboriginal people."

"So these survivors eventually began worshipping the remains of the ship?"

"Something like that. The ship itself is long gone, but the treasure and a number of other artifacts were taken to a large cave next to the Punchbowl. It's still there."

"The Punchbowl?" Finn asked.

"It's what makes the whole place tick, so to speak." Winchester smiled.

"You'll have to explain that," said Billy.

"Better if I show you," answered Winchester. "Tomorrow, after we get some rest."

Finn slept dreamlessly and woke to the unearthly smell of bacon and eggs. She sat up, blinking, and found a bright-eyed Winchester huddled over a frying pan made out of the bottom of a large tin can and a bamboo stick. Billy was already up and about as well, a simple wooden plate in each hand.

"Mozambique guinea fowl eggs," said Winchester. "One of the old admiral's better castaways. They seemed to have prospered here. The bacon's cut from one of the warthog variants I mentioned to you. Sunny-side up or overeasy?"

"Any way they come." Finn yawned, blinking the sleep out of her eyes. She sat up. "Too bad there's no coffee." She took a loaded plate from Billy and a utensil carved from wood that was a combination fork and spoon.

"But we do have coffee," said Winchester,

handing her a steaming mug with his free hand. Surprised, Finn took a swallow. It was delicious.

"It tastes just like Starbucks," she laughed.

"It is Starbucks," said Winchester. "Sulawesi, from Torajaland. A whole container of it washed up a week or so ago. Some freighter in trouble, no doubt. It happens more often than you'd think. I ground the beans myself, the old-fashioned way—mortar and pestle."

"Starbucks, bacon and eggs, and Chinese treasure," said Billy, spooning up his breakfast with the wooden utensil. "Will wonders never cease?"

"Early days yet, my boy. Eat up and we'll be on our way."

By the time they finished their meal, the sun was well up and the sky was clear. Before they began their expedition, Winchester gave them both strips of dried and roughly cured goatskin to wrap around their lower legs like his own makeshift puttees. "Keeps the nasties out," he told them. "And believe you me there's lots of them about." Thus prepared, they left the cave.

The pathways along the ridge were dry and the soil was thin. The trees were mostly massive maharanga and mahogany, their trunks huge and straight for a hundred feet, their upper-spreading limbs covered in a rainbow spray of fruit.

"It's like walking in paradise," breathed Finn, taking in the rich, rain-forest scents.

"That's all fine and good," said Winchester dryly, "until you step on a pit viper. They like this kind of jungle. Bite's fatal in about ninety seconds."

"What do they look like?" Finn asked.

"The ground," said Winchester. "Almost impossible to spot."

"Full of good news, aren't you?" Billy said.

"Centipedes, millipedes, black scorpions, even a few dangerous plants. Not a place for the faint-hearted, the jungle."

They kept walking for the better part of an hour, mostly upward and mostly following well-marked paths. According to Winchester they were animal trails, but Finn wasn't quite so sure; here and there she was fairly certain she could see the recent marks of some kind of blade cutting through the undergrowth.

"What about trying to escape?" Billy asked. "Ever tried it?"

"I thought of it at first," said the professor. "Building a raft, finding the shipping lanes."

"And?" said Finn.

"And then I sat down and had a good think about it. I asked myself why there were still people on this island, and why I've never seen any evidence of any sort of boat building or rafts anywhere. I finally figured out that the locals had almost certainly tried it themselves, and failed for some reason."

"What reason?" Finn asked.

"Many years ago there was a movie called *Papillon*," said Winchester, "about a man trying to escape from Devil's Island."

"Steve McQueen playing a Frenchman," said Billy. "Dustin Hoffman as a counterfeiter who was almost blind," he added. "Didn't really work for me."

"I wasn't talking about the acting," said Winchester. "I was talking about the escape."

"Didn't he float away on bags of coconuts?"

"Yes," said Winchester. "In reality of course it never would have worked. Believe me, there's enough coconuts on this bloody island for everyone here to float away a hundred times. Only they didn't, you see. They couldn't. Simply because the currents and the tides would make it entirely impossible."

They suddenly stepped out of the jungle and found themselves standing on a rocky, windswept promontory. They were at least a thousand feet above the shore where Finn had washed up. Directly in front of them and far below, they could see the heavy line of surf that marked the reef at least a mile distant. Even from where they stood, the sound of the waves was like rolling thunder.

"When I was a young lad at school I excelled in maths. I was one of those rare swots who actually understood trigonometry. I made a transit out of bamboo and actually triangulated the height of those waves down there a year or so ago, just to keep in practice. Even on a calm day they break at close to thirty feet. At low tide the water's even rougher. No raft could ever get past the reefs even in the calmest weather, and trying to launch a raft on the cliff sides of the island would be suicide."

"There has to be a break in the reef," said Billy, holding a shading hand over his eyes and squinting. "There must be. At least if what you've been telling us about Zheng He is true. If the treasure junk made it to shore, there must have been a way for it to get through the reef. We got through."

"In the middle of a typhoon," said Winchester. "And that's the rub."

"What do you mean?" Finn asked, looking down the steep hillside to the beach far below and then out to sea. There was nothing except the distant joining of sea and sky and the delicate curvature of the earth itself. Finn suddenly felt very small and lonely in the face of so much space. To spend years alone in a place like this must have been terrible. She turned to Winchester, about to say something, then noticed the small tear in the corner of his eye as he looked out across the sea. She kept silent.

"Sometimes when I come here at night, I wish I'd been an astronomer instead of a biologist," said Winchester softly. "You can see every star in the heavens on a clear night, like the sparkles of billions of diamonds on an infinite black velvet sky."

They stood for a moment longer, looking toward the sea, lost in their own thoughts, and then Winchester turned away. Finn and Billy followed him back into the jungle, following a different path through the undergrowth, heading inland.

"What did you mean about the typhoon being the problem?" Billy asked, panting behind the man in his goatskin outfit as they climbed through the dense forest.

"Not the problem, really," responded Winchester. "It almost certainly saved your life." He paused and turned, stopping on the path. "Know much about typhoons?"

"No."

"They create something called a 'storm surge,' an upwelling of water in the eye of the storm that can create a sort of bump or hill in the ocean. Depending on how shallow the approach to land is the results can be devastating."

"The storm surge from Katrina was twenty-eight feet," Finn said with a nod.

"Katrina?" Winchester asked. "Did I miss something?"

"A hurricane in the Gulf of Mexico. It virtually destroyed New Orleans."

"That was always a disaster waiting to happen," Winchester said with a knowing inclination of his head. "Anyone who knows anything at all about hurricanes or typhoons knew that." The professor shook his head. "Well, twenty-eight feet was about half of the surge that took you. I made it close to fifty feet. A supertyphoon without a doubt."

"I think I see now," said Finn, visualizing the storm. "You're saying the surge raised the water far enough above the reefs to take us through, but when the water receded, the ship was left aground."

"Something like that," said Winchester. "This whole island is like a giant lobster pot or fish trap. The topography is like a huge funnel with the island as the center of the trap. Once in, never out. You'll see it better when we reach the top of Spyglass Hill and you get a look at the Punchbowl."

Another hour passed, the heat of the day increasing as the sun rose over the arching canopy of the trees. Sweat began to pour and the air was thick with mosquitoes and swirling clouds of tiny flies. The jungle around them was alive with sound, from the faint sighing of a light breeze in the treetops high above their heads to the smaller chirps and rustles of insects, to the sudden, startling cries of a dozen different exotic birds. It was like being in the middle of the noisiest Tarzan movie ever made.

Finally the trees and undergrowth began to thin and Winchester made a warning gesture with his hand.

"Keep low," he said quietly. He tapped the binoculars hanging on a strap around his neck. "I don't know for sure if the locals or the Japs have a pair of these, but I'd rather not take the chance of being silhouetted on the top of the hill."

Winchester crept forward and Finn and Billy followed. They reached a sloping, almost bare patch of ground at the summit of the hill and peered over. The view was unbelievable.

Fifty yards from where they were perched, a waterfall sprang out of a narrow cleft in the rock and soared down a cliff that had to be as high as Half Dome in Yosemite, a sheer wall of some dark, shining stone that reared up out of a lush, immense jungle valley like a weathered ax blade.

The valley was at least twenty miles across. At its base was a bright blue jewel: an invisible lagoon in the interior of the island connected to the sea by a keyhole rift perhaps half a mile wide, its cliffs as sheer as the one that made up the valley-facing side of Spyglass Hill. A giant teacup with a crack in the side.

The lake, several miles across in its own right, seemed to be dotted with dozens of small misshapen islands—a model of the larger sea beyond. The shore of the lake was ringed with wide, brilliant white beaches lined with stands of palms. It was almost perfectly round. Finn commented on the fact.

"It's a caldera," explained Winchester. "The remains of an explosive volcano. Like Krakatoa, or Crater Lake in Oregon, Rotorua in New Zealand."

"How big is this place?" Billy asked, awestruck.

"By my calculations it's approximately forty-five miles across at its widest point and about sixty miles long."

"But that's incredible!" Billy said, stunned. "Surely it must show up on satellite photos and charts!"

"I'm sure it does," said Winchester mildly. "But so what? Half the time it's covered in cloud and there's no obvious sign that it's inhabited. The island is almost impossible to get to without enormous risk and under just the right conditions, so who'd bother to come?" He made a face. "The madmen who run the governments hereabouts aren't quite greedy enough to deforest this little place like they have the rest of Malaysia. Not quite yet anyway."

"This is the place," said Finn, suddenly understanding. "This is where Willem Van Boegart was shipwrecked back in Rembrandt's time. This is where his treasure came from. Somehow he found a way off the island and went back to Holland to found his empire."

"And this is where Pieter Boegart came looking a few hundred years later," said Billy.

"The Dutchman?" Winchester asked, surprised.

"You knew him?" Billy said.

"I saw him taken," said Winchester. "The locals got him."

"When?" Finn asked, surprised at the depth of emotion she felt for a man she'd never met.

"About a month ago." Winchester shrugged. "Hard to keep track, but I'd say it was about a month."

"How did he get here?" Billy asked. "I thought you said it was impossible without a storm surge."

"It is. He got here the only way you could without cracking up on the reefs. He flew." The goat skinned professor pointed a filthy, bony finger down toward the huge lake. "He landed down there. It was an old Norseman single engine from the war. They have them all over the Pacific. They've got a range of about six hundred miles, so he must have island-hopped, looking for the place."

"What happened?" Finn asked, looking down at the distant circle of blue far below them.

"He circled the island a few times at low altitude. I heard it clearly enough and so did the locals. I made it down to the water in time to see the plane land. By the time he put down, there was a war party waiting. They dragged him out and sank the airplane, all without a by-your-leave."

"They didn't kill him?"

"Not that I saw," said Winchester. "They bundled him out of the plane, threw him into one of their big war canoes, and took him to shore. That's the last I saw of him."

"You didn't try to help him?" Billy asked.

"Help him how?" Winchester said. "I've been trying my best to avoid those people for three years. They're not cannibals but they're not civilized either and they definitely like to chop off people's heads and put them onto bamboo poles. I've seen it. I have no intention of joining them."

"How did you know he was Dutch?" Billy asked suspiciously.

"Because the name *Boegart Line* was written across the fuselage in orange letters five feet high," answered Winchester. "Did I jump to the wrong conclusion?"

"I would have gone after him," said Billy hotly.

"This is their island. Their customs. They've been here for six centuries. I haven't even been here six years and you haven't been here so much as six days. You have no idea what you're up against." He took off the binoculars and handed them to Finn. "Take a look," he said. She raised the glasses to her eyes and followed Winchester's pointing finger.

"My God!" Finn whispered. What she'd thought to have been small islands in the lake were something else altogether.

"What is it?" Billy asked impatiently.

"Ships," said Finn. "Hundreds of them. It's a graveyard of ships." She could still see the names on some. M.V. *Marcalla*, SS *Docteur Angier*, SS *Sebago*, SS *City of Almaco*, SS *Norma C.*, USS *Geiger*, MV *Coolsingel*, SS *Morgantown Victory*. They were everywhere, broken islands of long-vanished vessels that time had forgotten. Some of them were military, like the *Geiger*, apparently a troop ship. *City of Almaco* was an enormous and very old-looking oil tanker.

There were even older ships, rotted wooden hulls, something that might once have been an early steamship, its huge mast turned to dark, waterlogged stumps, all the wrecks thrown hither and yon across the lagoon, some packed tightly together, others standing off by themselves. At the far end of the lake, two or three hundred yards offshore, she saw what she took to be the remains of Pieter Boegart's plane. In front of the half-sunken aircraft was something that looked like a PT boat, the hull smashed in at the bow. She swung the glass around and her passing eye caught a familiar shape. She focused the glasses and stared.

"It's the *Queen*!" The freighter was close to the neck of the lake at the reef end, beached on the sand and listing a good sixty degrees to one side, her rusted hull below the waterline fully exposed.

There was no sign of life anywhere. The whole

bridge section had been crushed and from where she lay Finn could see that the forward hatchway had been sprung and that the cargo crane in the forward section had almost been torn away by the savagery of the storm.

The entire hull sagged in the middle as though her back had been broken. The bow of the *Batavia Queen* had been driven a good thirty feet into the palms and jungle at the edge of the beach. It was a pitiful, unhappy end for any ship, let alone one you knew and cared for. It was almost like the death of a friend.

"Let me see," said Billy. Finn handed him the binoculars.

"No sign of your friends?" Winchester asked.

"No," said Finn.

Billy scanned the wreck of the *Batavia Queen*. He lowered the binoculars.

"Could they have survived?" he asked.

"Anything's possible," answered Winchester. "The two of you managed it."

"If the local people got them, where would they have been taken?" Finn asked.

"They have three settlements, all on the far side of the island."

"Which one would they have been taken to?" Billy asked urgently.

Winchester pointed to a broad craggy hill almost directly across from them. "There's a river that flows down from that mountain to the sea.

Their main village is close to the mouth. I don't know if it has a name."

"Do you know how to get there?" Billy asked.

"Well enough to stay away from it."

"Could you take us there?"

"To find your lost Dutchman?" the man in the goatskins scoffed. "Your friends?"

"To rescue them," said Billy "What's wrong with that?"

Winchester reached across and tapped the brass-cased binoculars. "What about these laddies?"

"What laddies?"

"The binoculars are Zeiss Feldstechers. Especially made for the Imperial Japanese Navy in 1942. Admiral Yamamoto had a pair just like them. Those laddies."

"We're supposed to worry about a few old castaways from World War Two?" Billy sneered.

"No, you're supposed to worry about their children," said the man in the goatskin cap. "The ones with the great bloody swords and the old-fashioned little caps with the flaps in the back. Those are the ones you're supposed to be worried about."

22

"It's a monster," said Billy, staring at the massive whale-sized hulk in the mangrove swamp. It was enormous, a four-hundred-foot-long bulbous tube of metal with a tumorlike hump that ran along its upper surface, the huge conning tower partially crumpled. The designation *I-404* was still faintly visible on the side beneath more than fifty years of rust, barnacles, and filth. The entire vessel was covered in a winding tangle of roots and vines.

"That's where your flag came from," said Finn.

Winchester nodded. "I've done a little investigating. The Japs won't come near it—some sort of superstition, I suppose."

They were lying on the grassy edge of a small sandy dune at the far end of the Punchbowl. To their right, below the sandy hummock, was the beach. In front of them was the swamp. Deepening jungle lay at their back, running in a steep slope into the ridges and hills at the far end of the island. "Enemy territory" as the professor called it.

"I've never seen anything like it," murmured Billy. "I didn't think the Japanese or anyone else had submarines this size during the war."

"They were the largest ever built before the nuclear ones," said Winchester. "The Sen Toku 400 class. They didn't make very many of them, only four or five, I think." He gestured toward the grotesque-looking wreck. "See that bump that runs along the front? That was to carry airplanes. Three of them, with folded wings. They're still in there. They were meant for special assignments, blowing up the Panama Canal, carrying high-technology material. I've had the occasional fantasy about resurrecting one of the airplanes and flying it out except there's no one to give me flying lessons." He laughed harshly. "This one was full of bullion. Probably heading for the German U-boat pens in France. The bullion was to pay for exotic raw materials the Japs were running short of. It wouldn't have been the first time for a Japanese submarine."

"Another video you saw on your research ship?" Billy asked.

"Stories my father told me," said Winchester, shaking his head. "He was an ANZAC . . . Australia and New Zealand Army Corps. He was a prisoner of war in a camp in Sandakan on the Borneo coast." The professor peered at Billy from under the sagging brim of his goatskin cap. "World War Two wasn't all Hitler and Nazis and Pearl Harbor, you know. The people down here were a lot more concerned about Tojo and Yamamoto than they were about the Luftwaffe and Rommel."

"None of that matters now," said Finn. "What matters is finding out what happened to our friends." She stared at the remains of the giant submarine entangled in the bowels of the swamp below them. "How many people do we have to be concerned about?"

"Hard to say," answered Winchester. "I think the submarine was carrying what my father used to call *Rikusentai*, the Japanese equivalent of Marines. The uniform rags they wear are green, not khaki like the ordinary Jap soldier. There must have been two or three hundred to start with. I have no idea how many survived originally. I've never seen more than three or four at any one time, and they don't seem to have any permanent homes like the Chinese here. They hunt in small groups."

"How could they possibly have survived?" said Billy.

Winchester shrugged. "By killing. They had more firepower than the locals originally, but not the numbers. They must have raided the Chinese villages for women and for food at first. Now everyone keeps out of one another's way." He lifted his shoulders again. "There's never been much love lost between the Japanese and the Chinese anyway. They each think the other is inferior and subhuman"—Winchester smiled—"rather like the Americans think of the Muslim races and vice versa."

"Or what the Brits think of the Australians," added Finn, defending herself.

"How are they armed?" asked Billy, getting back to the point.

"I've found all sorts of rusty old Nambu pistols and Arisaka rifles lying about, but they must have run out of ammunition long ago," said Winchester. "The only things I've actually seen them carrying are ceremonial *katana* swords the officers must have had and old bayonets. Spears, bows, blowguns maybe. The locals have a strange sort of crossbow device I've seen once or twice."

"They hunt?" Finn asked.

"They hunt, and they kill from time to time. Not for sport or as a test of manhood like the old headhunter clans in Borneo and elsewhere in Malaysia and the Philippines. The two groups seem to have made up their culture as they went along. The local Chinese are organized into family units. The Japanese seem to promote complete self-sufficiency, a kind of solitary socialism if you like. I've watched small children out hunting with their friends. If one catches something they all share equally. They don't seem to have specialties, either. Everybody hunts. Everybody cooks. Everyone builds huts, gathers firewood. Men and women alike. Very efficient."

"You sound as though you've studied them carefully," said Finn.

"I'm a scientist, so it's in my nature. And it's a matter of 'know thy enemy,' as well. It's in my best interests to keep track of them, and to keep away from them," he added pointedly.

"Do they know you're here?" Billy asked.

"I'm not sure," said Winchester. "I've never had them track me that I know of. As I said I've done my best to keep a low profile."

A breeze blew over the dune, bending the pale dense grasses at the summit and bringing the salt tang of the lagoon to their nostrils. Finn turned and looked out over the huge, lakelike expanse, ringed on every side by the high, jungle-shrouded sloping walls of the ancient volcano. The metal and wood islands of the old ships rose like the skeletons of ancient dinosaurs in the dark, flat water. A few hundred yards out the upended fuselage of Pieter Boegart's floatplane stood like an immense child's toy, tossed aside and forgotten.

In the far distance Finn could see the hazy, funnellike entrance to the hidden lagoon. Above her little puffballs of fleecy cloud moved slowly across the bright blue sky. She tried to imagine what the island would look like from a satellite. Winchester was right. A speck in the middle of an empty sea. At best it would look like exactly what it was: the jungle-covered remains of an old volcano with an inner lagoon and a ring of dangerous, protective reefs.

She was pretty sure that people had come here out of curiosity from time to time over the years and she was just as sure what had happened to them. Sailors, desperate for food or water, would have found a way to bring a small boat through the reefs and they would have paid the price once they reached the shore. Kids looking for Leonardo DiCaprio's beach or the perfect place to scuba, a childless couple sailing around the world—the locals almost surely posted lookouts, and except in the storms like the ones that had brought Winchester and the *Queen* here, they would be aware of any unwelcome visitors. In the end it was the center of a spiderweb and she was trapped in it.

"I wonder how Willem Van Boegart managed to do it," said Finn. He'd been shipwrecked here exactly the same way as she, Billy, and Winchester. "He was washed up here and he managed to get away again. Not only that, he managed to escape with a fortune."

"I'm not sure I catch your meaning," said Billy.

"How did he do it?" Finn asked rhetorically. "The professor says it's impossible, but Willem managed it four hundred years ago, loaded down with treasure. There must be a way off the island that you don't know about, Professor. One that the locals are unaware of, as well as the survivors of that submarine down there. It's the only thing that fits."

"There is no way," said Winchester emphatically. "Believe me, my dear, I would have found it by now."

"Maybe you haven't looked hard enough," said Finn.

"Maybe we should put that aside for the moment," whispered Billy. "We've got company." He gestured with his chin.

Five figures walking in single file were trudging down the beach. The one in front was dressed in a pair of ragged shorts and an equally ragged shirt, salt bleached but still holding a bit of faint green coloration. A Japanese army kepi with a sun flap down the neck was perched on his head. There was an embroidered star on the crown, once red, now pale pink.

He carried a sword freely in his right hand and a bamboo spear in his left, the tip edge with some kind of copper-colored metal that glinted in the sun. His jet-black hair was shaven to the skull. He wore heavy boots and puttees like Winchester's although his were made of what appeared to be cotton, not goatskin. He was clearly the leader of the group and the forward lookout, his eyes scanning back and forth carefully.

Behind him two more figures carried a heavy-looking net on a pole between them. The net looked as though it was closely woven from some kind of coarse string. Probably rattan, Finn thought; she'd seen the stubborn vine growing around lots of the forest and jungle trees they'd passed. A useful crop in a place like this. Both were women dressed in simple sarongs and ragged shirts the same green as the man in front. They wore hats made of broad leaves and they were barefoot and unarmed.

A fifth figure came behind, dressed in a rough patchwork loincloth and carrying a bamboo spear. He appeared to be much younger than the others, barely more than a boy. Across his shoulders on a thin bamboo yoke, he carried the day's catch— a dozen large fish strung with the bamboo through their gills.

"If they turn up off the beach, we're toast," whispered Finn, watching the group approach. Her heart began to pound.

"Then we're toast," said Billy, "unless they happen to be going into the swamp over there."

"Follow me," said Winchester. He slithered down the backside of the dune and ran toward the mangroves, keeping to the heavy grass and trying his best to avoid open areas of sand where his tracks would show. He paused at the edge of the swamp, gesturing for them to hurry. They ran down the slope of the dune and into the tall grass, not stopping until they reached Winchester, crouching low with his back to the dark, putrid water of the mangroves.

"Down!" Winchester hissed. "Cover yourself with the mud!" He looked at Finn's flaming hair. "Especially that!" he said.

Finn and Billy did as they were told, following Winchester's example and dropping full length into the shallow, stinking water. Finn reached both hands into the muck and quickly plastered it into her hair and over her face. Keeping low in the water, and trying not to think about what might be swimming around in the slimy ooze, she raised herself just enough to keep her eyes on the top of the dune. A moment later the little troop appeared, one by one, and marched down the near side of the sandy hummock. They appeared to find some path or trail into the jungle beyond, but suddenly the lead man stopped. He looked around, raising his glance to the canopy of trees just in front of the group, then briefly stared into the swamp.

"He's seen something," whispered Billy, his voice thin.

"Don't move a muscle," warned the professor.

Finn kept watching. The lead man barked a series of instructions and the rest of the group disappeared up the jungle path. The leader stayed where he was, continuing to look around, keeping his attention on the trees overhead. He cocked an ear, obviously listening for any signs of movement. There was nothing except the faint sighing of the wind in the trees and the thudding of Finn's heart within her chest. Finally, he turned slowly through three hundred sixty degrees, the long ceremonial sword pointing like the extended hand of a clock, searching. Then he turned and followed the other four into the protective shadows of the jungle.

"Wait," Winchester said softly. There was only silence.

"Now what?" Billy said.

"Wait," repeated Winchester. "It may be a trick."

"We should go back to the cave," said Billy urgently. "We shouldn't have come out here without weapons. We should have had a plan." The only thing they had that could have been considered a weapon was a long, thick piece of bamboo that Winchester used as a staff.

"I think he's gone," the professor said finally. He rose up out of the mud, dripping. Billy helped Finn up and they stared at each other, grinning.

"Very attractive," said Billy, laughing. Finn used both hands to slick the soggy mass of her hair away from her face. She swept away as much of the ooze from around her eyes, wrinkling her nose at the smell.

"I'm afraid your friend is right," said Winchester. "Our little voyage of discovery was ill advised. We should return to the cave at once. If that man spotted something we could be in serious trouble. They may send out a patrol to look for us."

Finn quickly checked herself over, looking for evidence of leeches, but Winchester's goatskin puttees seemed to have done the trick. They moved through the grass to the foot of the dune.

"We'll leave tracks if we go down the beach," said Finn.

"Not if we stay in the shallows. The tide is coming in," said Winchester. "It will wash away any tracks."

"Let's get moving," said Billy. He stepped forward out of the tall grass. There was a sudden, startling shout from only a few feet away.

"*Otaku! Teiryuu! Sate!*" The partially uniformed leader of the little band of fisherman stepped out of the shadows, sword at the ready. Behind him came the others, including the young boy with the spear. They eased to the left behind the leader, cutting off any chance at escape toward the dune. Finn, Billy, and Winchester were trapped; they either moved forward onto the point of the sword or backward into the dense mangrove swamp.

"Now what do we do?" Finn said.

The man with the sword took a step forward, the sword moving back and forth hypnotically. The young boy swung farther to the right, flanking them, his spear raised. Winchester moved to the right, making a small feint toward the dune.

"Yamate kudusai!" screamed the Japanese man in the hat. *"Wakamare-wasu?"* It wasn't really a question. Finn couldn't understand the words, but the intent was clear. *"Da-me!"* the young boy with the spear yelled. Both he and the man with the sword moved closer. Finn took a step back toward the swamp.

"We're in big trouble," said Billy. "He's not interested in negotiations here."

Suddenly the man with the sword made his move, charging toward Winchester, the blade upraised, an incoherent scream of rage erupting from between his clenched teeth. Winchester raised his stick to block the savage cut, realizing a split second later that the overhead blow had been a trick. Instead of bringing the blade directly down the man spun on his heel like a dancer, swinging the blade around in a sweeping arc aimed at cutting the professor in half from the side.

Winchester tried to back away from the swing, but it was hopeless. At the same time the young boy raised his spear, cocking his arm back, aiming the copper-tipped weapon at Finn's midsection.

There were three harsh cracking sounds in quick succession. The man with the sword stopped in midswing, his hat flying back off his head in a fountaining spray of blood and tissue as the whole top of his head from the bridge of his nose upward vaporized in a gory blur.

Magically two patches of rose-red color appeared in the center of the young man's ragged uniform blouse and he crumpled to the ground. The man with the sword, dead on his feet, fell backward in a heap, the sword still clutched in his fist for the killing blow. The sound of the shots echoed all around the deep expanse of the Punchbowl.

"What the hell?" said Billy, astounded, staring at the bodies. He turned to the equally startled Winchester. "I thought you said these people ran out of ammunition a long time ago."

"They did," said Winchester.

"I did not," said a voice in heavily accented English. From the jungle appeared a squat man wearing camouflage with a long bolo machete on his belt and carrying a very large automatic pistol in his right hand.

"My name is Fu Sheng," said the man. "Come with me quickly if you wish to free your friends."

23

Fu Sheng told his story. It was much like their own. He was a castaway as well. Caught in the typhoon while piloting *Pedang Emas* toward the position the fat pirate Lo Chang had finally revealed to them, he'd let the boat ride out the storm only for it to be thrown through the secret island's funnel like gap on the lip of the sweeping storm surge and then dashed to pieces on the far shore of the lagoon. According to him, he and his master, a man the Chinese man called Khan, were the only ones on board the old sardine boat who survived the storm and its aftermath.

After recuperating from their near drowning, the two men had separated to look for a source of fresh water. Returning to their rendezvous point, Fu Sheng had been just in time to see his friend and fellow survivor being carried off by what he first took to be wild men of some kind.

Following them at a distance, Fu Sheng watched helplessly as his friend was taken to a compound close to a river that flowed down from the mountains and emptied on the far side of the original mangrove swamp Finn had seen when she'd awakened on the beach. According to Fu Sheng, the village was occupied by at least two hundred of the natives.

"Is he talking about the Japanese or your so-called locals?" Billy asked Winchester quietly.

"The locals," answered the professor.

"How are we supposed to take on two hundred people?" Finn asked.

"Not to mention the Japanese," added Billy. "Those shots must have woken up everyone on the island."

"Those shots also saved our lives," said Finn. "I don't much like his looks, but he's got the gun and he seems to have the know-how as well."

"We still need some sort of plan," said Billy.

"I rather think this Fu Sheng fellow makes it up as he goes along," murmured Winchester, following the squat man in his camouflage fatigues as he moved quickly through the dense undergrowth. They climbed steadily through the jungle, keeping the Punchbowl at their backs and moving west, skirting the perimeter of the swamp.

They kept walking for more than an hour, pausing every few minutes to listen for anything other than the constant screeching chatter of the island's birds and monkeys. There was nothing; if the Japanese had sent out patrols to look for the missing fishing party they were being quiet about it.

Eventually they reached a wide, boiling stream that surged down from the Punchbowl's high rim, its course strewn with large tumbled boulders. The banks were steep and slippery looking, turned to slick eroding mud by the constant spray of water dashed onto the rocks.

"There," grunted Fu Sheng, pointing. Finn looked. There was a heavy rope tied to a protruding tree root and dangling down the stream bank. It was made out of several tightly wrapped strands of rattan and knotted at foot-wide intervals. Through the spray Finn could also see another rope contraption that spanned the stream itself. It was a crude bridge with one strand of rattan rope to hang on to and a second lower strand to put your feet on, the lower strand twice as thick as the upper. At intervals were heavy-looking lengths of bamboo woven between the top and bottom ropes to keep them taut and separated.

"Ingenious," said Winchester, impressed.

"Ratlines," said Billy, smiling. "They've turned ratlines on their side."

"Ratlines?" Finn asked.

"Those ropes like ladders on pirate ships," explained Billy. "Sailors used them to climb up and lower the sails."

"They would have had something like that on Zheng He's treasure junks," said Winchester. "A remnant from the past."

"Cross," instructed Fu Sheng. "One at a time."

Finn went first, dropping down the knotted rope and out onto the twisting bridge. She wavered at first and slipped, then got the hang of it, shuffling sideways, gripping the upper rope firmly with both hands. Watching her go, Fu Sheng kept the heavy automatic ready in his hand, his dark eyes scanning the surrounding walls of noisy jungle, searching for a hint of anything out of place. Finn reached the far side, turned, and waited. Billy came next, followed quickly by Winchester. When Winchester was halfway across, there was a sudden gust of wind that shook the trees and the man's hideous-looking goatskin cap flipped off and swirled down into the water.

"Damn!" the professor cried. "My best hat!"

"No great loss." Billy grinned, standing with Finn on the far bank. The gust of wind was followed by an equally sudden dark screen of cloud and an abrupt deluge. Within seconds the pounding rain became a torrential downpour, sheets of flailing water shrouding the other side of the stream like a heavy curtain, catching Winchester in midcrossing and instantly soaking Finn and Billy to the skin.

They ran back into the protective cover offered by the enormous canopy of a gigantic gnarled jungle tree and watched as Winchester struggled across the wildly swing bridge. He made it at last, then stumbled through the downpour, slipping wildly on the muddy ground, and joined Finn and Billy under the tree.

"Bloody hell!" the professor breathed. "That's quite something!" He turned and watched as Fu Sheng shoved the pistol into his belt, slithered down the knotted rope, and then stepped out onto the bridge. The rain continued to pour down, the hammering of the drops on the broad-leafed jungle foliage drowning out anything but shouted conversation. At least it had stopped the endless annoying symphony of the birds and monkeys.

The pirate was more than halfway across the rope bridge, barely visible in the fog of rain. There was a brief sound like the buzzing of some whirring insect and an instant later Fu Sheng staggered on the rope ladder and gave a sudden cry. A foot-long sliver of bamboo magically appeared, jutting from his shoulder. Its shaft was fletched with brightly colored feathers, startling in the sheeting rain like Technicolor smears. Blood blossomed on the pirate's chest, a darker stain against the green camouflage.

Finn whirled, trying to see the person who'd shot the arrow. There was nothing. The attacker was invisible. Finn jumped forward, heading for the bridge, but Billy grabbed her by the arm and pulled her back.

"Are you out of your mind!" he yelled. "You'll get yourself killed!"

There was a second buzzing sound and an arrow tore through the foliage no more than a foot from where Billy stood. He dragged Finn down to the floor of the jungle. Winchester followed. They stared out at Fu Sheng, swinging on the ladder. Another arrow whizzed past, narrowly missing him.

Fu Sheng reached up, grabbed the shaft of the arrow in his shoulder, and snapped it off. Obviously in terrible pain, teeth clenched, he hurled himself across the last few feet of the ladder and headed up the shallow embankment. This time Finn got to her feet and ran toward him. She managed to get one arm around his waist as another arrow came perilously close, flicking through the underbrush by her side.

"Help me!" Finn said.

Billy and Winchester surged upward, then pulled both Finn and the pirate into the relative safety of the jungle undergrowth at the foot of the big tree. Finn propped Fu Sheng against the trunk and looked at the arrow in his shoulder. Remembering her first year of anatomy in art class, she saw that the shaft had missed the chest and impacted in the deltoid, slicing through it and pushing out through his back.

It wasn't quite as serious as it looked. Painful,

but at least it hadn't pierced the lungs or struck any major arteries.

Two more arrows in quick succession sliced through the leaves on Finn's right. One of the arrows struck the trunk of the tree and skidded off.

She pulled Fu Sheng forward to look at the exit wound. Then she reached for the arrowhead, intending to pull it out through the wound, when a bark from Winchester stopped her.

"Don't!"

"Why not?"

"They poison their arrows. I've seen them killing wild boar that way."

"You're sure?"

"Do you want to take the chance?"

"I can't leave it in there!"

Fu Sheng was fading, eyes fluttering, his lips pale.

Finn reached down, pulled out a handful of grass and leaves from the ground, and wrapped it around the sharpened end of the arrow. Grabbing firmly she pulled out the broken shaft in a single swift motion. It came out with a horrible sucking noise and Fu Sheng gasped with the pain. His eyes fluttered open and he attempted a smile.

"Thank you, lady," he whispered. One thick hand reached down to the waistband of his fatigues. He pulled out the automatic and pushed it into her hand. It felt like it weighed twenty pounds.

"Do you have any idea how to use that?" Winchester asked. The weapon was an Egyptian Helwan knockoff of the 1950s-model Beretta 91. Finn remembered her friend Michael Valentine showing her how to work his big old Colt .45. She flicked off the safety and popped the fire selector to SEMI.

"Yes, I know how to use it," she said.

"My breast pocket," instructed Fu Sheng. "There are three more magazines. Ten rounds each."

He'd used three shots on the group of fishermen. That meant seven shots already in the weapon and thirty more in the spare magazines. Thirty-seven rounds against two hundred natives. She had a flashing memory of the child she'd seen murdered in the Cairo slums the year before and the body of the young boy on the beach today. Knowing how to shoot a gun wasn't the same as taking a life with it. Finn clicked the safety back on and pushed the weapon into her jeans at the hollow of her back. There were no more arrows.

"An unlucky patrol?" Billy said, still keeping low, his eyes looking into the jungle. The rain began to lessen almost as quickly as it had begun. Beside Finn Fu Sheng gasped with terrible pain, sat forward with his eyes staring, and clutched at his chest with his free hand. Then he was still. Finn put her finger on the carotid artery bulging in the man's thick neck. There was no pulse. He was dead. She looked at her watch. Whatever poison they used on their arrows had taken less than three minutes to kill him after spreading from a nonlethal wound. Something very nasty.

"It wasn't any patrol. They were waiting at the bridge. They must have heard the shots. They knew we had to come this way," said the professor.

Finn stared at Fu Sheng's body, then turned to Winchester. "You know what village he was talking about?"

"Yes. It's the largest of them. I've seen it from a distance. It has bamboo walls on three sides and the river on the other. There are two gates that I saw."

"How high are these bamboo walls?"

"Not high. Five feet perhaps, but it's useless to try and scale them. The tops are sharpened like that arrow." He pointed to the bloody stump of the broken shaft that Finn had taken from the pirate's shoulder. "They might even be poisoned."

Finn carefully picked up the broken shaft and sniffed the point. There was nothing. She could see faint pale smears of some white, sticky substance caught in a thin crack in the bamboo. "Where do they get the poison?"

Winchester reached out and tapped the gnarled trunk of the tree. "Right here. Cut through the bark and you get a thin kind of latex called 'upas.'

Antiaris toxicaria, I believe. It's a cardiac glycoside. It's called *Antiarin* if I remember my botanical studies from the university. It's quite common hereabouts." He made a face. "Rather like getting a huge dose of Digitalis. It's related to deadly nightshade. His heart exploded in his chest."

"It's thin," said Finn, "and probably fairly labor intensive to harvest. It would wash off in the rain. I doubt if they use it on their palisade walls."

"Doubt all you like," said Winchester. "But I can assure you I won't be joining in any attempt to scale them."

"What about the waterside?" Billy suggested. He stared back across the stream, the way they had come.

"Some very unpleasant creatures in that water. You'd have to swim at least three hundred yards—something I simply am not capable of doing—and then you'd find yourself right in the middle of the village. From what I saw of the place their whole life is centered on the river."

Finn said, "Not capable of swimming three hundred yards?"

"Not capable of swimming at all," said Winchester. "I never learned."

Billy stared, unbelieving. "And you're a marine biologist?"

"It wasn't a requirement for my doctorate as I recall," the professor answered stiffly.

"How did you survive your ship going down?" Billy asked.

"I always made sure my life jacket was within reach. The crew used to tease me about it. On the other hand I was the only one to survive."

"Well, we can't just stay here arguing," said Finn. "We have to come to some sort of decision."

"We should go back to the cave," said Winchester. "The odds are entirely against us and thanks to our dead friend here we've lost the element of surprise."

"I think that's the whole point," argued Finn. "They know we're here now, both the Japanese and the natives. They'll come looking for us, and eventually they'll find us, one group or the other."

"We don't even know if your lost Dutchman is still alive," responded the older man. "He could be dead by now and so could this Khan fellow."

"There could have been other survivors from our ship," said Billy. "We have to try."

"And then we have to figure out a way off this island," said Finn.

"I've already told you," said Winchester, exasperated. "It's impossible. It can't be done."

"Yes, it can." Finn stood up. The rain had stopped and the sun was shining down hotly again. Warm mist began to rise. "There's a way. There has to be."

24

They reached the ridge that marked the summit of the Punchbowl by the middle of the afternoon and found the river an hour after that. They climbed down through the jungle forest, following the river course, the broad expanse of the sea far below occasionally visible through the trees. In another time the hike might have been idyllic, a nature lover's dream of exotic plants, birds, and wildlife. As it was, each step was bringing them closer and closer to a confrontation none of them wanted.

"This may well turn out to be a fool's errand," Winchester grumbled as they threaded their way down a steep jungle trail beside the river. "Your Dutch uncle or whoever he is may be long dead and there's no guarantee that the natives captured anyone else."

"What about Fu Sheng's friend?" said Finn. "Are we just supposed to abandon him?"

"Survival of the fittest if you ask me," said Winchester. "He means nothing to me."

"He saved your life," said Billy harshly.

"And now I'm supposed to sacrifice mine?" Winchester scoffed. "This isn't some remake of *Beau Geste*, my young friend. This is the real world we're living in. I've managed to survive here for three years by keeping a low profile, not charging after faint hopes." He shook his head and poked his long bamboo staff into the dirt. "We should be back in my cave worrying about filling our bellies with food, not poisoned arrows."

"Look," said Finn, exasperated. "At the very least, we have to see what we're up against. I'd like to do it before it gets too dark to see my hand in front of my face. I don't think any of us want to be out in the open when it gets dark." She continued on, picking her way along the path, still slick and muddy from the rain. By her calculations and rough line-of-sight bearings, they'd circled halfway back toward the cave.

By cutting directly cross-country, they'd run into the ridge above the valley with an hour or two of hard hiking. That left them with an hour of daylight to check out the native village and formulate some sort of plan. She tried not to look at Winchester or Billy. So far she was talking a good line, but she didn't really believe any of it. She was out of her depth, exhausted, and afraid.

Her mind wandered for a moment and she suddenly had a sharp, vivid memory of the onion rings at Pick More Daisies in Crouch End. If Lord Billy and Willem Van Boegart hadn't come into her life, she could be sitting in her flat chowing down on a sloppy Joe with a side of rings and fries right this minute, watching reruns of *The X Factor* on her unlicensed and illegal television.

That and a glass of cheap red wine plonk from Emir's shop across the way would be just about perfect right now. Instead she was hiking through a steaming jungle on a desert island in the middle of the South Pacific and wondering if the faint tickling sensation she could feel on the back of her right leg was a giant, bloated, bloodsucking leech or just a very large mosquito drinking her dry. She silently vowed to herself that if she got out of this mess alive, her adventuring days would be over. So far the only good thing that had happened was not stepping on some horribly venomous snake.

"Give it time," she muttered to herself.

"Pardon?" Billy asked politely, walking just behind her.

"Nothing." She reached down and slapped the back of her leg, then kept on walking, the phantom aroma of onion rings in her nostrils.

They reached the outskirts of the village as dusk

began to fall. From a mile upstream the first signs were clear: a fish trap set into the fast-flowing water. The trap was made of closely woven strips of bamboo, the pattern close enough to capture fish of a useful size yet open enough to let out the immature fingerlings; a clever, natural method of environmental control. On the nearby rocks was evidence that fish had been gutted and skinned, and farther down they found a small hut raised on bamboo stilts and fitted with closely packed, oily racks that smelled strongly of wood smoke.

At that point they headed inland away from the riverbank, moving slowly through the thinning jungle, carefully watching and listening. More and more they saw evidence of human occupation: small patches of cultivation, felled trees, another smokehouse, and well-trodden trails that intersected on the forest floor. They even found a fruit rind from somebody's casual snack tossed into the undergrowth beside the trail. And they saw smoke, then smelled it. Cooking fires. Eventually the jungle thinned absolutely and they saw a broad, cleared perimeter of dark earth and a densely built wall of bamboo, the broad stakes sharpened at the top and held together by thick rattan ropes. Beyond the palisade they could just make out an assembly of high-pitched roofs, thatched in heavy layers of some kind of bunched, split-cane bundles. They squatted at the edge of the jungle and looked out across the clearing.

There were no signs of any panic or activity. They could hear faint sounds, a hollow hammering of a mallet, laughter, childish squeals of pleasure, and the high-pitched commands of a mother to her child. There was no doubt that the language was Chinese of some sort, a harsh, almost guttural dialect completely unlike the singsong music of Malay or Philippino Tagalog.

"Now what?" Billy said, looking out across the clearing.

To the right of the enclosing, the fortlike palisade was nothing but jungle. To the left they could see how the land led down to the river. Outside the wall they could see some sort of rough dock and several long, canoe-shaped dugouts, each one apparently created from a single log. One of them was made out of two immense tree trunks bound together by a complex web of bamboo poles making a catamaran. This vessel was also equipped with a central mast and a dark brown sail bundled closely into a heavy fanlike shape. The furled sail of a junk. The sail was made from some sort of pounded vegetable fiber and reinforced by dozens of thin bamboo strips. Beneath the mast and between the dugouts was a large platform made from more bound bamboo poles. Powered by the sail or by at least two dozen paddlers, the whole contraption looked as though it could easily carry thirty or forty passengers, or warriors.

"Is that the war canoe you were talking about?" Finn whispered.

Winchester nodded. "Yes. Except it was fitted out with some kind of big throne at the stern end. That's not there now."

"You'd think a great bugger of a thing like that could get through the reefs," said Billy.

"Just what I was thinking," said Finn. "But then again perhaps they didn't want to leave. Maybe they liked it here and decided to stay. We'll never know."

"I must say they don't seem too worried about us," commented the professor. I don't see any guards and we didn't run into anyone except that archer by the rope bridge."

"Why worry?" Billy said. "We're kind of a captive audience, don't you think? And they know it."

Winchester turned fidgety. He looked over his shoulder, frowning, then up at the darkening sky. "It's getting on," he said. "We should be on our way. We've seen the place."

"I want to get inside," said Finn.

"Don't be a mad fool!" Winchester sputtered. "You can't be serious!"

"We've come a very long way looking for Pieter Boegart. I'm not just going to walk away from him now."

"He may very well be dead."

"Then we'll know. And there could be others in there."

"We don't know that!"

"Then maybe we should find out."

"How do we get in?" Billy asked, scanning the palisade.

"You said there are two ways in?" Finn said, turning to Winchester.

"By the river and on the far side of the compound," said the professor, sulking. "But you'll never get through that way."

"Why not?"

"Because they have bloody guards, and they have gates that they close." He shrugged. "It's not as though we can just walk in and take a look around."

"We can't climb the fence," mused Billy. "Even from here they look wickedly sharp. And they could be poisoned, like the arrows, even though it's unlikely."

"So?" Finn asked. "Where does that leave us?"

"We could cut through the fence easily enough," said Billy. He hefted the big bolo machete he'd removed from Fu Sheng's body.

"They'd hear you," said Winchester. "It's impossible."

"Not if we had a distraction," offered Finn.

"Such as?"

"A lot of noise. Firing the gun into the air or something."

"How about a fire?" Billy grinned.

"I have a burning glass," said Winchester. "But there's not enough sun to make it work. Sorry."

"And I didn't bring my handy-dandy blowtorch with me," said Finn.

"But I did," said Billy. He reached into the button pocket of his faded shirt and brought out a bright blue, very ordinary Bic lighter.

"Where on earth did you get that?" Finn asked.

"It was just about the last thing I remember before the wreck. The pilot light on the stove in the galley went out and Toshi asked me to relight it. After I lit the pilot light again I must have put the lighter in my pocket and buttoned the flap. Then we went aground and it was lights-out, so to speak."

"Does it work?"

Billy clicked the Bic. It sparked and flared into life. Finn took the lighter from him and tried it herself. Flame jumped in the gathering darkness. Thirty-nine cents at the Kwiki-Mart, right beside the beef jerky. The huge difference such a small thing could make. The difference between civilization and the Stone Age. The cooked and the raw. She put anthropology out of her mind and handed Billy back the lighter.

"This is the plan," said Finn.

25

The torch whirled through the gloom, trailing sparks, and did a twisting somersault above the sharpened teeth of the palisade. Then the second bundle of bound, dry branches flew over the fence followed by two more in quick succession. The last two let out clouds of oily, foul-smelling black smoke.

The two final bundles had been soaked in the thin white gum flayed with the machete from the woody trunk of a tall upas tree just outside the cleared perimeter of the village. If the rubberlike substance was as poisonous as Winchester thought, there was a chance that the smoke would provide an even more powerful distraction than the flames.

A hundred yards away, close to the river, Finn and Billy waited in the looming shadows for the alarm to be raised. A few moments after they'd seen the whirling flames of the torches, they heard the first frightened cries.

"Look!" Finn said breathlessly. Even from this distance, they could see the rising flames. A torch had landed on the thatched roof of one of the buildings, burned through the damp top layer, then ignited the dry straw beneath. Within seconds the whole building was ablaze. "That should keep them busy for a while."

"Come on!" said Billy. Together they raced across the clearing, ghosts in the dusky light and protective shadows of the jungle sunset.

They reached the base of the palisade and paused there, listening to the rising commotion and the crackling of the distant flames. To the left, out of the corner of her eye, Finn could see the flat black surface of the river and the shapes of the dugouts drawn up on the shore, long carved paddles neatly left across the thwarts. Nobody was guarding the boats.

"Now," she whispered to Billy. Her friend raised the heavy, half-curved blade of the lethal-looking machete and began to hack at the bamboo, chopping a rough hole through the fence. It didn't take long.

Billy leaned down and squinted through the newly fashioned opening. He turned back to Finn. "There's a big square building on bamboo stilts about two feet off the ground. More buildings to the left and right, smaller ones."

Finn closed her eyes, trying to remember the layouts of the ancient village sites she'd roamed through as a kid with her mother and father in the Yucatan, wondering if they had any relevance here. Those villages were usually built around a central plaza or ceremonial altar, the buildings—residential and otherwise—laid out in closely built concentric circles. Where would they keep prisoners if they had them?

"Buildings with people in them will have god windows," she said finally, remembering the old tales her mother used to tell her. "Look for any building with its doors and windows shuttered and closed."

"God windows?" Billy asked.

It was common to most cultures in one form or another—the Ainu natives in Japan had small windows in each of their simple houses to give spirits free access and, just as important, an easy escape route. Ancient Europeans called them "ley lines" or lines of force.

The Nazca had them in Peru. Romans built their roads according to them and hundreds of thousands of pilgrims followed one particular "spirit path" called the Way of St. James through the mountains of Spain. The Chinese had them as well—the pseudoscience of feng shui, the "resting dragon," was based on making sure the spirits had free passage through any structure. To close the doors and windows would mean that something was imprisoned within.

"Look for any building with its doors and windows closed," she said.

"That's it?"

"That's all I can think of unless they're tied to a stake in the village square."

"Ever the optimist," grunted Billy.

"I'll go first. Stick together. If we get separated you know what to do."

"Never argue with a woman who has a very large gun stuck down her pants," said Billy solemnly.

Finn gave him a look, drew the pistol out of her jeans, then bent down and scuttled through the hole in the palisade.

The village within the bamboo wall was remarkably neat and tidy. There were about twenty small buildings, all raised on three-foot lengths of thick bamboo, and several larger buildings that looked as though they might have some sort of communal purpose. All of them had plaited rattan walls and heavily thatched roofs, the roofs pitched very steeply. As Finn had guessed all the buildings had small open windows on one side and open doorways.

Thanks to Winchester's efforts, the three buildings farthest from Finn and Billy were in flames, as was a whole section of that end of the palisade.

They could see the silhouettes of people crowding around the burning structures, trying to beat out the fires with big bamboo mats. They weren't having much success.

"There!" Billy said, pointing. Twenty feet away, close to the palisade wall, was a large hut on stilts with its side window covered and its entrance firmly shut. There was an awkward-looking set of steps leading up to a porchlike affair that ran around three sides. At the top of the steps was a stocky figure dressed in an ornately designed woven tunic and carrying an astounding-looking battle-ax with a brightly gleaming blade that flickered nastily in the rising glow of the flames.

The ax head was fitted onto a heavy length of bamboo as high as the man's head. He looked like a wrestler with long jet-black hair and a straggly black beard that covered most of the lower part of his face. A face out of the past, the features those of an ancient Chinese warrior. As they watched a voice called out of the darkness. The guard stepped forward, called out again, and then ran down the steps and headed for the blaze at the far end of the compound.

"We just got lucky," whispered Finn. They waited until the man rushed by, then scuttled toward the hut. They went up the steps and threw open the door.

The room was ten by ten, the floor covered with thin woven mats. A lamp flickered on a small table. Four men were bound hand and foot on benches at the far end of the room, their arms pinioned and trussed with bamboo poles threaded behind their elbows.

"Well, I'll be a sheep-shagging bum pot! *Pogue Mahon* and God save me for a *braw Tumshie heid*! It's our Miss Ryan!" Run-Run McSeveney shook his head, beaming up at her from the bench. "Almost gave me the skitters comin' in like that!"

"What's going on out there?" Briney Hanson asked.

"A diversion. Cut them loose," Finn said to Billy. The third man on the bench was Eli Santoro, first mate on the *Batavia Queen*. He gave Billy a huge grin as he was cut loose from the chafing rattan ropes. The fourth man, dressed in ragged camouflage fatigues and with a native Dyak haircut, was silent.

"Is this everyone?" Finn said.

"I'm afraid so," said Hanson, climbing to his feet, wincing as he rubbed his wrists.

"We don't have much time," said Finn. She hefted the automatic in her hand. "We have a friend outside waiting for us and a hole in the palisade wall. Head for the river. We're going to steal one of their canoes."

"They'll come after us," warned Hanson.

"Not if our friend has done his job," answered Finn. "He should have pushed all but one of the boats into the river by now."

"Miss Ryan," began Hanson, "there's something you should know . . ."

"Save it till later," said Finn. "Come on!"

Billy slashed through the last of the ropes with the machete. With Eli's help he pushed aside the bench and started hacking a hole in the woven matting of the rear wall. The hut would provide a little cover as they made their way back to the breach in the palisade. There was the sudden sound of footsteps and Finn whirled, lifting the pistol in her hands.

Standing in the doorway was a tall figure in padded leather armor, a long, leather-wrapped bow over his shoulder, and a huge flat sword in his right hand. Like the guard at the door, he resembled something out of the distant past. In the center of his chest was a huge twisting dragon on a medallion the size of a dinner platter.

The huge medallion glowed in the small light from the sputtering lamp on the table. He lifted the sword in his hand and took a step forward. His eyes locked with Finn's. She stared. The face, the hair, and the Viking beard were unmistakable.

"Pieter Boegart!" she whispered.

"I know you," said the warrior, stopping in his tracks. He stared at Finn, a strange expression on his face.

"No, you knew my mother," said Finn. "Maggie Ryan. Lyman Ryan's wife."

"Maggie," said the man. "You're Maggie's little

girl. We met once, a long, long time ago. You'd just learned how to walk. Maggie was very proud of you." There was a terrible ache of memory in the man's voice. "I didn't really think you'd come."

"They didn't take you prisoner," said Billy.

The red-haired man looked confused. "Prisoner? Why would they take me prisoner?"

"The plane—Winchester saw it. They captured you."

"They rescued me. The float caught a deadhead when I landed." The man frowned. "Who's Winchester?"

"Never mind," said Finn urgently. "We're getting out of here."

The red-haired man looked over his shoulder. "They're coming. Go now. They won't understand why I let you escape. Hurry, before it's too late."

"Come with us!" Finn said urgently.

"I came back here to stay. This is my place, my home. These are my people."

"That's insane!" Billy said.

"Then I'm mad," said Boegart. "If I don't protect them the world will reach out and destroy them. That's why I came back."

"Then why did you want us to come looking for you?"

"I thought that if you were the kind of people who could find me, you might be the kind of people who could understand what I'm endeavoring to do here. To save at least one small part of the

past, keep it safe from your so-called civilization."
He turned and looked over his shoulder again,
then turned back to Finn. "You must go now!" he
pleaded. "Get off the island."

"And just how are we supposed to manage
that?" Billy said.

"The same way I did," said Pieter Boegart. "The
same way Willem Van Boegart did four hundred
years ago. *Fugio ab insula opes usus venti carmeni,*"
he quoted.

"The motto above the door of the cabinet of
curiosities," said Finn.

"Good girl!" said Boegart. "Now go!"

Billy had chopped a big enough hole in the rear
wall of the hut and everyone was dropping
through it and disappearing into the darkness.
Billy was the last out. He paused and turned to
Finn.

"It's time to leave," he said.

"All right," she answered. "I'll meet you at the
river." She turned back to the doorway.

Pieter Boegart smiled, raising the huge sword
in a final valedictory salute. "I will see you again.
I promise," he said. He paused, the smile quickly
turning into something else. "You look just like
your mother," he whispered finally, and then he
was gone, into the night, back in time. Something
tugged at Finn's heart for an instant, and then she
followed Billy through the hole in the wall and
disappeared.

She went after the others, their figures nothing but shifting shadows against the flickering palisade. With her way lit by the roaring bonfire of the burning huts, she made her way behind the line of buildings to the opening and ducked through. There was no sign of pursuit; the villagers' attention was securely fixed on the fire.

At the river she saw that Winchester had done his job perfectly. A half dozen canoes were floating away on the gathering current and were swiftly being taken downstream. The others were already scrambling into the remaining dugout, while Eli held the narrow craft steady, looking anxiously for Finn as she ran toward him.

Silently she scurried aboard, then felt the sudden shift as Eli pushed them off and threw himself into the stern of the canoe. Someone in the darkness pushed a paddle into her hands. She cut the long, beautifully crafted blade into the dark water and felt it dig in. Tears finally coming freely, the memory of the tall, bearded man in the ancient padded armor clear in her mind, she helped maneuver the dugout into the center of the hurrying river, heading toward the distant sea. They'd done it. For the moment at least, they were free.

26

The river current, swollen by the recent rain, carried them swiftly down to the sea. On their left, foam bright and phosphorescent in the darkness, the never-ending breakers pounded at the distant reefs. On their right, two hundred yards inshore from where they paddled, was the looming jungle, no more than a darker shadow in the perfect blackness of the total tropical night. There was no sound except for the line of glowing breakers and the pounding of the surf on the nearby beach. Three hours had passed and still there was no sign of anyone following them.

By midnight they were exhausted and the tempo of the paddling slowed. The tide was running against them now and it was all they could do to keep from being swept out onto the reefs. Finally, with the sky brightening to a golden smear that turned the black expanse of jungle to a sharp-edged silhouette, they reached the keyhole cleft that marked the entrance route to the Punchbowl deep in the center of the island.

"There," said Winchester from the rounded prow of the dugout, pointing toward the shore.

Finn stared, bleary-eyed, into the rising dawn. At first she couldn't see anything except the beach and the dense jungle beyond, but then her eyes adjusted and she could make out a narrow slice of weak daylight between the steep hills.

"The tide is turning again," said Billy quietly from his position midway up the narrow canoe. "If we just keep to the path of the current, it should carry us into the Punchbowl without any trouble."

Finn and the silent man with the native haircut put the blades of their paddles into the water on either side of the canoe, steering into the tidal sweep that steadily carried them toward the shore. In minutes they were slipping easily between the high walls of the gap and into the steep, hidden canyon that lay beyond. The water burbled along the sides of the dugout, and beyond, in the jungle growth that shrouded the ancient volcanic walls, the first chattering, screeching sounds of morning could be heard.

"He said something in Latin," murmured the man with the strange haircut, speaking for the first time since they'd escaped from the village.

"That's right," answered Finn.

"He seemed to think it answered your question about leaving this place."

"Yes," said Finn. She'd been thinking about it herself for most of the night as they paddled along the perimeter of the island.

"What did he say?" asked the man. The tidal rush was pulling at them even more rapidly now, swirling around them, carrying them dangerously close to the near rock wall. There was no beach here, only jagged rock, the fringe of jungle hanging precipitously in the thin soil. The man dug in hard with his paddle and the others did the same, carrying them back into the center of the passage to the interior.

"*Fugio ab insula opes usus venti carmeni,*" said Billy, irritation in his voice. "Escape to my hidden island of treasure on winds of music," he explained.

"No," said the man with the native haircut. "That's not correct."

"What would you know about it?" Billy said.

"It's from Homer's *Odyssey*," the man answered without inflection. "I spent a number of years in boarding school translating huge sections of it as punishment for skipping class." He laughed softly. "That particular passage refers to Circe and her island. Some scholars believe Homer took his ideas from the eastern epic of Gilgamesh in which the hero escapes from the island by going through a tunnel where the sun comes into the sky."

"So how do you translate it?" Billy said.

"Escape *from* my hidden island of treasure on winds of music. The word 'ab' means 'from,' not 'to.' " He shrugged. "It would seem to have more relevance."

"He's right, you know," said Winchester. "About the Latin, I mean. Studied Homer myself. *'Virtutem paret doctrina,'* and all that. 'Let education make the all round man.' Scot's College."

"I stand corrected," said Billy stiffly.

"Is there a place like that here?" Finn asked, calling forward to Winchester, sitting in the front of the dugout.

"A place like what?" Winchester asked, digging in with his paddle.

"A tunnel where the sun appears. Something to do with wind. Music. I don't know," she said, frustrated. It wasn't much to go on.

Then, suddenly, the fjordlike confines of the keyhole slot leading to the Punchbowl ended and they were swept into the huge, almost perfectly circular lagoon that had once been the raging heart of a volcano.

Winchester spoke. "There was a cave I saw once, during my first year here," he said. "I didn't think much of it at the time. A blowhole, I suppose you'd call it."

"Blowhole?" Run-Run McSeveney muttered. "Sounds like some *bowffing cack erse* people I've known in the bluidy past." He dug his paddle into the water, scowling as usual.

"A blowhole is a volcanic leftover," explained Winchester. "A vent tunnel." He paused in his paddling, looking upward to the far side of the enormous circular valley, scanning the jungle forests rising from the misty dawn. "I was hunting when I happened to find it," he said. "Quite shocked me actually. At first there was nothing and then it was like standing next to an exploding steam pipe."

"There's a place like that in your South Dakota," said Billy. "My parents took me there when I was young. Wind Cave or something."

"Could you call it music?"

"I suppose," said Winchester, "if you weren't too musical. More like a bloody great whistle."

The incoming tide swept them into the Punchbowl's sinister graveyard of hulks, looking even more ghostly in the early morning half-light. They slid silently past the moldering wreck of some ancient ironclad schooner, the masts long rotted, the hull a dark, gap-toothed wreck of barnacles and crusted sea life. The old vessel was anonymous now, the name on her upended transom long since worn away. To the right, rising out of the fog, they could see what was left of the *Batavia Queen*. Ahead of them were a dozen other wrecks and the shattered remains of the old single-engined aircraft that had returned Pieter Boegart to the island.

"Can you remember where it was?" Finn asked.

"Certainly," said Winchester. He stopped paddling for a second and pointed up the side of the steeply sloping caldera. "It's just there, where those two hills thrust up. I call them the lions." Just then the sun rose fractionally higher, throwing the two crouching shapes into sharp relief. Winchester was right. The two hills looked exactly like crouching lions facing each other.

"A tunnel where the sun comes into the sky," said Khan.

"That could be it," said Billy, excitement rising in his voice. "It fits."

"We're going too fast," said Briney Hanson, looking out over the water. There were ripples and eddies everywhere marking unseen hidden obstructions; the remains of vessels captured by the deadly wrecker's island. "We should warp up to the lee side of one of these old wrecks and wait for the tide to slack. It's too dangerous to go on like this. We could hit something."

"Aye, he's right about that," cautioned McSeveney, peering over the side.

"That's ridiculous. I can see perfectly," said Winchester from the bow of the dugout. "It's clear water. I can almost make out the bottom." There was a sudden swirling in the water as the tide pushed them past the listing wreck of the old oil tanker, *City of Almaco*, the tall, rusted stack over her rear superstructure and the stumps of her derricks all that were visible in the mist. The sheering currents fought against each other for a moment, swinging the canoe around like a swirling leaf in a rushing gutter, and the goatskin-clad professor found himself facing back the way he'd come. Panicking, Winchester clutched the low thwarts and tried to stand.

"Sit down!" Hanson bellowed. "You'll tip us over!"

"Ye *numpty cludge*!" McSeveney yelled, trying to steady the boat. "We're tipping!"

It was too late. Winchester's sudden movement pushed the dugout in another direction. The fighting currents slammed the boat against the side of the old oiler and they spun around a second time, tilting heavily to one side. Winchester lost his paddle, made a desperate grab, and then everyone was in the water.

The full horror came without warning as Finn hit the water and went under. For a moment she didn't know what was happening. Then she was aware of a lashing pain across her cheek and then another whiplash against the bare skin of her stomach where her shirt had pulled up. She gagged at the sudden pain, thrashing to the surface, fighting for air. There were more excruciating lashes to her arms and legs. Through the pain she was faintly aware of Winchester's screams that he couldn't swim. She managed to lift one hand, sweeping whatever it was away from her face, feeling more stinging pain across her palms and cheek. She blinked and saw the horror that lay in front of her.

The water all around her was a solid mass of bubbling, undulating slime. Attracted by the warm shallow water and the recent rain, a huge, roving colony of box jellyfish had made their way on the incoming tide to the Punchbowl's interior. The mindless nightmare now lay like some obscene, translucently pulsing blanket across the surface of the sea.

Horrified by the sight, Finn thrashed at the water with her arms, trying to beat the pulsing creatures away from her body. A dozen burning filaments dangling beneath the oozing bubbles of jelly stroked the flesh of her legs and she screamed again, rearing up out of the water, trying to do anything in her power to get away.

Spinning in the water, Finn was dimly aware that the colony had formed itself into a giant crescent flowing toward the shallows closer to the beach, the two outer arms of the arc spreading out on either side. Turning, choking, she tried to find the shape of the overturned dugout. She swam toward it, now at least fifty feet away, surrounded by the purple-humped monstrosities. The colony, a hundred fifty yards long and twice as deep, was a death trap, oozing all around her like some grotesque minefield, waiting to entangle her completely.

A small patch of straggling organisms on the

forward edge of the swarm lay in her path and she arched her back in a desperate attempt to avoid them. They were small, their slightly squared bubble sails still immature as they pulsed toward her, the strings of sensory eyes around the bubbles, perimeters clearly visible like black specks in the clear mucosa of the body.

Their stingers swept lightly against her and she gasped with the burning pain. She cried out again, batting weakly at the creatures, just managing to keep her head above water, and then the numbing cramps began as the deadly venom reached her bloodstream. She knew that she was weakening and soon she'd be unable to swim.

Dimly, at the edge of her awareness, she thought she heard Billy calling her name, but help was too late in coming now. The jellyfish had completely surrounded her, each gentle motion of the swell and their own pulsing energy bringing the colony close around her so that the feat would be shared equally among the ever hungry creatures. Finn began to sink under the water, the last of her strength draining from her body as their poison took hold.

Eyes open, she saw what lay beneath the surface and recoiled in unholy terror as all hope vanished. In the faint morning light, the hideous flotilla had been terrible enough; beneath the blue-green water, it was a vision straight from hell. Millions of tentacles, some light as a human hair, others thick as twisting ropes, dangled from the bellying domes above, an endless hypnotically swaying forest of deadly threads that had already wrapped themselves completely around Ben Winchester's body in a monstrous tangle, slowly but surely pulling him upward into the very center of the swarm, his corpse slowly drained of nutrients until finally everything that had been the man would be absorbed within the colony.

Finn remembered hearing once that drowning had been called the death of dreaming, but this was a death of nightmares everlasting, and even as she sank downward her hands fluttered, some last instinct trying to push her back toward the surface.

She felt a clutching pain deep within her chest as the last of the air exploded from her lungs. Vision blurring as she died, she saw the last of Winchester's pale face in front of her, Medusa-like, his hair a mass of serpent strands like some mythical creature caught within the colony of roving jellyfish. Then the vision faded and darkened. Pain was swept away, she heard her name called one last time, and then there was only darkness and the pounding of her final desperate heartbeats echoing faintly and fading in her ears.

She awoke in paradise. Directly above her head the dappled sun sparkled through bright green leaves and there was the flush, rich scent of something spicy and exotic in her nostrils.

"*Mijn kind.*" The words were spoken softly, gently. She let her head fall to one side and saw the red-bearded face of Pieter Boegart. He was kneeling beside her. They were in a large clearing almost at the summit of the Punchbowl, a sloping meadow of gently waving grasses surrounded by a ring of flowering trees.

"*Mijn kind,*" he said again. There were tears in his eyes and she tried to smile, but the dull pain took her for a moment and she gasped with the intensity of it. "You've been sleeping," said the red-bearded man. She turned her head slowly in the other direction.

She was lying with her head in Billy Pilgrim's lap. He was sitting beneath a tall upas tree at the edge of the clearing. Far below, through the seething jungle, she could see the bright blue-green circle of the deadly lagoon. "They gave you medicine. Sweet cane vinegar to ease the pain. You almost died."

"How did I get here?" She blinked.

"We carried you," said Billy, smiling down at her. There were a half dozen cruel red welts across his face where he'd been stung by the lethal jelly-fish. Finn saw now that the others were nearby, looking exhausted, along with several of the locals who were bathing their stings with something they were ladling from rattan-wrapped pottery urns. None of them seemed to be armed. Two were women, their jet-black hair tied back with elaborate leather thongs. Everyone from the dug-out was there. Everyone except Winchester.

She shivered, remembering her last sight of him. "Where are we?"

"Winchester's 'lions,' " said Billy. He stroked a strand of hair back out of her eyes. "Can you stand up or do you want to rest a little longer?"

"I'm okay," she said. "I think." She tried to stand up with Boegart's and Billy's help. She staggered to her feet, felt faint, and leaned on Billy. Boegart kept a careful eye on her condition. Of the others Khan was the only one who rose to his feet. Because his arms and legs had been bare when he'd gone into the water, he seemed to have received the worst of the stings.

"He's the one who got you out of the water," said Billy. "He saved your life actually."

"You would have died," said Khan simply. "The jellies were young, most of them, but you were the smallest and they would have killed you as they did your friend in the goatskin. I could not let that happen."

"Thank you," said Finn. There was nothing else to say.

"And you?" Finn asked, turning to Pieter Boegart, not sure what to think of this strange, red-bearded man who might or might not be her natural father. "Why are you here?"

"One of our scouts saw the jellyfish. I knew you'd be in danger." He paused. "I wasn't sure if your Latin was good enough to translate *Grootvater* Willem's instructions."

"Mine wasn't," laughed Billy.

"Come," said Pieter, gently taking Finn by the arm. "I have something I must show the two of you." They walked across the clearing and along a sloping path that wound up through the jungle for a hundred yards, bringing them out to a small rock outcropping that overlooked the entire caldera.

At the far end of the outcrop was an almost invisible opening in the rock.

"Step through," he said.

She twisted sideways and slid through the narrow passage into a wider area beyond. It was a small, bare cave with a shadowed area of darkness on the left that marked an exit to another cave and an almost perfectly circular passage that opened at the far end of the chamber. She could hear a faint sighing sound and felt a soft, salt breeze against her face.

"As the tide falls, the sound recedes," explained Pieter Boegart. "When the tide comes in, the air pressure builds and the whole cave resonates, sometimes very loudly."

"Escape from my hidden island of treasure on winds of music," said Finn. "The tunnel leads down to the sea?"

"And another cavern. You'll find a boat there. Not large, but large enough to take you all. She is old, the boat, but seaworthy." He laughed. "Not so old as the one *Grootvater* Willem must have built for himself, mind you!" He twinkled. "The cave can't really be seen from the sea unless you're looking for it. There's no real foreshore to land on, but the way is clear. There are no rocks or reefs or anything to hinder you." He turned to Billy. "I heard you were a sailor. Can you navigate with the stars, young fellow?"

"Yes." Billy nodded.

"Keep Ursa Minor at your back and Sirius and Canus Major ahead on the horizon. Sail four days and you'll reach the coast of Sandakan, and safety. *Grootvater* Willem did it and so did I." The red-bearded man paused. "I need your trust," he said at last. "What you see can go no farther than this, the two of you." He gestured, then stepped toward the dark shadows to the left. Finn and Billy followed. The shadows formed into a dark passage that led into yet another cave, this one much larger than the first. A crack in the spiny rock above let in a single bright beam of midday sun. It was enough.

The golden treasure was piled everywhere. Suits of ancient armor made from thin gold plates threaded with gold wire clothed life-sized figures carved from jade. Ingots were piled to the ceiling; golden plates and drinking vessels were stacked in rows. A hundred steel chests, each one the size of an old-fashioned steamer trunk, stood with their lids thrown open, gold coins and wafers piled to the rim.

Ebony figures of forgotten African kings, a crystal elephant the size of a watermelon that crackled and glowed with diamond brilliance in the faint light. A line of crystal skulls, a pile of javelin-length golden spears, a huge coffin sheathed in thin sheets of the gleaming metal. Twinkling emeralds and sapphires and rubies in golden eyes. Tall silver heads tattooed in chased gold. Inlaid plaques and small ceremonial tables of fantastic beauty.

A perfect human hand, three times normal size, held in a two-fingered sign of prayer. A strange, bearded figure of a standing bull with human eyes, carved from lapis lazuli and clothed in golden robes. Africa, India, and everywhere in between, pearls diamonds, ivory, and still more gold. The room was endless.

"The treasures of an empire," said Pieter Boegart. "Willem's legacy."

"Legacy for who?" Billy said, his words choked, his eyes wide with the terrible beauty of the hidden room. "This is like searching for the Maltese Falcon, then finding out it's real. This is too much to deal with."

"This is death to the people who live here," said Pieter. "It marks them as certainly as though they were a target in a shooting gallery. The contents of that Japanese submarine are almost as bad. Three tons of bullion bound for the Nazi coffers in the Reichsbank in Berlin or, worse, to secret vaults in Berne and Geneva for the future. There is enough treasure here to drive men mad. Who claims this place? Borneo, Malaysia, the Philippines? Muslims, Christians, your companion out there with the Dyak haircut and hard features?" He paused again. "Do you know who he is?"

"The man behind the people who tried to kidnap us in London. The people who blew up my boat." Finn paused. "The man who came here hoping to find this."

"His name is Khan. El Piligroso, Tim-timan, the Faithful One, the Philippinos call him. The next Fidel Castro or Che Guevara. A man of principle whose only way of doing good is committing violence. An honest fanatic. An insane seeker for truth. With this wealth he would start a war, and perhaps win it."

Pieter spread his arms and slowly turned around. "And in the process the people on this island would all die, either sacrificed to his cause, or to other people's greed. Subject for a reality television show or a *National Geographic* special. A ride at Euro Disney."

"Then why are you showing us this?" asked Billy. "Why are you telling us these things?"

"So you will know the consequences of telling anyone of its existence. So you will not be tempted to return to search for it." He gave Finn with a look of excruciating finality. "So you will never come back."

"We've lost everything," said Billy. "The *Batavia Queen*, my boat . . ." The young man's eyes trailed across the immense heaps of glittering treasure.

Pieter Boegart smiled. "You still have my house on the *Herengracht*," he said. "Willem's cabinet of curiosities. There's more than enough there for everyone." His smile broadened. "You said it yourself, my boy: like the Maltese Falcon, only real. It is an apt comparison, I think."

From outside the cave there was a sudden, strange thundering sound, a familiar beating at the air that Finn recognized instantly.

"That's a helicopter!"

The three people rushed out of the cave and out onto the little rocky outcropping. The helicopter was clearly visible, arcing in across the breadth of the Punchbowl, coming directly toward the plateau where the others were gathered. It flew without any hesitating motion in a perfectly straight line, losing altitude steadily as though it knew exactly where to look.

In the meadow below, Khan watched the approaching aircraft. It was a Westland Gazelle with its familiar elongated teardrop fuselage and enclosed "fin-in-the-fan" tail rotor. It was painted in the blue and gold of the Singapore Air Force, complete with the big gold lion's head on the side, but Khan knew the livery of the approaching chopper was a lie. The helicopter could hold four or five heavily armed troops and carried everything from miniguns to HOT missiles and twenty-millimeter cannons. They were tank killers and sub chasers and they were deadly.

"Aragas," said the dark-haired freighter captain who'd been a prisoner with him in the village.

"You know him?" said Khan, keeping his eyes on the helicopter. Less than five hundred yards and closing steadily. If they were going to run it had to be now. The middle-aged ship captain didn't move.

"He followed me here," said Hanson. "Looking for you."

"For me?"

The ship captain nodded absently, watching the helicopter approach. The others had struggled to their feet and were watching as well. The natives had melted into the surrounding forest. "He gave me a satellite phone. Blackmailed me. It's somewhere on the wreck of my ship. No doubt it was fitted with a GPS transponder and led them right to us. I'm sorry."

"I'm not," said Khan. "In fact I'm thankful for the confrontation. It's been a long time coming. I'll be glad to see it over."

Hanson looked at him. Or glad to die? he thought. Not that it mattered to him now anyway. With the *Batavia Queen* gone, he had nothing and not much reason to do more than survive. And he was damned if he was going to run from a sadistic little maniac like Senor Lazlo Aragas, the chubby policeman with the Dracula smile.

"Is it really you he's coming for?"

"Me, and the gold he thinks is here. There's always been a rumor of a Japanese submarine full of bullion that disappeared in this area."

"I wouldn't be surprised," said Hanson. "Look at that lagoon down there. It's possible."

"It's a dream," said Khan. "A fool's dream. A dreamer's dream. The Isle of Storms."

As the helicopter roared overhead, it made a swinging turn to land upwind, the rotors chewing up the air in angry jet-fueled screams, flattening the jungle canopy as it slid to earth like some enormous bubble-headed insect. Finn, Billy, and the red-haired native leader appeared along the track leading from above. The helicopter finally dropped its skids to the ground and the rotors began to slow. The big Turbomeca turbine wound down in a noisy blur of sound.

For a moment nothing moved as the rotors whickered slowly to a stop. The side hatch in the canopy opened and Aragas appeared in his white suit and sunglasses, his Borsalino hat gripped in one hand. He looked wildly out of place in the jungle clearing. Behind him four men slid out of the helicopter in the black suit and full-face-mask balaclava uniforms of the Singapore Special Tactics and Rescue, or STAR, Team. Each of the four men carried either an SAR21 Assault Rifle or an MP5 machine gun. On their belts they wore Glock 17 automatics in quick-release holsters.

"So nice of all of you to come out to greet me," said the dapper man in his blindingly white suit. As the rotor came to a complete stop, Aragas dropped the Borsalino onto his head.

"You would be Miss Ryan," he said, bowing slightly as he stopped in front of her. He held out a well-manicured forefinger and waved it in the direction of her cheek. "Not pleasant," he murmured solicitously. "Most painful by all appearances."

"Who are you?" Finn asked.

"A thug," said Hanson. "A blackmailer."

"You know him?" Billy asked, turning to Hanson.

"We've met once or twice."

"A Judas should be more ingratiating to his new master," said Aragas. He made a little noise under his breath. "I'll have to teach you manners." He moved slowly along the line and stopped in front of Pieter Boegart.

"Ah," said Aragas. "The proverbial prodigal son. The heir to a fortune living like some sort of new white rajah in the back of beyond." Aragas shook his head. "The colonial mind never ceases to amaze me." He paused, reaching out with one hand, trailing his fingers across Pieter's ancient, padded armor. "An interesting costume." He smiled. "I'd like to see the treasure that goes with it."

"*Zwijn*," said Pieter.

Aragas let out a little hoot of delight. "You call me a pig? I'll have you know I'm a devout Muslim. I pray six times a day."

"Your only god is your greed," said Khan, standing at Pieter's side.

"As your only god is war."

"Revolution," corrected Khan.

"Rhetoric," replied Aragas, sneering as he turned away. He went back to Finn and smiled widely. "Tell your uncle or whoever he is to tell me where the treasure is or the four men you see behind me will kill all your friends and then rape you."

"Touch her and you die," said Pieter. His voice was frosted with authority.

Aragas reached into his suit jacket and took a small snub-nosed revolver out of his clamshell shoulder harness. "I have helicopters. I have men with machine guns. I have people in London who do my bidding. In Holland too. You are no match for me, I'm afraid, Mr. Boegart."

"It was your people," said Finn, suddenly understanding. "Outside the Courtauld."

"You blew up my boat!" Billy said.

"Of course," said Aragas. "I had Khan's contacts abroad under surveillance. They led me to you. I thought you would lead me to your wandering uncle here and to the treasure I've been searching for all these years. My gold."

"You're insane," said Hanson grimly.

"Who cares?" Aragas replied. "I'm the one who is about to blow off the top of Miss Ryan's charming little head unless her relative speaks up." He lifted the barrel of the pistol and pulled back the hammer. He half turned his head and barked a terse order to the men ten feet behind him. "If anyone interferes, kill them."

With unbelievable speed, Khan swept the heavy automatic out from under his shirt. The automatic Finn had been carrying when he pulled her from the colony of jellyfish. His swift hand squeezed the trigger once and the right lens of Aragas's sunglasses shattered into sun-twinkled powder. The front of the policeman's suit turned pink in the haze of blood that erupted from the rotund man's head. The Borsalino flew off and huffed into the bright blue sky.

Pieter Boegart yelled loudly. "Down! Everyone, down!"

One of the four soldiers standing behind Aragas's slumping corpse managed to get out his Glock and fire a stream of bullets that stitched across Khan's chest, killing him instantly, but that was all. Everyone else did as Pieter Boegart ordered and dropped to the floor of the clearing.

The *gonne*, a primitive hand-cannon, was being used by Chinese infantry as early as A.D. 1300 and perhaps even earlier. Together with technological developments, like the invention of the repeating crossbow, it changed the face of modern warfare forever.

The first *gonnes* used bamboo tubes but they were quickly replaced with iron and bronze barrels roughly eighteen inches long and fitted with heavy wooden stocks that could be braced in the fork of a tree or some other stable object, including specially made rest cradles.

Filled with black powder, tamped and wadded, the *gonne* fired an iron ball weighing between six and sixteen ounces, fired by applying a slow match to a touchhole at the rear of the barrel. The *gonne* was generally accurate over a range of a hundred meters or slightly more than three hundred feet. Roughly half the distance from the screening trees at the edge of the clearing.

Six hundred years before the four elite soldiers from the Singapore STAR unit set foot on the island, such weapons were capable of blowing a hole the size of a human fist through polished steel armor and chain mail. The thin Kevlar vests worn by the four men offered absolutely no protection at all as the twenty men fired off their *gonnes* in a grisly volleying progression that rattled across the clearing and sent up huge clouds of reeking yellow smoke.

Within the cloud of smoke and flying iron, the four men were eviscerated, flayed, and turned inside out, transformed from living human beings to scattered bloody offal on the ground in a matter of seconds. More than half the round shot tore into the soldiers, but the *gonne*, not being the most accurate of weapons, totally missed what was left of the soldiers and several scattered pounds of red-hot metal skipped through the smoke and struck the waiting helicopter.

The canopy disintegrated, along with the pilot, and after a split second, a thousand pounds of high-octane jet fuel exploded, vaporizing what was left of the machine in a white-hot instant. The earsplitting explosion carried off across the huge echo chamber of the caldera, the aircraft's dying moments repeating themselves again and again in a fading roar.

The smoke was carried away, and coughing in the sulfurous haze, the survivors climbed to their feet as the score of hidden soldiers came out of the surrounding forest to stand by their leader. The Island of Storms had claimed one more wreck and a half dozen new victims.

"Dear God," said Briney Hanson, looking at the spot where the four men had been. There was nothing but a huge red smear and behind it the scorched pyre of the burning helicopter's shattered remains.

"It's time for you to go," said Boegart, helping Finn rise to her feet.

She stared down at the torn body of Khan, the automatic still in his dead hand. "What about him?" she said. "He saved my life."

"We'll take care of him," said the red-bearded man gently. "Come with me."

With the ancient, silent soldiers flanking them in two lines the little group of survivors went back up the path and slipped into the narrow mouth of the cave. Looking straight ahead, Pieter led them to the blowhole and down the long sloping vent tunnel to the sea.

As promised the boat was there, an old-fashioned clinker-built design with eight oars, two sails, and a mast that was easily raised into place. It waited for them on the rising tide that filled a broad low-ceilinged cave that looked out to the open sea, moored to a natural stone bollard that rose out of a long, narrow ledge. There was water for ten days in tall jars and food for twice that long.

"Which one of us takes the helm?" Billy asked Briney Hanson.

"We'll take turns," answered the older man, smiling.

"You remember my directions?" Pieter said.

Billy nodded. "Small bear behind, Sirius and the big dog ahead."

"Second star to the right and straight on till morning," said Finn. She leaned over and kissed the red-bearded man on the cheek.

As the tide rose higher, the wind began to sigh and Finn felt the salt breeze stinging her eyes. Old Willem's music. "There wasn't enough time," she said to him as the others clambered into the longboat.

"There never is, child. That's just the way of the world, I'm afraid."

"It isn't fair," she said, the tears coming freely.

"Life isn't fair. But it's precious, so hold on to it as long as you can, right to the end of the adventure." He kissed her softly, then smiled. "Tell my nephew he was right about the bird." He touched her cheek. "Good-bye."

"Good-bye," she answered, but he was already gone.

EPILOGUE

It was raining in Amsterdam—a hard rain, tapping with bony, insistent fingers at windows and roofs and doors. An unhappy downpour of the kind that might lead some people to spend the afternoon alone in a bar, thinking dangerous thoughts.

Finn and Billy stood in Willem Van Boegart's cabinet of curiosities, the room that he'd asked the great Dutch master Rembrandt to disguise for him when he painted the merchant's portrait. The portrait that in the end had sent them halfway round the world.

True to Pieter's word, four days of sailing with Sirius over the bow had brought them to the northern coast of Sandakan, and from there, after enduring a few days of notoriety in the news, that had been the end of it. Hanson, Tomi, and Run-Run McSeveney were beached in Jakarta, looking for another ship with little hope of finding one, while Finn and Billy had returned to Amsterdam to wrap up Pieter Boegart's affairs and sell the *Herengracht* house to recoup the losses Billy had suffered when his sailboat was blown up. Derlagen was on his way to the house with documents for them to sign. Neither Finn nor Billy had said a word about the island or the vast treasure hidden there.

Billy wandered around the little room, idly picking up items and putting them down again. He hefted a gigantic leathery egg that supposedly belonged to some extinct bird, then put it down again. Finn stood by the secret doorway into the room, watching her friend and thinking about the recent past.

"I had a fantasy, you know," said Billy with a wistful note in his voice. "From the moment your friend at the Courtauld . . ." He searched his memory for the name.

"Professor Shneegarten," prompted Finn.

"That's the fellow!" Billy said. "Shneegarten!" He picked up the bell jar with the mummified head inside and peered through the glass. He put it back down on the display table and moved on.

"A fantasy," Finn reminded him.

"That's right," said Billy, nodding. "Ever since your professor peeled back that dodgy canvas and revealed the real Rembrandt underneath, I had this fantasy that we'd find old Willem Van Boegart's fortune, then go off and buy some wonderful salvage ship and sail the seven seas looking for buried doubloons and pieces of eight and high adventure. I even had a name. We'd call ourselves the Treasure Seekers and make television documentaries about our voyages. We'd have sponsors like your American race car drivers. A French wine company to give us a lifetime supply. Endorsements for hair gel and tooth powder and fast cars, that sort of thing. Buy a parrot and call it Captain Flint. Johnny Depp would go deep-sea fishing with us."

"A little more treasure and a little less adventure," laughed Finn. "I'd take the hair gel. Forget the parrot. They make too much mess."

"It was such a lovely dream," sighed Billy.

Finn's gaze traveled around the room. She frowned. "He mentioned it twice," she said finally.

"What?"

"On the island. You said it was like the Maltese Falcon, only real. And then just before we left he said, 'Tell my nephew he was right about the bird.'"

"I don't get it," said Billy

"In *The Maltese Falcon*, everyone runs around looking for a bird they think is really a thinly disguised treasure, paint over solid gold or diamonds or something. They're all willing to kill to get it, and in the end, it turns out to be a phony.

The fat man starts hacking away at it with a pock-etknife but it's just lead."

"Sidney Greenstreet. He plays the fat guy, Kaspar Gutman."

"You said the treasure in the cave was like the Maltese Falcon, only real."

"I still don't see," said Billy, looking at her quizzically. "You're talking in circles."

"Not circles," said Finn, excitement rising in her voice. "Layers. Like ghosting the Rembrandt with a cheap phony . . ."

Billy stared. He looked around the room at the ornate, heavily plastered ceiling and the walls. Vines, birds, all sort of creatures, large and small. "A jungle," he whispered.

"A treasure in the jungle." Finn grinned. "He told us. He said we still had the *Herengracht* house, that the cabinet of curiosities should be more than enough for everyone." Finn found a long midshipman's dirk that might have been used by young Willem Van Boegart on his first voyage. She took the slender knife to the wall and dug down through the plaster. The powder spilled. She dug away at a large plaster gem, scraping deeply. Suddenly a deep ruby slash appeared against the white surface of the wall.

Working cautiously now she scraped carefully down revealing a bloodred gem the size of a robin's egg. A fortune by itself, and there were a hundred, no, a thousand more. She dug the needle

blade into a flat piece of the wall between orna-
ments and scraped away a six-inch square. It
gleamed bright gold beneath the plaster covering.

"This was what Rembrandt hid," said Finn,
staring. "It's the room itself! The whole room is
the treasure!" She scraped harder with the dirk.
The six-inch square became a foot.

Somewhere in the distance, a doorbell rang.

"That must be Derlagen," said Finn.

"I'll tell him to go away," said Billy. "We've got
some renovating to do." He paused at the secret
doorway. "I wonder what time it is in Jakarta."

Sunday, the Fifteenth of July, A.D. 1733
Cayo Hueso, Florida

Friar Bartolome de las Casas of the *Ordo fratrum
Praedicatorum*, the Order of St. Dominic, heard the
giant wave before he saw it. The surging breaker
came out of the storm-racked darkness like a
howling beast, a savage, climbing monster that
suddenly appeared behind the treasure-laden galleon, *Nuestra Señora de las Angustias*, its belly black
as the night around it, the wave's huge, driving
shoulders a livid sickly green, its ragged, curling
head white and torn with ghostly tendrils of
wind-whipped spume and spindrift.

It rose like a toppling wall above the stern of
the groaning ship, pushing the galleon ahead of
it like a chip of wood in a rain-swollen gutter,

the seething wave rising until it could climb no more, filling the dark sky above the terrified monk, then reaching down like some malevolent screaming demon of the seas. Seeing it, Friar Bartolome knew without a doubt that his life was about to end.

He waited for death helplessly crouched in the waist of the vessel with the few other passengers who had come aboard in Havana, including Don Antonio de Escheverz y Zubiza, the governor's son on his way home to Spain for the proper education appropriate to a young man of the nobility. Some of the crew were desperately trying to unship the *Nuestra Señora*'s small boats from the skidrails over the main hatch cover while the rest of the men huddled by the fo'c'sle deck. No one stayed below in such desperate weather—better to see fate approaching, no matter how terrible, than to seal yourself blindly within a leaking, unlit coffin.

Above them all the rain came down in torrents and the remains of the fore staysail and the foresail hammered in the terrible wind, the lines and rigging beating like hailstones on the drumheads of torn, ruined canvas. The rest of the sails had been ragged to tatters and the jibboom was gone entirely and the bowsprit splintered away.

There had to be a hole somewhere deep within the hull because the *Nuestra Señora* was moving more and more sluggishly with every passing moment and taking water in the stern, the missing sea anchor forcing them to run before the wind, any remnant of control long since vanished. The mainmast groaned and creaked, the hull moaned and the seas pounded mercilessly at the schooner's flanks. Everyone knew the ship wouldn't last the hour, let alone survive the night.

Turning his head in time to see the deadly, bludgeoning wave, Friar Bartolome had a single heartbeat of time to take some measure to save himself and his precious cargo. With barely a conscious thought, he dropped to the sodden deck and wrapped his arms tightly around the anchor chain that lay between the capstan and the bitt, holding on for dear life as the breaking monster pummeled down upon him.

The wave struck with a thundering roar and there was an even more terrible sound from within the belly of the ship: a deep, grating screech as the keel scraped along a hidden line of reef and then stuck fast, hard aground, wedged between two invisible clutching jaws of coral, stopping the *Nuestra Señora* dead in the water. There was an immense cracking sound and the mainmast toppled, carrying the yards and spars along with it into the raging sea.

The wave, unhindered, swept along the deck of the schooner, swallowing the cowering crew, demolishing the ships boats and burying Friar Bartolome beneath tons of suffocating water. The wave surged on, the suction pulling at his straining arms and heavy cassock but he managed to keep his grip long enough for the great green wall to pass. He came up for air and saw in an instant that he was the only one alive left on the deck. Everyone else was gone except Don Antonio, who lay broken like a child's doll, tangled in the pins and rigging of the foremast fife rail, his head crushed, gray matter oozing wetly from beneath his cap, eyes wide and staring toward the dark heavens, seeing nothing. There would be no school in Spain after all.

Friar Bartolome looked back toward the stern but saw only the dark. Struggling to his knees, he began tearing at his cassock, realizing that if he was thrown into the water the drenched fabric would doom him, dragging him down to the bottom. He managed to relieve herself of the heavy robe and then the next wave struck with no warning at all.

Without the anchor chain to hold him, the monk was immediately swept up, turning head over heels and thrown toward the snarled rigging at the bow, striking his head on the rail and feeling a piercing tear at his throat as a splinter of wood slashed into him. Then he was overboard, pushed down so deeply within the wave that he felt the rough touch of the coral bottom as it smashed into his shoulders and back. Crushed by the huge weight of water, he felt the remains of his clothing torn away, and he tumbled helplessly within the wave across the seabed. He forced himself to hold his breath and pushed toward the surface, his arms windmilling underwater, his face upturned.

Finally he broke free of the wave's terrible grip and gulped in huge, gasping lungfuls of air, retching seawater, feeling the tug of the next wave as he was swept forward and down again with barely enough time to take a breath before the deluge swallowed him again. Once more he was pressed down to the bottom, the rough sand and coral tearing at his skin, and once more, exhausted, he clawed his way to the surface for another retching breath.

A fourth wave took him, but this time, instead of coral, there was only sand on the sloping bottom, and he barely had to swim at all before he reached the surface. His feet stumbled and he threw himself forward with the last of his strength, staggering as the sea sucked back from the shore in a rushing rip current, strong enough to bring her to her knees. He crawled, rose to his feet again and plunged on, knees buckling, in despair because he knew in some distant corner of his mind that another wave as strong as the first could still steal his life away with salvation and survival so tantalizingly near.

He staggered again in the treacherous sand that dragged at his heels and almost toppled him over.

He took another step and then another, blinking in the slanting, blinding rain. Ahead, farther up the broad strip of shining beach, was a darker line of trees, fan palms and coconuts, their trunks bent away from the howling wind and the lashing rain, unripe fruit torn away, crashing into the forest like cannonballs. His breath came in ragged gasps and his legs were like deadweights, but at least he was free of the mad, clutching surf that broke behind him like crashing thunder.

Struggling higher up the sandy slope he finally reached a point above the wreck and turned back to the sea, sinking down exhausted to his knees, naked except for the ragged remnants of his linen stockings and undershift, still badly frightened but weeping with relief as he stared into the shrieking night. By the grace of God, and by the continuing miracles of the most secret and terrible Hounds of God, he had survived.

Through the rain he could see the heaving broken line of frothing white that marked the reef they'd run aground on, but nothing more. Somewhere out there, invisible in the darkness the *Nuestra Señora de las Angustias* was dying, breaking apart on the teeth of the coral shore, her crew and captain gone to whatever their fate, leaving Friar Bartolome alone in this terrible place. Remembering suddenly he fumbled under his remaining clothing and felt the oilskin-wrapped parcel and its precious contents still strapped securely around his waist. The codex had survived, and the last and greatest secret left by the fiendish heretic and enemy of God, Hernán Cortéz, Marqués del Valle de Oaxaca, was safe.

National Bestselling Author
Paul Christopher

MICHELANGELO'S NOTEBOOK

While studying art history at New York University, brilliant and beautiful Finn Ryan makes a startling discovery: a Michelangelo drawing of a dissected corpse—supposedly from the artist's near-mythical notebook. But that very night, someone breaks into her apartment—murdering her boyfriend and stealing the sketches she made of the drawing. Fleeing for her life, Finn heads to the address her mother had given her for emergencies, where she finds the enigmatic antiquarian book dealer, Michael Valentine. Together, they embark on a desperate race through the city—and through the pages of history itself—to expose an electrifying secret from the final days of World War II—a secret that lies in the dark labyrinthine heart of the Vatican.

BESTSELLING AUTHOR
DANIEL SILVA

PRINCE OF FIRE

Gabriel Allon faces his most determined enemy—
and greatest challenge—in the stunning novel from
the "world-class practitioner of spy fiction"
(*The Washington Post*).

"Those in the know are calling Daniel Silva the new
John le Carré. Those who are reading him can't put
him down." —*Chicago Sun-Times*

"A first-rate thriller." —*Rocky Mountain News*